TO STEAL THE SUN

THE FOUR KINGDOMS AND BEYOND

THE FOUR KINGDOMS

The Princess Companion: A Retelling of The Princess and the Pea
(Book One)

The Princess Fugitive: A Reimagining of Little Red Riding Hood
(Book Two)

The Coronation Ball: A Four Kingdoms Cinderella Novelette

Happily Every Afters: A Reimagining of Snow White and Rose Red
(Novella)

The Princess Pact: A Twist on Rumpelstiltskin (Book Three)

A Midwinter's Wedding: A Retelling of The Frog Prince (Novella)

The Princess Game: A Reimagining of Sleeping Beauty (Book Four)

The Princess Search: A Retelling of The Ugly Duckling (Book Five)

BEYOND THE FOUR KINGDOMS

A Dance of Silver and Shadow: A Retelling of The Twelve Dancing
Princesses (Book One)

A Tale of Beauty and Beast: A Retelling of Beauty and the Beast
(Book Two)

A Crown of Snow and Ice: A Retelling of The Snow Queen (Book Three)

A Dream of Ebony and White: A Retelling of Snow White (Book Four)

A Captive of Wing and Feather: A Retelling of Swan Lake (Book Five)

A Princess of Wind and Wave: A Retelling of The Little Mermaid
(Book Six)

TO STEAL THE SUN

A RETELLING OF EAST OF THE SUN AND WEST OF THE MOON

FOUR KINGDOMS DUOLOGY BOOK 2

MELANIE CELLIER

LUMINANT PUBLICATIONS

TO STEAL THE SUN – A RETELLING OF EAST OF THE SUN AND WEST OF THE MOON

Four Kingdoms Duology Book 2
First edition published in 2024 (v1.1)
by Luminant Publications

ISBN 978-1-925898-93-4

Luminant Publications
PO Box 305
Greenacres, South Australia 5086

melanie@melaniecellier.com
http://www.melaniecellier.com

Cover Design by Karri Klawiter
Editing by Mary Novak
Proofreading by James Packer

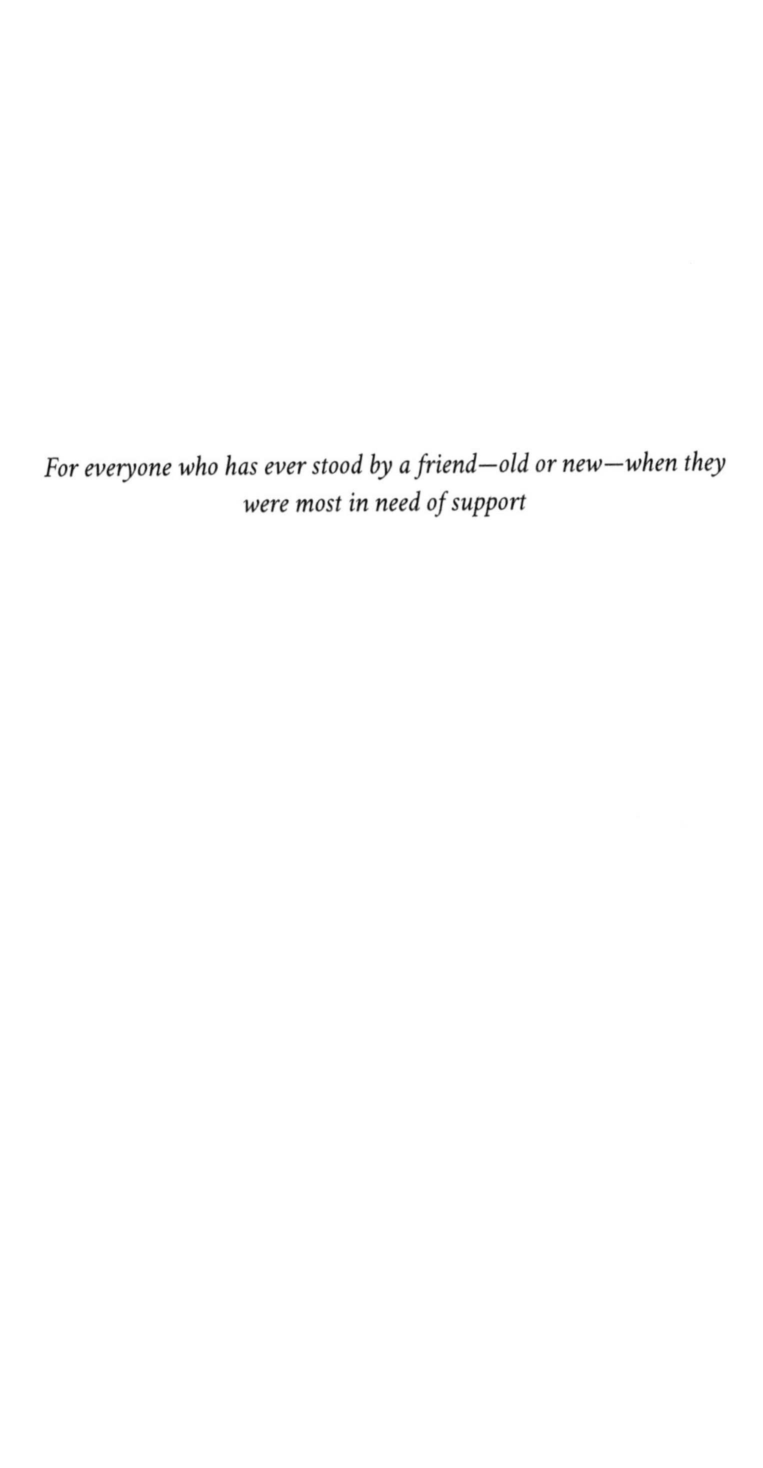

For everyone who has ever stood by a friend—old or new—when they were most in need of support

Four Kingdoms
Northhelm
GREENHOLD
NORTHGATE
RANGMEROS
Rangmere
Arcadia
Kuralan
KAREMA
MADOS
The Great Desert
ARCADIE
LANARE
Lanover
SIKKALA
Ardasira
CATALIE
INVERNE
BANISHMENT ISLAND

PROLOGUE

GWEN

$\mathcal{I}$t wasn't hard for Gwen to appear lost and confused as she walked down the street toward the palace. Not only was the route new to her, but she had never walked any street alone in her life.

I'm not really alone, she told herself, calling up the memory of Charlotte's farewell hug, the strength of Count Oswin's handshake, and the look in Easton's eyes as he told her to stay safe.

But the appearance of a squad of guards sent the memories fleeing. The men approached her with steely determination, and there was no one to face them at her side. She *was* alone.

Every instinct told her to run—to flee far and fast. To run until she reached the safety of Easton's arms.

She forced herself to freeze instead, letting go of any hold on her fear and anxiety and giving the emotions free rein to flood through her. By the time the guards reached her, she was visibly trembling. A distant part of her was even impressed at her own performance. The other part was afraid it wasn't a performance at all. But she had assured the others she could be their double agent in the palace, and she was determined not to fail before she even began.

When the guards reached her, she braced herself to be seized by rough hands. But no one touched her at all. Instead, the men formed a protective square around her, their focus on the surrounding streets, as if fearing she might come under attack.

Gwen frowned. What game was her mother playing now?

She licked her lips, her mouth almost too dry to talk. "There's no one following me," she managed to get out.

The oldest guard—the one who seemed to be in charge—turned to give her a sympathetic look. With a flash of recognition, she realized it was the older of the guards she had met at dusk in the gardens. It had only been weeks ago, although it felt like a lifetime.

He had seemed brusque and rough at the time, but she knew now he had been protecting her. And afterward, he had reported to someone other than her mother.

Another shock flashed through her. The guard who led the men intercepting her was one of Oswin's men—a man who, like the count, had changed allegiances over the years, turning against her mother. Her eyes roamed across the other guards. Were they all loyal to Oswin? Was this what he had needed to organize when he had left during the night? Had he somehow maneuvered the situation to send friendly forces to escort her back?

She shook herself. Without confirmation, she couldn't risk so much as a look or gesture that might betray her. She would drive herself mad if she started trying to second guess the loyalties of everyone who lived in the palace.

"I'm ready to go to my mother," she said softly, her voice faltering over the final word.

The guard captain threw her another look but limited his response to a single nod. Even so, within seconds, the group was en route to the castle.

The structure loomed over the city in a way that felt threatening, although Gwen suspected the original builders had intended a different effect. Had they meant the mountain palace to be a protective presence? Perhaps some of them had even dreamed of making it beautiful, like the airy storybook palaces found in children's tales. Gwen had read the Arcadian palace was built in that style.

Whatever the intentions of the original inhabitants, Gwen felt nothing benevolent in the presence of the castle now. Every step closer felt heavier than the last until she wasn't sure if her own feet could carry her all the way inside.

But such thoughts were only a fancy in her mind, and within far too short a time, she was once again within the walls that had been the confines of her whole life. Each time they turned a corner, she looked for any sign of the captive servants. There was none.

She tried not to let her foreboding grow any greater. The count had said they were all still well. Her mother hadn't discovered their involvement in Gwen's liberation, and they had been continuing their duties as normal. She would have liked a glimpse of a friendly face, though.

The guards led her directly to the throne room, but when they opened the doors, the large space held only a single person. The queen sat on her throne in solitary state, as if presiding over an imaginary court.

A shiver ran through Gwen, but her legs carried her forward. She crossed the cavernous space without faltering, registering only faintly that the guards had remained outside.

When she finally reached the stairs that led up to the dais, she stopped and gazed upward, meeting her mother's eyes. Gwen had been afraid that when she came face to face with her mother, she wouldn't be able to conceal the secrets boiling inside her. She had been afraid that her face, her manner—maybe even her words— would spill the truth of her hatred and defiance.

What happened was even worse. Standing in the presence of her mother, a lifetime of habit took over. Her body ceased trembling, and her face became a pleasant mask as she stepped into the role of the dutiful Princess Gwendolyn. She had thought it outgrown, but it fit without a wrinkle, as if it were a second skin.

Shame filled Gwen, although it didn't show on her face. *This is how you survived,* a voice said in the back of her mind. *This is how you can still survive.*

Gwen acknowledged the truth of the thought, but it was soon overwhelmed by another. When she was finished playing her role, how much of her true self would be left to retrieve? If she let herself be subsumed by her mother again, would she lose herself completely this time?

But those thoughts too were followed by another, more final one. *There is no other way.*

CHARLOTTE

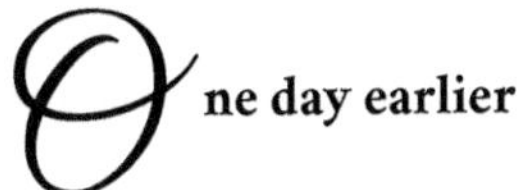

"But have you seen Henry yourself?" Charlotte pressed, trying to keep the desperation out of her voice. "Have you spoken to him?"

The man in front of her—the one Gwen had introduced as Count Oswin—hesitated, and her heart contracted. What had the mountain queen done to Henry?

"As far as I know he is well enough," the count said at last. "But I haven't actually exchanged words with him. Queen Celandine has been keeping him in solitary confinement since his abrupt appearance the night before last. I only know he reappeared because a number of us were together at the time, in consultation with the queen."

"You think she would have hidden his arrival if she could?" Gwen asked, and Charlotte tried to focus on their conversation instead of her overpowering fear for her husband.

At least Henry was still alive, and she now knew where he

was. Her determination to rescue him had already brought her further than he had believed possible.

"I'm certain she would have preferred to conceal him," Count Oswin said without hesitation. "She's still pretending you're in the castle—in seclusion as you recover from a bout of ill health. But since you're not there, the presence of the prince creates a significant problem for her."

"Because they're supposed to get married," Charlotte said in a flat voice.

The count threw her an uncomfortable look. "Precisely. Of course we didn't know about your existence…" He trailed off, clearly uneasy with the situation.

They all fell silent momentarily, and the count gathered himself, returning to his previous polished air.

"Why don't we all sit down?" He looked behind him at the selection of seating, his face puckering slightly in distaste.

Charlotte echoed his sentiments. The threadbare nature of the furniture didn't bother her, but everything in the basement looked like it needed a good clean.

No one protested aloud, though, so the count quickly had them organized in a loose circle. He sat directly across from Gwen while Easton sat at her side, pulling his chair as close as possible to her. That left Charlotte to fill in one of the gaps with their guide across from her.

The girl—who looked several years younger than Charlotte—gazed unabashedly back at her, clearly fascinated by the young woman who had just been introduced as a princess. Charlotte wished the girl would look elsewhere. Whatever she was expecting from Charlotte, she was going to be disappointed. Charlotte was no princess.

She avoided the girl's gaze, looking around the dim basement. She had spent the journey through the mountains in a state of constant tension. Not only had they been literally riding the wind while it tried to buck and throw them to their deaths, but she had been braced for a dramatic and possibly violent confrontation with the queen on arrival. She hadn't expected to find herself sitting in a basement with no idea what was supposed to happen next.

She refocused on the count. "Do you have a plan? For freeing my husband, I mean."

The count cleared his throat and looked toward Gwen. Charlotte followed his gaze with a sinking feeling. Had the rebels just been waiting, expecting Gwen to arrive with a plan? Because Charlotte was certain Gwen didn't have a plan. Only that morning Gwen had been on her way to Henry's castle to check on Charlotte.

She rubbed her temples. Had it really been less than a day since she had run into Gwen in the forest? Less than two full days since she had lost Henry? It felt like a lifetime. The Charlotte who had returned to the castle on Henry's back, eager to see her husband's face, had been a different woman—one who seemed impossibly young and naive.

Given the way Gwen straightened in her chair, she had also noticed that the count was looking to her. And from the way she was biting her lip, she felt as lost as Charlotte. Charlotte felt a surge of pity for her. If two days of suffering had aged Charlotte, how ancient must Gwen feel?

On impulse, she took her friend's hand. Charlotte had come to the kingdom east of the sun and west of the moon to rescue her husband, but she had also come to help her friend. She wasn't going to let some old man berate Gwen for not having a solution to a problem he hadn't managed to solve in a decade.

GWEN

Gwen looked down at Charlotte's hand, some of the stiffness leaving her body. She didn't deserve her friend's sympathy, but she drew strength from it anyway. The count's expectations were like bricks heaped on her shoulders, but Charlotte gave her support freely, and it lightened Gwen's load to know she wasn't alone.

She didn't have a plan, but she knew what needed to happen. Surely if they all worked together, they could come up with a way forward.

"My mother—" She stopped sharply and drew a firm breath. "No. That woman is not my mother." Some things mattered more than blood. A woman who had spent years using, manipulating, and abusing Gwen without a second thought didn't deserve the title of mother.

It was still hard to look up and meet the eyes of the others, and Gwen braced herself to hear a lecture on what she owed the woman who had given her birth. But Easton's warm hand slid into her free one, giving it an encouraging squeeze at the same time as Charlotte firmly gripped her other hand.

Gwen drew another, freer, breath. Was it really that easy?

The past twenty-three years unrolled through her mind, over-shadowed by the constant, looming presence of the queen. Even now, Gwen could feel Celandine's poisonous words burrowed deep in her mind, not yet fully uprooted. No, it hadn't been easy at all, and it wouldn't be easy in the future. But here, encircled by people who saw her as something more than the queen's shadow, she had made a start at least.

She started again. "Queen Celandine has to be stopped. But if you're hoping I flew in here with a plan for how to do that, I'm sorry to disappoint you. I came back because I knew I had to do something to help my people." Her eyes flicked to the young girl on Easton's other side. "I'm sorry that I'm not what you were hoping for or expecting."

The girl shrugged. "He's the one who said we needed you and told me to keep watch." She gestured toward the count with her head. "I could already see how it was that time I went looking for you at the palace."

"Excuse me?" Gwen stared at her, utterly confused.

The girl smiled, a look of combined sympathy and pity that was almost amusing on her youthful face. Almost. Instead, it made Gwen ashamed of what little use she'd made of her extra decade of experience.

"I suppose it's understandable enough," the girl said in a voice that suggested she didn't really understand. "After all, you grew up with *her* for a mother." Her face twisted at her mention of the queen. "And my family appreciated the gold you gave us. My mother is healthy thanks to you." Her eyes slid away. "But it was obvious you weren't going to be good for much else. That's why I found him instead." She nodded at the count. "But then he insisted we had to wait for you. That we needed you." She rolled her eyes and fell silent.

The count gave her a stern look—the kind he must have used many times on his own children and grandchildren. The look of someone whose extra years of experience had been used instead of wasted.

"Of course we need Her Highness," he said. "This is a delicate enough matter as it is. If people think I'm trying to seize power for myself, our side will break into factions and start in-fighting. It will destroy everything we're working toward." He softened slightly, looking between each of the three newcomers. "But I will acknowledge that Natalie is the one who found me. Many among the court have become disillusioned over the years, and I was already their leader, but she's the one responsible for connecting the rebellion at court with the rebels in the city."

Natalie shrugged like it was no big deal, and the count chuckled softly.

"Oh, for the confidence of youth," he murmured.

"You did all that?" Easton gave Natalie an impressed look. She was only a little older than he had been when he had confronted the queen and been banished for his effrontery. Was he wishing he had handled himself more like her back then?

If he had responded differently, he might never have been forced to leave. But at the same time, a small part of Gwen had always warmed whenever she thought of him storming in to confront her moth—no, the queen—on her behalf. She appreciated his passion and loyalty even if she hated the separation it had caused.

"It wasn't as hard as you might think." Natalie shrugged at Easton before turning to Gwen. "Do you remember how those guards were coming our way, and you distracted them so I could sneak out? I was shocked to see guards manhandling the princess like that. And you'd seemed so timid and terrified as we were sneaking out, too. After I got home, I kept worrying about what they'd done to you after I left. So I snuck back into the palace grounds the next day to find out what punishment you'd received. That's the sort of thing people are guaranteed to gossip about. But no one was talking about the incident at all. It was suspicious." She shrugged again. "I found the same guards, and once I'd managed that, I didn't have to follow them for long before they led me to Count Oswin."

"You're the one the guards reported to?" Gwen cried, staring at the count. "That's why my mother never heard I'd been out in the grounds so close to nightfall! Some of the guards are loyal to you over her."

"Thankfully they were the ones to find you that night," the count said. "Of course actually confronting me was a far riskier move than Natalie seems to realize. But happily it turns out we're all on the same side."

"That's not surprising, is it?" Natalie said cheerfully. "The people of the city are on the side of anyone who opposes that woman and her taxes and her bears." She shuddered at the final word.

"I will refrain from pointing out that I'm one of those bears," the count muttered. Gwen shifted uncomfortably. As little as she liked to think of it in those terms, she was one of Queen Celandine's bears too.

"You *were* one of them," Charlotte said, looking unaccountably sad. "The enchantment is broken now."

Instant silence and stillness seized the room as all four of them stared at Charlotte. She blinked back at them.

"Isn't it?" she asked hesitantly. "Henry's enchantment broke, and I thought that was the point of including him in the first place. When it broke for him, wasn't it supposed to break for all of you?"

The count half rose before sinking back into his chair. "The lowlander prince no longer turns into a bear during the day?"

Charlotte gaped at him. "You didn't know?"

He shook his head. "Like I said, he appeared at night, and the queen has had him locked away in solitary confinement since."

"Her specialty," Gwen muttered.

"But wait, are you saying you all still turn into bears at night?"

Charlotte gazed wide-eyed between Gwen and the count. "Were you a bear last night, Gwen?"

Gwen shifted uncomfortably. She still wasn't used to the reality of her nightly transformations herself. Her eyes flashed to the count, remembering the deception her mother had perpetrated on the court. He didn't look surprised to hear Gwen also became a bear, though.

"Why do you think I was out in the forest so early when you found me this morning?" Gwen asked Charlotte with a sigh. "It's true I was on my way to your castle, but I had a head start since I spend all my nights outside." She glanced at the dirty half-window in the basement wall. "And talking of nighttime, it must be close to sunset now." She glanced uncertainly at the count.

"You don't need to be concerned," he said calmly. "I sometimes spend the night at my manor in the city, so my absence won't cause any alarm at the palace. And my own people are utterly loyal to me. None of them would dream of mentioning that I didn't spend the night at home."

"But..." Gwen looked uncertainly at the other three. That hadn't been her concern. She had never transformed in front of anyone before, and the idea of doing it in front of Easton made her stomach churn. How could he look at her the same after that?

Charlotte frowned. "I don't understand. Henry definitely turned back into a man. He said he'd never be a bear again. He broke the enchantment. Why are you all still bears at night?"

Gwen forgot her fear for a moment, staring at the count for an answer. He stared back at her, his expression equally blank and confused.

"I was definitely a bear last night," she said slowly. "And you?"

The count nodded, his eyes narrowing in thought. "The idea of including the prince in the enchantment came from the queen, and it obviously didn't work as she intended since it was reversed for the prince—his days as a bear, his nights as a man. I suppose that wasn't the only thing that didn't work to plan."

"No wonder she's been hiding him." Gwen shook her head. "She's already made so many mistakes with these enchantments—each new mistake must make it harder for her to hide her errors."

The count nodded slowly. "Plus, if he's a human all the time now, there's nothing stopping him marrying the princess during the daytime—except for the fact the queen doesn't actually have Princess Gwendolyn stashed in a room at the palace like she claims." Charlotte made a wordless sound of dissent, and he winced. "Well, there's nothing preventing his marriage in the minds of the courtiers. Of course they don't know he already has a wife."

"But how did he break the enchantment?" Gwen asked eagerly, looking toward Charlotte. "If we know that, we might be able to find a way to break ours as well." She carefully didn't look at Easton. Perhaps it would be possible to release herself before he ever had to see her as a bear.

Charlotte's cheeks turned slowly pink. "According to his godmother, the enchantment did need a royal wedding to be broken, but it also took love. He said..." She paused before rushing on. "He said the enchantment would be broken when he looked into his wife's eyes in his human form and felt nothing but love."

The count ran a hand over his head. "Well." He shot a surreptitious glance at Gwen and Easton, who still sat too close together. "Well, then."

It was Gwen's turn to flush, but she resolutely ignored it. "The queen must know that's how the enchantment is broken. She mentioned Prince Henry's godmother to me—about hearing what she said to him—so she must have found a way to overhear when his godmother told him how to break the enchantment." She looked at Charlotte, feeling embarrassed, although she knew she wasn't responsible for the queen's actions. "She was monitoring you somehow. I went into her rooms once, and she had a giant portrait of you and Henry as a bear. She seemed to know he would be returning here soon as well."

Charlotte paled, pressing her hands to her face. "She knew I would…"

She trailed off and went silent, not explaining to the rest of them the terms of the second enchantment—the one that had transported Henry back to the queen. Although the two had broken the original enchantment, they hadn't succeeded in breaking the second one due to Charlotte seeing Henry's human face before the necessary three months had elapsed. Charlotte's visible anguish sent a shaft of pain through Gwen's heart. It hadn't been Charlotte's idea to use that candle, it had been Gwen's. And she still hadn't found the courage to confess it to her friend.

Gwen spoke quickly, trying to distract the others from Charlotte's state. "So the queen's followers believe—"

"Get back!" The count spoke sharply, his words overlapping the sudden itchy sensation that had sprung up beneath Gwen's skin.

She sucked in a sharp breath, her eyes jumping to Easton.

"No. No, no, no," she breathed, frantic but unable to work out what she should do. Should she run out of the basement? Where would she go?

The count surged to his feet, not showing any inclination to scratch the tingling itchiness that must also be sweeping through him. "You all need to stand back." He spoke forcefully, gesturing to the other side of the basement.

Natalie glanced toward the window. "The glass is so dirty, it's hard to tell if it's day or night." She sounded disapproving but unafraid.

Unlike Charlotte and Easton, she showed no bemusement at the count's sudden actions. She must know what was happening. Standing, she stretched out her arms and swept the other two along with her toward the far wall.

"There's no need to be concerned," she said, perhaps in response to their expressions. "They're not actually turning into wild animals. They're just going to become a lot bigger. But they don't always have full control of their movements during the change. If we're too close, we might get hurt."

"You've seen it before?" Charlotte gasped, and it took Gwen a moment to place the emotion in her voice. Was it envy?

"Henry never let me see him change," she added, confirming Gwen's impression.

Gwen's eyes went to Easton again, but the tearing feeling—as if she were coming apart all the way up the center of her body—had already begun, and she couldn't stomach seeing his expression as she changed. She lowered her head, squeezing her eyes shut as she dropped to all fours and waited for the dizziness to pass.

When she opened them again, she saw white fur.

She stared at the other bear across from her. The count had moved back from the chairs, putting space between them, and she was grateful for it because he was huge. Even larger than she was. The sight of his bear form made her instincts twang, shouting at her to run and hide. Her instincts kept forgetting she was a bear as well.

"Gwen?" Easton's tentative question made her wince and turn further away from him. He moved with her, though, circling until he could see her face. "Is that really you?"

He sounded unnerved. How could he not?

Gwen wished she could hide her face in her hands, but she didn't have hands. She had paws. And her face was not her own. The princess Easton loved was gone, replaced by a bear.

CHARLOTTE

"**T**hat was amazing!" Charlotte breathed. "I can't believe Henry never gave me the chance to watch!"

"I can," Gwen said in a muffled voice, angling her face away.

Charlotte frowned, moving slowly toward her friend. Easton stood close beside Gwen, but Gwen appeared to be straining away from him.

Charlotte realized the issue and rushed the rest of the way forward. Throwing her arms around Gwen's large, furry neck, she put her mouth near her ear.

"Don't worry," she whispered. "Once I got over the first surprise, I never had trouble with Henry's bear form. I always knew it was him, whatever body he was in. I still loved the man inside. Easton will be the same. I'm sure of it."

Gwen stiffened at first, but the longer Charlotte talked, the more she relaxed. When Charlotte finally stepped back with a last squeeze of Gwen's neck, Gwen shifted, facing them all without flinching.

Easton offered her a smile and tentatively extended his hand. Gwen glanced at Charlotte before looking back at him and visibly swallowing. Only when she nodded her head, did he reach gently forward and placed a hand on her large shoulder.

"It's so soft," he murmured, and Charlotte nodded enthusiastically.

"Isn't it?" she agreed. "I was amazed the first time I felt Henry's fur."

Gwen relaxed even further, and Charlotte was grateful she was present to smooth over the awkward moment for her friend.

"Their fur might be soft, but they also have claws. And teeth." Natalie's voice was hard.

Charlotte threw an inquiring look first at her and then at the count.

"The queen has her guards patrol the city after sundown," the count said. "Anyone fool enough to be caught outside gets scars to remind them of their mistake."

Gwen sucked in an audible breath.

"The queen has no friends in the city," Natalie said. "But there are plenty of people who are too scared to oppose her." She lowered her voice to a mutter. "Cowards."

"Or perhaps they just have more sense than you," the count replied, his tone long-suffering.

Did he resent being forced to work with someone so young? Based on Gwen's brief introduction, he was used to consulting with monarchs.

"Does that mean we're stuck here until sunrise?" Easton asked, his focus on practicalities.

"That would be wisest," the count said. "But don't worry, my grandson will be here soon with food."

Easton raised his eyebrows. "I thought it wasn't safe on the streets at night?"

"My grandson is…distinctive," the count said in a flat voice. "The guards all know him, and none would dare harm him."

Natalie gave a dramatic sigh, in sharp contrast to the count's carefully emotionless face and voice.

"You didn't tell me Emmett was coming," she said. "I would have left before dark if I'd known that."

Charlotte threw her a questioning look, and the girl leaned closer, talking in a loud whisper.

"Emmett is seven. And he has a crush on me." She rolled her eyes.

Charlotte tried and failed to hold back her smile.

"My grandson does not have…" The count sighed, giving up on his denial—either because he knew her claim was true or he knew there was no point trying to reason with Natalie. Charlotte found both options appealingly amusing. It was hard not to like Natalie despite how outrageous she was.

As if on cue, there was a quiet knock on the basement door, giving a moment of warning before it opened. A small figure slipped inside, but his presence was bulkier than his frame warranted thanks to the crutches he maneuvered inside with him. They didn't slow him down, though. He wielded them like someone with long experience.

"Emmett." The deep rumble of the count's bear voice still managed to sound soft and welcoming. The courtier obviously held his grandson in deep affection.

"Did you bring us something yummy, at least?" Natalie asked, her focus on the bag slung over the boy's shoulder.

From the way Emmett's eyes brightened as they fell on her and the way his gaze quickly flitted away from her again, Charlotte gathered Natalie had been right about the crush. Her mouth tugged upward. Poor boy.

Emmett unhooked the bag and offered it to Natalie. The older girl took it and immediately began rifling through the contents, muttering to herself. When it became obvious she didn't have anything else to say to him, Emmett turned to his grandfather.

"Did she really come back? Is she here?" He glanced doubtfully at Charlotte. Despite the late hour, there was enough light in the basement to clearly illuminate her golden coloring. And while he was apparently unfamiliar with the details of his princess's appearance, he must at least know she was dark-haired.

"I am Princess Gwendolyn," Gwen said calmly, her bear's voice lower than her human one although still recognizable to Charlotte's ear.

Emmett started so badly, he nearly lost his balance. Charlotte's instinct was to rush forward and help, but the boy had recovered before she could move.

"But…you're a bear," he said.

"I hope we can trust you, Emmett," the count said in a heavy voice.

The boy's eyes widened even further, and he cast another look toward Natalie as he nodded vigorously.

"Of course, Grandfather. I would never say anything, you know that." He faltered. "But…why is she a bear? I thought…"

"That I was a princess so pure the enchantment couldn't touch me?" Gwen interjected in sour tones.

Charlotte made a revolted face, knowing Gwen was repeating her mother's words. Gwen might be attempting a façade of calm, but Charlotte knew how deeply her mother had hurt her, and how much Gwen hated being the tool the queen had used against her people.

Emmett stared at Gwen in bewilderment, and Easton drew even closer to her, his air protective. Charlotte couldn't help smiling at the incongruous sight given Gwen's size and current possession of sharp teeth. She had known Easton for less than a day, but he was clearly as devoted to Gwen as the princess was to him.

The thought of the pair's reunion after so many years gave Charlotte joy, but it came hand in hand with an uncomfortable pang. How long would her separation from Henry be? Even if it took years, she would endure it—although she wasn't sure how.

She didn't want to think about being separated from him for so long.

"You're a dependable lad, Emmett," Count Oswin said, "but you're still a child. There are a great many things I haven't confided in you."

"You obviously knew," Gwen said quietly to the count. "About me turning into a bear like everyone else."

The count nodded. "Not initially. But my son was the one leading the expedition that brought Prince Henry across the mountains. Although Queen Celandine kept his presence as quiet as possible, she had to allow a few of us into her confidence. We were pressing for a wedding to take place immediately since she had claimed that was what would free us all from the enchantment. She countered by insisting that he needed to be included in the enchantment first. And then when it went wrong and turned him into a bear during the day, she had to explain why the ceremony couldn't be performed at night when he was human."

Natalie had extracted all the food from the bag while he spoke, and she soon had everyone seated in approximation of their previous circle as she distributed the meal. There were a few moments of silence as everyone began eating, but Charlotte was too confused to let the conversation drop.

"Why couldn't the ceremony happen while one of them was a bear?" Charlotte asked, not understanding the issue. "Henry and I were married while he was in his bear form."

The count raised his eyebrows. "Then I can only assume valley weddings are much simpler affairs than mountain ones."

Charlotte suddenly remembered Henry's initial question to her—back when she had only known him as a bear. He had even mentioned that some places had more elaborate ceremonies.

"Among other things," the count continued, "a mountain bride and groom must each wash a dirty shirt belonging to the other."

"Your marriage ceremony includes washing dirty clothing? By

hand? On the spot?" Charlotte realized too late that her astonishment might seem rude. Thankfully the count responded stoically.

"As you can imagine, it isn't something that can be done with paws like these. However, it is an essential part of our ceremony. It symbolizes starting a new, fresh future together."

"That's what they say," Easton interjected. "But I'm pretty sure it's an ancient conspiracy to make sure no mountain lady finds herself married to a man who doesn't know how to do his own laundry."

He delivered the words with such a serious air that they surprised a giggle out of Gwen, the vaguely threatening rumble reminding Charlotte of Henry.

Easton smiled back at Gwen, his eyes warm. "I've missed your laugh," he said softly, his words clearly meant for her ears only.

Charlotte looked away, uncomfortable to be intruding on their moment. Tears built up behind her eyes. She ached for the sense of familiar companionship that existed between Gwen and Easton—the closeness she had experienced for herself for a few short months. She ached for Henry.

"I think it's silly." Natalie wrinkled her nose. "You put on the nicest dress you're ever going to wear in your life and then you have to do laundry?"

"I'm surprised the queen didn't just change the law about weddings," Easton said.

"That assumes she actually wanted us to get married," Gwen said. "But since she had lied about my marriage to a prince breaking the enchantment, the last thing she wanted was to have the wedding actually happen and be proved a liar in front of the entire kingdom. She's been using delaying tactics for the last ten years, so she must have been delighted when it affected Henry differently. She was trying everything possible to delay, hoping something would come up to her advantage, and it did. The reversal in the enchantment for him was a convenient tool for her."

"And now she knows the truth of breaking the enchantment thanks to Prince Henry's godmother, but she still wants the wedding to go ahead," the count mused. "At least she's searching for you as frantically as if she wanted it to. Why is she still committed to the marriage?"

"I don't think that has anything to do with the enchantment." Gwen drew her words out, as if she didn't want to say them. "Or at least, only a little. Our potential marriage has become about what she intends to do after the enchantment is broken."

The count's whole body went still, and it was somehow more intimidating than if he'd made a threat—a reminder that he was currently wearing the form of a very large predator.

"She wants to send you away to Arcadia, doesn't she?" the count asked slowly. "She doesn't intend to ever give you the mountain throne. It's what we've been afraid of for years, but we didn't have any choice. At least we thought we didn't have a choice if we wanted to break the..." His voice trailed off, and his eyes moved to his grandson.

Charlotte frowned. She was definitely missing something here. Possibly multiple somethings.

"Actually, she wants me to marry Prince Henry so I have a claim to the Arcadian throne," Gwen said, eliciting several gasps. "Obviously she intends for us to be puppet rulers, and it doesn't seem like her ambition ends with Arcadia. She sees herself in the role of empress. She talked about her kingdom stretching to the sea."

The count surged upward to stand on four feet. "Queen Celandine dreams of conquest?" A low, menacing growl rolled through the room.

Charlotte gulped, her back straightening. She had never lived in Arcadia, but she had spent years in Northhelm and Rangmere and had met honest, friendly, hardworking people in both places. Were their lives about to be overrun with war? Was Henry's kingdom about to be attacked?

She wanted to jump up and do something, but what could she possibly do? Her best hope to help Henry's kingdom was the same thing she had been aiming for from the beginning—rescue him from the mountain queen.

"So that's it." The count paced the width of the basement, only managing a few strides given his enormous size. "She hasn't been able to move forward with plans of conquest all these years since the enchantment has tied us to the mountains. No wonder she's getting desperate to break it."

Gwen sighed. "Sit down. Please. You're making me dizzy."

To Charlotte's surprise, the count complied. Maybe he really saw Gwen as an authority in the kingdom, and not just as a figurehead. The possibility must be even more overwhelming to Gwen than it was to Charlotte, but there was no question Gwen would make a better queen than her mother.

At least, that fact seemed obvious to Charlotte. But weren't the courtiers supposed to be loyal to the queen?

"Why are you all so desperate to break the enchantment?" Charlotte asked the count. "If you're not interested in conquest yourself, is it so bad to be stuck here or to be a bear if it's only at night?"

Natalie snorted, and Charlotte winced. "I understand why the people of the city must want it to end," she hurried to add, "but is it so terrible for the court? You seem to be fully in control of yourselves still, and you're only bears at night which is much better than it used to be for poor Henry. And isn't your bear form the only reason you're able to get through the mountain passes? What's the reason for the court being so desperate to free themselves?"

"It's me," Emmett said softly, inserting himself into the conversation for the first time. "I'm the reason." He looked down at his right leg where the trouser was pinned up just below his knee.

"You are not the reason," the count said firmly. "You are the miracle." He sighed, looking across at Charlotte with eyes that conveyed the sorrow of years. "Changing nightly appears to have no ill effect on our bodies—even the children who are caught in the enchantment have been able to grow in a normal way. Unfortunately, the same cannot be said for the unborn. We didn't realize initially, but as time passed it became increasingly clear that it was extremely difficult for an enchanted woman to become pregnant. And those babies that did manage to cling to life were harmed somehow in the process of the daily transformations. The effect has been different for each one, but..." He sighed again, glancing at his grandson's missing leg.

"I always wanted a brother or sister." Emmett shrunk in on himself, his food uneaten in his hand.

The count gave a rough growl in the back of his throat. "My son and his wife are desperate for more children but have been unsuccessful all these years. It grieves them greatly, although my daughters consider them fortunate to have even one. Neither of them has managed as much. I expected to have a bevy of grandchildren at my knee by now, but so far Emmett is the only one. And the years keep passing. We have to find a way to break the enchantment before it's too late for them to think of future children. But we cannot allow it to lead to war. I want to save my future grandchildren, but I have no desire to see my children pointlessly slaughtered in the process."

Gwen's mouth fell open, and Charlotte could tell this information was as new to her as it was to Charlotte.

"I understand why you don't want war," Gwen said. "I'm guessing your son would be expected to lead our forces. But the court not being able to have children of their own...How did I not...Is that why I saw so few children at court? I always thought the courtiers were just keeping them away. I never saw Emmett at court, after all."

The count nodded. "We do keep them away. Anyone fortunate enough to have a child tends to be protective of them. And no one wants to risk one of them saying the wrong thing and—" He broke off and looked at Easton.

"You don't want them to end up like me," Easton said grimly. "And my parents."

"I think your parents might be the fortunate ones," Charlotte muttered. "Didn't the queen exile them from court? Sounds like a reward from where I'm sitting."

"A reward for some, punishment for others," Natalie muttered.

"I think they're nice," Emmett said and then immediately looked mortified, the tips of his ears going red.

Easton looked between them. "Huh?"

Natalie glanced back at him and gave an exaggerated sigh. "They live with us now."

Easton straightened, his eyes widening. "My parents live with your family? Wha—how—?"

"That's a coincidence," Charlotte said lightly, looking between them.

"Not really," the count said. "I'm not denying Natalie did well for a girl her age, but there's a reason she went to the palace in the first place, and why she was able to find and connect with me. She knows a lot more about the palace and court than most fourteen-year-olds in the city."

"My parents are at your house right now?" Easton looked like he wanted to bolt straight out of the door.

Natalie rolled her eyes. "Relax. They'll still be there in the morning."

"But how did they end up—" Easton clearly couldn't relax.

"It used to be the other way around," Natalie said, sounding softer. "When I was very little, my parents both worked in your family's city mansion. Your parents treated them well, and when my mother first got sick they supported her, helped her get early treatment—although the doctors here didn't know how to treat it properly. So when your parents lost everything, my parents took them in without question." Her eyes narrowed. "That's why I've always had to share a room with my younger sister, you know. Our house isn't a mansion like your old one."

"Thank you." Easton held her eyes, his face and voice sincere. "Thank you from the bottom of my heart. I always hoped they were all right, but I feared…" He drew a deep breath. "Thank you. Will you take me to see them?"

Natalie softened even further, giving him a small smile. "I suppose I could manage that. It will be fun actually to see the lost son return." She brightened immediately, bouncing on her seat. "They're going to be so pleased with me for bringing you home. The count kept insisting the princess would return, and of course my parents believed it because they've always put their hope in her, and they wouldn't believe me when I said—" She cut herself off and glanced at Gwen. "Well, never mind that. The point is that no one was expecting *you* to return. They're going to be so surprised." Her grin spread across her face. "I bet our mothers will cook up a feast."

"You can take Easton to see his parents once it's daytime," the count said. "Just make sure he isn't seen by anyone outside the household." He looked across at Gwen. "Easton's parents have been a big part of gathering the rebellion in the city—such as it is. Natalie's home is a central location for our network. No one there will betray us."

"It will be good to see them again," Gwen said with what might have been a tentative smile. For all the remarkable expressiveness of the transformed bears, there were some subtleties of expression lost.

"I said Easton can go," the count said sharply. "Obviously you can't go, Your Highness. You have to return to the palace."

GWEN

There had been debate on the matter, naturally. Easton had taken more offense than Gwen herself over the count issuing her orders. Although his incensed response might have had more to do with the idea of Gwen putting herself in harm's way than any affront to her rank.

Charlotte had mostly stayed silent, but Gwen could read her thoughts in her eyes. She wanted Gwen to go to the palace because that was where Henry was being held. Her only issue was that the count was insisting Charlotte couldn't accompany her. But Charlotte wouldn't speak up, not when going might put Gwen in danger. Instead, she sat silently, leaving the debate to the count.

Natalie had weighed in once—she thought Gwen should do what needed to be done because no one else could do it. It was a sentiment so complete and final that Gwen wasn't surprised when Natalie immediately wandered away, losing interest in the conversation.

The count had plenty of arguments in favor of the plan, but in the end, Gwen agreed because of Natalie's simple statement. It was the same thought that had taken residence in her mind from the moment the count outlined his plan. Gwen had returned to the mountain kingdom to help her people because she was the heir to her mother's throne and therefore the one most able to help them. What was the point of her return if she shied away at the first hint of danger?

"I'll go," she said quietly. "Of course I will."

Easton went still, looking down at where she sat. He had stood some time ago, facing off with the count's enormous shape.

She could see he wanted to protest, but after a moment of eye contact, he ran his hand through his hair and collapsed back into his seat. Gwen wished she could take his hand.

"I can see why you were originally planning to send Gwen back," he said to the count. "When you still thought she needed to marry Prince Henry to break the enchantment, it made sense. But now we know the wedding isn't the answer, and yet you still want to follow through with the plan for Gwen to return to the palace undercover. What's the point of that when the queen also knows the wedding isn't the answer and even that Henry is already married? You seem convinced she isn't looking for Gwen just to get revenge or to eliminate her, but how can you be sure of that? If Gwen is needed as a spy to gather information, that tells me you don't actually know what the queen is thinking after all. So how can you guarantee Gwen's safety?"

Gwen sighed. The count had already explained his thinking, but Easton was finding it hard to accept. If Gwen was honest, she was as well. It didn't matter, though. She had to confront her mother. She could feel it down to her bones.

"Of course Queen Celandine needs Gwendolyn," the count snapped, his frustration finally breaking free. "That much is obvious. She's the center of all her plans."

Gwen frowned. She wanted to argue, but her mother had said basically the same thing.

The count looked warily between them before sighing. "You're right, there is more to my plan than I've said. I just wasn't sure…It seems obvious, but…"

Easton's eyes narrowed. "What plan?"

The count glanced at Emmett, who had lost interest in their circular dispute and gone after Natalie. The two were involved in some sort of conversation, but the count still lowered his voice.

"From what you've told us, Your Highness, I think the queen will still want to go ahead with your marriage to Prince Henry. She has too many plans for it. She won't hurt you because she needs you to make a public spectacle of the wedding."

"Prince Henry is already married," Charlotte said through her teeth, but the count barely looked her way.

"I hardly think that's likely to stop Queen Celandine from going after what she wants. Nothing has ever stopped her before."

"How will she maintain her position when the wedding takes place but the enchantment remains?" Easton asked. "It doesn't make any sense. She won't even be able to carry out her plans for conquest since you'll all still be tied to the mountains. Gwen marrying Prince Henry is the last thing we want." He glanced at Charlotte before suddenly stiffening. "Or is that your plan?" He swung back to face the count. "You want the kingdom to see that nothing changes when Gwen marries this prince? But even if you don't care about throwing away Gwen's future like that, what about the actual solution to the enchantment? Charlotte said it requires a royal marriage made with love. If you're ever going to be freed, then Gwen needs to—"

"That is exactly my new plan," the count said, watching first Easton and then Gwen with a careful expression, apparently unaffected by Easton's fresh indignation. "The princess returns to the palace and pretends compliance. We encourage the queen to make the wedding as grand and public an event as possible, and then—at the last possible second—we exchange the grooms. The queen has played into our hand by keeping the prince hidden away, and no one knows what you look like these days either, Easton. As long as we find a way to restrain Queen Celandine herself at the crucial moment, none of her loyal supporters will know the difference. And once the marriage is official, the enchantment will be lifted. It will be too late then to take back the marriage. Her plans for conquest will be dealt a crushing blow since you'll have a mountain husband with no tie to any of the lowland thrones."

Gwen's mind went blank. She stared straight ahead, afraid to move in case she caught Easton's eye. For the first time, she was glad she was in bear form since she didn't think bears could blush.

Gwen knew her marriage to Easton would successfully lift the enchantment. If all that was required was for her to look into Easton's eyes and feel nothing but love, then their wedding would be enough. She couldn't remember a time when her heart hadn't been filled with love for Easton.

But that didn't mean he wanted to marry her. He had always held her in affection, certainly, and his kiss back at Ranost suggested his affection had evolved beyond childish friendship. But they had been interrupted by Charlotte, and everything had moved so quickly since that there had been no time to discuss their impulsive moment and what it meant. How could the count just assume…

"You want me to step in and marry the princess?" Easton sounded as dazed as Gwen felt.

"Am I saying you're the king I would have chosen?" the count asked bluntly. "Hardly. But ending the enchantment is more important than choosing a king with connections. And you're not a total disaster. Given your parents' presence in the city, you've acquired an almost mythical status among the ordinary people: the boy who faced off against the queen and lived to tell the tale. You wouldn't believe some of the rumors about where you supposedly are and what you've been doing all these years. The people of the kingdom will accept you as king, and the courtiers will accept anyone who freed them from the enchantment."

Gwen finally looked up and took in the shock on Easton's face. Feeling affection for his playmate Gwen was one thing. Marrying Princess Gwendolyn just as her people conspired to put her on the throne was another matter entirely. She knew Easton loved her as a friend, and he had given her some indication he was interested in her as a woman as well, but that didn't mean he wanted to marry her—not when that meant finding himself jointly responsible for a kingdom in crisis.

He hadn't even explicitly said he intended to relocate to the mountain kingdom. He had a new life in Ranost. What if he had planned to return to it after he'd finished helping her?

She looked around the dirty basement, her eyes skating over her silent, wide-eyed friend and the determined count before resting on her own giant paws. Nothing about the setting was ideal for this conversation. This was not how she and Easton were supposed to talk about their feelings or their future plans.

When she looked up again, she found him looking at her. Their eyes caught and held, and Gwen was doubly glad a bear couldn't blush.

"Well?" the count asked brusquely. "If you marry Easton, will it release us from this enchantment?"

Gwen swallowed, tearing her eyes from Easton to face the other bear. "Yes," she managed to say, the word rough and awkward. As much as she hated the way they were being swept along, the stakes were too high for her to play coy.

She took several steadying breaths before she glanced back at Easton. His expression had changed to one of acceptance and determination, and nausea rose through her. Easton understood the stakes as well as she did. Whatever his personal feelings, he wouldn't refuse the role forced on him by her emotions. And he would never do anything to make her feel bad about it. So how was she ever going to find out his true wishes now?

"If Gwen and Easton getting married will release the enchantment, why don't you have them get married immediately?" Charlotte asked, startling Gwen out of her dark thoughts.

Gwen stared at her, somehow even more shocked than she'd already been. Marry Easton immediately? The idea was at once thrilling and terrifying.

"Why go to the risk of involving the queen and a bunch of subterfuge?" Charlotte continued. "If you do it as soon as it's light out, nothing can prevent the marriage taking place."

The count was already shaking his head before she finished. "If our only aim was to break the enchantment, that would make the most sense. But Queen Celandine is a powerful opponent with a trove of enchantments at her fingertips. If we quietly break the enchantment now, she'll easily take credit for it. That will weaken Princess Gwendolyn's position. As it is, the queen has set our chance up for us. She's the one who built up the princess's position as the kingdom's future savior, and we need to play into that narrative. As soon as the wedding takes place, we intend to put Gwendolyn on the throne—as we were promised—and we need to do everything we can to minimize any opposition."

Gwen swallowed. She had come back to save her kingdom because she was the heir, so she had understood what that meant, but it had felt like a distant and amorphous thing when she stood on the cliff in Ranost. Back in the mountain kingdom, talking specific plans with a senior member of court, it felt entirely too real. If they succeeded, she would become queen.

"So you want the spectacle for more than just the deception,"

Charlotte said slowly, sounding almost embarrassed at not having seen that for herself.

Gwen wished she could take her friend's hand and give it an encouraging squeeze as Charlotte had done for her. Given her own current feelings, it was easy to read Charlotte's emotions on her face. The girl from the valley had no experience with politics or intrigue and hadn't even known about her new title until two days ago. At least Gwen had always known she was intended to take the throne one day—even if that reality had seemed impossibly distant. How much more lost and out of her depth must Charlotte be feeling?

"But all of this still assumes the queen will go ahead with the wedding," Easton said. "How can we be sure she'll do it, knowing what she does about the enchantment?"

Gwen reminded herself that Easton had always been against the plan. He was worried about Gwen's safety, not looking for any excuse to get out of the proposed marriage.

"Actually," Charlotte said in a small voice, "I've been thinking about that." She turned to face Gwen. "What does Queen Celandine think of love?"

"Love?" Gwen frowned. "I..." She faltered, unsure how to answer the question.

A lifetime of interactions with her mother unfurled in her mind. Celandine had never shown Gwen a mother's love—she had only experienced warmth like that from Nanny. But it wasn't just Gwen. Celandine had always been there overseeing Gwen's life, but that meant Gwen had observed her mother's life for the last twenty years as well. And Gwen had never seen Celandine show love to anyone. On the rare occasions she had spoken of love, or the relationships of her own past, she had always used a scathing tone as if...

"I'm not sure she believes in love at all," Gwen said.

Charlotte swallowed, clearly uncomfortable. "I wondered if that might be the case. From everything you've said of her, and…" She paused again. "You said she knew about my existence and Henry's marriage, and she knew his godmother had told him a way to free himself from both enchantments, including the one tying him to her. And yet she claimed to know he would be returning soon. It sounded like…like she knew I would fail at the test of trust." Charlotte's eyes shone with unshed tears, but she pushed herself to continue. "But not even I knew that until the last moment. It was a rash decision, not a longstanding one. And the queen doesn't know me at all. That's why I've been sitting here wondering—maybe it has nothing to do with me specifically. Maybe she doesn't think anyone would have that kind of trust—she doesn't think anyone could love like that. And if she doesn't actually believe in love…"

"You think she's discounting that part of the godmother's words as…as meaningless fluff," Easton said thoughtfully.

Charlotte nodded. "If she thinks all that's needed is the actual marriage—followed by the two looking at each other, human eyes to human eyes—she may well believe that marrying Gwen to Henry will break the enchantment. It wouldn't have worked when he was a bear in the day and she was a bear at night, but now that he's free of the enchantment…"

"That lines up with everything I've seen of Celandine over the last two decades," the count said heavily. "She likes concrete realities and doesn't put much stock in emotions." His voice dropped to a mutter. "Sometimes it seems like she doesn't even have them."

"Then that's her mistake," Gwen said fiercely. "She'll never truly understand other people if she discounts emotions, and if she doesn't understand us, maybe she'll underestimate us."

"We're still making a lot of assumptions," Easton said. "We can't send Gwen to face her alone on the back of nothing but guesswork."

"Then what do you suggest instead?" the count asked sternly. "Did you perhaps bring an army across the mountains with you?

One that you've previously failed to mention and that won't be intimidated to face a force of giant bears?"

Easton shifted his weight, staying silent.

"I don't want to put anyone at risk, let alone the princess," the count said. "But we can't avoid all risks. The queen has pinned too much on her heir to eliminate her now. I'm confident she won't kill Gwendolyn, no matter how angry she is."

"I agree." Gwen tried not to think of what her mother might do instead. If she started thinking of small, dark spaces while they were stuck inside the basement, she might lose it.

But even if her mother did lock her up, she would have to endure it. An entire kingdom was depending on her.

Easton fell silent. From the look in his eyes, he still wasn't happy about the plan, but he knew when he was past hope of convincing the rest of them.

"What about me, then?" Charlotte still sounded subdued. "I came here to rescue Henry, but I'm just supposed to sit in this basement instead?"

"Not here." Natalie suddenly reappeared, her nose wrinkling. "This place isn't set up for long term anything. You'll have to come back to my house with Easton." She looked Easton up and down, her lips pursed and eyes narrowed. "But if the plan revolves around no one knowing he's returned or what he looks like, we can't go waltzing through the front door."

"The plan...?" the count asked carefully.

Natalie rolled her eyes. "I was standing on the other side of the room, not down the street. If the plan was supposed to be such a big secret, you shouldn't have talked about it right in front of me." She propped both hands on her hips. "And it's a good thing you've got me anyway. You and the toddler over there will be heading back to your fancy manor soon, and it's going to be up to me to keep these two under wraps."

"Hey! I'm not a toddler!" Emmett protested, but Natalie ignored him.

"We'll have to go before it gets light," she said.

"I thought bears patrolled the streets overnight," Charlotte said cautiously. "Aren't we supposed to stay inside until morning?"

"They do, but come on—they're not on every street at once." Natalie eyed the window consideringly. "If we leave just before dawn, there will be even fewer because some of the patrols always cheat and head back early. On the other hand, if we wait until after sunrise, the people will flood out of their houses and there really will be someone on every street. If we want to get back unseen, we need to go while it's still dark. It would be one thing if I had brought giant cloaks or something to disguise you all, but I didn't know I'd need to do that."

"Is that really wise?" Easton looked to the count.

He sighed. "It's not ideal, but she might be right. I don't spend a lot of time in this part of the city during the day, but the streets have been busy whenever I've come."

"Relax." Natalie snorted. "I'm not suggesting you hand your plans and your whole future over to a fourteen-year-old. I'm just going to sneak you through five streets and across one square. Then I'll hand you over to the grown-ups."

Something about her tone told Gwen they wouldn't get rid of the younger girl so easily, but she stayed silent. Natalie was Gwen's opposite in so many ways, but Gwen couldn't help wondering if she might have turned out more like the other girl if she had been free of her mother's influence. It was an unanswerable question, but Gwen liked Natalie all the same. At least someone was willing to take bold action and state their opinion without hesitation or pretense.

"If the plan is settled, Emmett and I will head home now," the count said. "I need to make some preparations before the missing princess returns. The rest of you should try to get some sleep. It will be many hours before it's time for Easton and Charlotte to head out. And Gwen, you'll be the last to leave. It's essential you not be seen until you're human again. Most of the kingdom still believe you escaped the enchantment."

"The pure princess who's going to save everyone," Gwen muttered, wishing she could say the words with any kind of conviction.

But it was too late for her to quibble now. She had committed herself to the count's plan, and she would have to see it through.

CHARLOTTE

*L*eaving Gwen alone in the dirty basement felt wrong. Especially when Charlotte was leaving with Gwen's… betrothed? She wasn't sure if that was the right term for them, but they had both agreed to the plan, so it seemed to fit better than anything else. Charlotte just wished she could have had a proper conversation with Gwen about it—one that didn't involve Easton and Natalie listening in.

"Are you sure…Are you sure we should just leave?" Charlotte asked instead, looking reluctantly at Gwen.

Her friend forced out a laugh. "Don't make me say it again! This is the plan. I'll be fine waiting in an empty room on my own."

But from Gwen's face, she was as aware as Charlotte that neither of them were worried about the extra hour or two of waiting. It was the part that came after. She wrapped her arms around Gwen's enormous bear neck and gave her a tight hug.

"You can do this," she whispered. "And you won't be alone once you reach the palace, right? You'll have Alma and the others?"

Gwen twitched beneath her arms, confirming Charlotte's

"

earlier suspicion. She'd noticed her friend hadn't mentioned her alliance with the captive servants to the count, and it hadn't taken much thought to come up with a reason why.

They had arrived in the mountain kingdom mere hours ago, and so far the only assurance they had that the count was telling the truth was Natalie's corroboration. Could they be one hundred percent sure it wasn't some elaborate scheme orchestrated by Queen Celandine? Charlotte couldn't think of a reason why the queen would do something so complex, but that didn't mean she entirely trusted the count either.

She couldn't say anything aloud—not in front of Natalie, and not in front of Easton. If it occurred to Easton this might all be a deception, he would never agree to leave Gwen.

"Don't worry," Charlotte whispered, too quiet for a human to hear, but knowing Gwen's enhanced bear hearing would pick up her words. "I won't say anything about them to anyone. There's no harm in having an extra card to play if something goes wrong."

Gwen nodded almost imperceptibly. "Thank you," she said aloud, and her words rang with sincerity.

Charlotte gave her a final squeeze and stepped back, thinking Easton might want to take her place. He remained where he was, however, merely meeting Gwen's eyes with an intense gaze.

"Stay safe." His voice was low and rough.

She nodded, appearing unable to answer with words.

Charlotte waited another moment, but when neither of them moved, she tugged lightly on Easton's arm. "Come on." It would only get harder the longer they lingered.

At first, Easton didn't budge, his eyes still fixed on Gwen. But finally he relaxed, bowing to the princess before he followed after Natalie and Charlotte with quick strides.

In the doorway, Charlotte looked back one final time at Gwen. The bear was looking at the small group of them.

"Don't worry," Gwen said with a faint smile. "I'll find your Henry for you."

Charlotte managed a return smile before Natalie pulled her out of the door.

After so long in the stuffy basement, Charlotte should have been glad for the open air and space. But she'd spent too many hours in growing fear of the strange city patrolled by giant bears. Now that she was standing in the street, she felt dangerously exposed.

At least dawn wasn't far away. The deep black of night had given way to dark gray, and regular streetlights broke the darkness even further. Or maybe she should be regretting the presence of streetlights? Weren't they supposed to be in hiding?

Charlotte shook her head. Subterfuge was outside her experience.

"Come on!" Natalie hissed, waving Easton and Charlotte forward. Charlotte wasn't the only one lingering near the door of the basement—although Charlotte suspected Easton had a different reason for being reluctant to move away from the relative safety behind them.

Charlotte reminded herself who she was doing everything for: Henry. If she couldn't even brave a dark street for him, how did she hope to snatch him from the mountain queen?

Scampering after Natalie, she caught up with the younger girl at the closest street corner. Natalie was peering around it, her other hand held up to signal for Charlotte to wait behind her.

Charlotte's nerves thrummed as she waited, wondering what Natalie could see. It was hard to resist the instinct to push forward and see for herself.

Easton's steadying presence arrived at her back, helping to calm her. She felt safer with someone on either side, even though she knew it was just an illusion.

Whatever Natalie saw on the other street must have satisfied her because she gestured them forward. The three crept onto the larger street in single file.

Charlotte tried to step quietly, but Natalie quickly outpaced her. Apparently the other girl was going for speed over silence. Charlotte increased her speed to match, cringing at every footfall.

When they reached the next corner, Natalie's check was much shorter. She had barely peered around the edge before she was gesturing them forward again.

"Wait," Charlotte whispered. "Shouldn't we be more..." She fell silent when Natalie ignored her. Reluctantly, she put on another spurt of speed to catch the other girl instead.

"Natalie!" Easton hissed from behind Charlotte.

She wasn't the only one confused and uncomfortable. Weren't they supposed to be creeping through the streets unseen?

But Natalie didn't pause again until they were on the edge of a cobbled square. This time Charlotte was able to peer over her shoulder, and she caught herself looking for the fountain that usually marked the middle of town squares. Instead of a fountain, however, this square held only the statue of an imposing woman wearing a crown. Charlotte grimaced. She supposed it made sense not to have a fountain in a place where the temperature must often be below freezing. But she would have preferred not to creep right under Queen Celandine's eyes—even if they were just stone versions.

Natalie glanced quickly up and down the square before shrugging and striding openly across its center.

"Natalie!" Easton hissed again, with more force if not more volume.

The younger girl didn't flinch or look back, though, so after a resigned shrug, Charlotte and Easton both hurried after her. As they crossed the open space, Charlotte flicked glances at the surrounding buildings. It wasn't only stone eyes that watched them but also the closed shutters of too many windows to count.

It didn't matter how many times she told herself she was being fanciful—they felt like a real presence tracking the progress of the small group.

"Shouldn't we stick to the edge?" she whispered to Natalie as she finally caught up with the other girl. They had made it more than halfway across the square, but Charlotte's skin was crawling so badly she could barely walk straight.

"I hear something," Easton whispered sharply, and Natalie finally responded.

Grabbing Charlotte's sleeve, she cried, "Run!" without bothering to lower her voice. Pulling Charlotte with her, she veered sideways. Instead of making for the continuation of the main road that had appeared to be their goal, she threw them both sideways toward what looked like nothing but a deep shadow.

Charlotte barely kept herself from screaming as they careened toward the black space. At the last second, she perceived a narrow alley, its entrance blocked by an abandoned cart missing a wheel.

Natalie let go of Charlotte's sleeve, glancing once over her shoulder to check Easton was with them. As Charlotte turned to look as well, Natalie was already leaping up the cart, cresting it in two bounds.

Behind her, Charlotte could hear the local girl hissing for her to hurry and follow, but she couldn't turn back around. Easton was heading their way, and he had obviously taken a few beats to grasp what was happening. He was no longer alone in the square.

Behind him, two large, white figures lumbered across the open space, closing the gap with terrifying speed. Easton saw the look on her face and faltered, turning to glance behind him.

"No!" Charlotte screamed, all her fear forgotten in the panic of the moment.

Their whole plan depended on no one knowing Easton's face. He couldn't let himself be seen.

Her cry brought his face forward again, halting his motion

before he had fully turned. She flung herself in his direction. Catching him off guard, she seized the front of his shirt and yanked him toward the alley with all her strength. She used the momentum, sending him behind her while she staggered into the square.

Their positions had now been reversed. Easton was at the base of the cart, being urged by Natalie to "Climb! Climb!" while Charlotte was bringing up the rear of the group.

She spun and dashed to follow him. When he faltered, one foot on the cart, one still on the cobblestones, she screamed at him to go.

He complied, pulling himself up with a grunt. He looked like he was going to stop at the top to help pull Charlotte up, but Natalie must have had the same realization as Charlotte. Her wiry hands appeared out of the darkness, pulling him down the other side of the cart.

Charlotte threw herself the final couple of steps, her hands reaching for the side of the cart. But as they made contact with the round wood, she felt hot breath behind her followed by a tearing pain down her left arm.

She screamed, the cry splitting the night as red splattered across the cart. Immobilized by pain, she froze, but the wiry hands reappeared, pulling her forward. Wrenched into movement, she lurched up, somehow finding the strength to climb the side of the cart.

A change in the air pressure and a panting breath made her duck instinctively forward. The second stroke of the huge clawed paw missed her, hitting the cart instead.

The entire structure crumbled, smashed to pieces by the bear's force. Charlotte tumbled down among the splintered pieces of wood. She twisted at the last moment, landing on her right side to shield her injured left arm.

The shock and pain of the landing held her still as the bear roared and struck at the cart again, reducing it even further into kindling. For a second, her eyes caught on his black ones, and then Natalie was behind her, hauling her to her feet.

"Come on!" she cried. "Run!"

The bear lunged forward, but the alley was even narrower than Charlotte had originally realized. She and Natalie could barely fit down it single file, her shoulders almost brushing the brick wall of the buildings on either side. It must have been a tight squeeze for Easton, who had already disappeared, presumably sent ahead by Natalie.

The bear roared again in frustration, and Natalie urged her to move faster, even shoving her in the back when she slowed. They burst out the other side of the alley onto a new street. Easton waited for them there, his eyes glued to the alley entrance, clearly having been debating if he should go back.

Natalie hissed at him wordlessly and took the lead. Abandoning the last of any pretense at quiet or subtlety, she sprinted down the street and careened around the second corner she encountered.

Easton took one look at Charlotte's injured arm and scooped her off her feet, running after Natalie.

"I can run myself," Charlotte wheezed through the pain. Her injured arm was jammed against his chest, and it was only increasing the agony.

"I know," Easton said through hard breaths. "It's your arm that's injured, not your leg. But there's no time to bind the wound, and we can't leave a trail of blood."

Charlotte fell silent, realizing why he had positioned her in such a painful way. She bit her tongue on the cries that tried to work their way out of her as he ran. She would be in worse pain if they didn't escape the bears.

When they rounded the corner, Natalie was waving them forward from halfway down the street where she stood in what appeared to be a public water trough for the city's horses. When

Easton reached her, he dumped Charlotte on her feet in the trough and climbed up after her.

Natalie nodded approvingly and sloshed through the water. When she reached the other end of the long trough, she clambered out again, landing on a long length of rough fabric. Charlotte attempted to follow, only to have her knees give out at a fresh wave of pain, sending her splashing down into the water.

Easton braced her from behind, putting his hands under her arms and lifting her over the edge of the trough in one swift movement. As soon as she had her balance, she shuffled forward on the material, making room for him to follow.

Natalie had already run the length of the material, disappearing down yet another narrow alley. Charlotte gritted her teeth and forced her legs to work, clasping the gash on her left arm with her right in an attempt to keep too much blood from oozing out.

As soon as she'd rounded the corner, she saw the material led to an open door. Natalie stood just inside, waving Charlotte forward with urgency. She half ran the final steps, staggering inside with Easton crowding in behind her.

He seemed to have understood what was happening much more clearly than her, because the second he was inside, he turned and began pulling on the material. Someone behind them seemed to be helping him, because it whisked inside impossibly fast. As soon as the last length made it past the threshold, Natalie closed the door behind them.

"Phew!" she breathed, sinking to the floor and breathing hard. "That was too close." She looked up accusingly. "How are you two so slow?!"

"We need help here!" Easton called down the dark corridor in front of them. "Someone's injured!"

He grabbed a towel off a nearby chair and folded it several times, pressing it to Charlotte's wound. She looked down, planning to take over with her good arm. But instead her head spun, and she nearly collapsed again.

This time Natalie propped her up from behind with an exasperated huff. "The cut didn't look that bad," she muttered, but Charlotte could hear the guilt in her tone.

"What. Was. That?" Easton asked threateningly, his eyes spearing into Natalie.

Charlotte didn't have the energy for his outrage, but she nodded supportively. "I thought we were supposed to be creeping through the city unnoticed." She wished she sounded more indignant and less exhausted.

"Unnoticed?" Natalie snorted. "I guess you two don't know much about bears. Do you have any idea how well they hear? Well, their hearing is nothing on how well they smell! It wasn't a matter of not being noticed so much as *when* we were noticed. I had to time it so we were most of the way across the square. Thankfully this city has a collection of ridiculously narrow alleys that date from before patrols were done by bears."

Charlotte finally caught up to what must have been apparent to Easton from the beginning.

"The water and the material…that was to throw off our scent trail? So it wouldn't lead them to this house?"

Natalie nodded. "When I first spotted you in the air, I sent word to both the count and my family. My family knew there was a chance I might have to return at night, so they had someone listening out. Thankfully, that fool guard made more than enough noise roaring away at us. So they got the material laid out before we reached the trough." She shook her head. "It wouldn't have been such a close thing if you two had moved a bit faster, though."

"Charlotte is injured," Easton said through his teeth. "And maybe we would have been more prepared if you'd considered *warning us.*"

Natalie looked between the two of them doubtfully before

shrugging. "Or maybe one or both of you would have refused to set foot out of the basement if you'd known you were about to be chased through the city by a patrol of bears. I don't know you that well, so how could I say?"

"You—" Easton stepped toward her, but the arrival of several people distracted him from whatever scolding he was intending.

"Someone's injured?" A woman bustled forward, her focus on Charlotte. "Oh, you are too! You poor dear!"

The man moved to Natalie instead, glowering at Easton. Easton met his gaze coolly, not backing down.

"I got the material laid out for you," the man said. "So how did someone end up injured? They're not about to break down our door, are they?"

"I told you, Da," a bored voice said from further along the corridor. "We got it pulled in well before any of the patrols worked out where they were. They're always confounded by those alleys." He had the superior tone of late adolescence, a youth hovering on the edge of manhood.

When he stepped forward into the light, Charlotte could place him instantly. There was no doubting he was Natalie's older brother given the similarity in their coloring and features.

The young man gave his sister a lazy nod, and she narrowed her eyes in response. Apparently his assistance in retrieving the material hadn't won him any points in her eyes. Charlotte could relate to the prickly sibling dynamic.

"Nice to see you helping—for once," Natalie said.

The youth's eyes narrowed. "What was the other option? Let you bring the bears straight to our door? I don't have a death wish, you know."

Natalie's voice turned mockingly sweet. "I know it's just that you love your family soooo much. Admit it! You've been worrying about me all night."

"Ew! Get off me!" The youth tried to fend her off as she surged forward and pulled him into a hug.

Charlotte's heart dropped. The prickly antagonism between Natalie and her brother was merely one layer of their relationship. But Charlotte's sister's taunts hadn't been a façade for a deeper well of affection.

She swayed, lightheaded. It was a struggle to fight against the pain and not make any embarrassing sounds of distress.

The woman—who must be Natalie's mother—tutted and pressed more tightly on the towel, which only made Charlotte sway again.

"How did you end up injured?" she asked, the question sounding much softer and more sympathetic on her lips than it had on her husband's.

But the reminder caused Natalie's father to throw another suspicious look at both Charlotte and Easton. Another male voice sounded from the end of the corridor.

"Dane, Patti, why don't you bring them in? There'll be time enough to hear how she was injured once they're settled."

Easton stiffened at the sound of the voice. For one lingering second, he continued to match stares with Natalie's father, and then he slowly turned to face the newcomer. "She was injured," he said, "protecting me."

A woman from further inside the house gave a muffled scream just as Natalie's mother removed the towel from Charlotte's arm. Charlotte looked down at the red that spurted from her gashed arm, felt a surge of pain, and blackness rushed over her, claiming all her senses.

CHARLOTTE

$\mathcal{C}$harlotte came around slowly, grogginess making everything fuzzy for several seconds. Logically, she knew she couldn't have passed out for more than a minute or two, but thankfully someone—or multiple someones—had used that time to move her the rest of the way into the house and lay her down on a sofa.

Natalie's mother—had someone called her Patti?—had even produced some bandages and was in the process of binding the wound properly. She tutted to herself quietly as she secured the final knot.

Charlotte sucked in a breath, but the pain quickly receded to a more manageable throbbing ache now she wasn't being jostled around.

"Does it need stitches?" she managed in a quavering voice.

"You woke up." Natalie stated the fact without emotion, wandering over to gaze down at Charlotte. "For a second, I thought you'd died."

Patti heaved herself to her feet, rolling her eyes at her daughter. "There's no need to be so dramatic, my dear. Of course she wasn't going to die over a little gash like that."

"Little," Charlotte repeated in the same faint voice, trying to get a proper look at her bandage. "Is it going to need stitches?"

"Don't you worry." Patti gave her a comforting pat. "It's bad enough I thought it might need stitches at first, but now that I've had a good look, I think you'll be all right after all. Which is a good thing since we don't have any doctors on hand. I've seen plenty of gashes in my time, and that one should heal up just fine. I've slathered it in salve—it's one we make ourselves from a plant found only in the high mountains. It's better than anything you have in the lowlands for healing wounds, or so I've heard. Our salve fetches a very pretty price when the traders take it through those new passes."

"Oh." Charlotte felt like her brain was packed with cotton wool.

She tried to pull herself up to a sitting position, and Patti swooped in to help her. Once she was upright, she had to wait a moment for another head rush to die down before she could get a proper look at the room.

She was sitting in a living room of medium size and full of furnishing that wasn't new but instead looked well used and comfortable. Overall it was a welcoming place, but her focus skipped over the room itself to the three people standing several steps away.

Natalie's father and brother had disappeared, so the only one of the three she recognized was Easton. And she nearly didn't recognize him since his back was to her and most of his body was obscured due to the hug he was receiving from the older woman. She had tears running down her face and appeared to have no plans to let go anytime soon.

The man looked equally shaken, standing close and alternating between patting Easton on the back and the woman on the shoulder. He was the only one whose face Charlotte could properly see, and he looked remarkably like—

"Are those Easton's parents?" she asked, feeling a sweeping

wave of emotion. No wonder the woman looked like she would never let him go again. They must have spent ten years fearing for him.

Natalie rolled her eyes, but she couldn't wipe the grin off her face. "I knew it was going to be satisfying to bring him home. Aunt Lydia is going to shrivel up after losing all that moisture."

Charlotte gave her a knowing smile. She had talked as if having Easton's parents in her home was a burden, but it was obvious she actually held them in affection.

She cackled. "Uncle Jett doesn't even know what to do with himself." She raised her voice. "Oi! She's awake! Are you finished over there?"

"Oh, leave them be," Charlotte protested, but it was too late.

Easton's mother finally broke off the hug, and Easton quickly turned to face the rest of the room. Charlotte bit back a grin when she saw his look of relieved rescue. He must have shared their concern that his mother was never going to stop crying.

His mother rushed immediately to Charlotte's side, dropping to her knees beside the sofa and warmly clasping her right hand.

"Thank you, thank you," she said wetly. "I heard you protected our Easton. I'm Lydia, by the way." She glanced up at her husband, who had followed her at a more decorous pace. "And this is Jett. You have our gratitude."

Charlotte smiled weakly and extracted her hand. "To be honest, I didn't really do it for him."

Lydia stood slowly, glancing between Easton and Charlotte. "You're not..." When Charlotte looked blank, she gestured between them. "The two of you aren't..."

"A couple?" Charlotte asked, finally realizing what she was trying to imply. "Oh goodness, no. I'm married. To someone else. Of course I didn't want the bears to hurt Easton, but I didn't jump in because of him. I did it for Henry. And Gwen too, of course. It's because the plan hinges on Easton not being recognized."

"The…plan?" Lydia and Jett exchanged a look of bewildered incomprehension.

Easton grimaced. "We hadn't gotten to the explaining part yet."

Charlotte grinned guiltily. "I'm gathering that." She tried to swallow the smile. "The crying part seemed to be lasting a while."

Easton rubbed the back of his neck, and she relented. "Of course it would! You haven't seen each other for ten years! I think you should be the one to explain everything, though."

"Wait!" Patti cried. "We should get Dane and Baden first. Natalie, you run and fetch them."

Natalie looked like she was about to protest but thought better of it and left the room. Within less than a minute she returned with only her father in tow. Her mother looked as if she was going to say something, but when she saw Natalie's defiant expression, she sighed and remained silent.

Natalie sat on the sofa beside Charlotte. "Fetch Baden? What a joke," she muttered. "When everyone knows he barely tolerates all this stuff." She waved around them.

"The rebellion, you mean?" Charlotte whispered back, eyebrows raised.

Natalie snorted. "He's at that age where he thinks he knows better than everyone. He's convinced we're going to get ourselves killed." She rolled her eyes contemptuously, while Charlotte stared at her.

Baden thought he knew better than everyone? She blinked several times in rapid succession wondering if there was anything to be said in response to such a statement from Natalie. She concluded there wasn't.

"You don't agree with him?" she whispered instead, curious. "You're not worried about the risk?"

Natalie gave her a contemptuous look. "The only thing I can't understand is why it's taken the grown-ups so long. If you want something to change, it's simple. Change it."

Charlotte sat back, not sure whether to laugh or cry. Had she ever possessed the naive certainty that exuded from Natalie? The girl was so clearly young, and yet at the same time, she'd already achieved more in her life than Charlotte had done. Could she really dispute Natalie's philosophy?

While the two of them were whispering, Easton had started the explanation to the older couples. When he got to the part of their plan where he married Gwen and became king, the story broke down, overwhelmed by their exclamations. He eventually had to start again and explain it all to his mother a second time.

"You will be king?" Jett asked, clearly incredulous. "Our son?"

"It wasn't my idea," Easton said, sounding defensive. "But if we want to break the enchantment..." He trailed off, running a hand through his hair. Clearly he lacked the confidence to baldly state that he was the only one Gwen loved and therefore the only one who could break the enchantment with her.

"It's not a terrible idea," Patti said thoughtfully.

Her husband threw her a look, and she shrugged. "You know how the people of the city talk about Easton. And even if their ideas are fanciful, it's true that at only thirteen he had the courage to stand up to Celandine. Who else in the kingdom can say that? And he and his family have suffered at her hands. They have the bloodlines to satisfy the courtiers and the credibility to be accepted by the city folk."

Dane nodded slowly. "As always, you speak wisdom, my dear."

Patti winked at Lydia, who smiled warmly back. "If we have any standing here in the city, it's because of your family's support."

"Support that you've earned," Patti said firmly. "And that you've worked tirelessly to repay. You haven't had an idle day since you came here."

Charlotte stood to her feet, unable to take any more.

"Speaking of idle days," she said. "Are we really supposed to sit around here and do nothing while we wait to see what happens to Gwen?"

As soon as she spoke Gwen's name, Easton tensed.

"No," he said shortly. "Obviously we can't do that."

"If you're going to be accepted as king, we'll need to make some discreet introductions," Dane said. "Let people know you're back."

"No," Charlotte said sharply. "That's the opposite of what we're supposed to be doing. We have to keep his identity—and even his return—a secret."

"A secret from the queen's supporters," Jett said. "But we have to think beyond the wedding. Just succeeding in the marriage won't be enough. We still need to put them on the throne. And for that we need supporters. We'll be careful and keep the circle small. Just the most influential among the rebels. The people we need to speak up in our support at the crucial moment."

Charlotte bit her lip. His words sounded sensible, but her instincts still protested. The more people who knew, the more likely someone would make a mistake. If this was their only chance to free Henry, then everything needed to go perfectly.

"What about me?" she blurted out instead of the protests she really wanted to make. "What am I supposed to do?"

No one answered, looks of discomfort on their faces. They felt for her situation, but they didn't need her for what they were trying to accomplish.

When they began a conversation about who to introduce first, an unexpected arm slid through hers. "You're with me," Natalie said quietly. "Someone has to plug the rather glaring hole in the count's plan."

"Hole?" Charlotte asked.

Natalie raised an eyebrow. "The bit where the queen is restrained at the crucial moment during the ceremony, of course. Were you thinking that would be easy to achieve?"

Charlotte blinked. "No, I'm guessing not. With so much going on, I hadn't thought yet about—"

"Exactly." Natalie gave a long-suffering sigh. "I'm fairly sure everyone is hoping one of the others will think of a solution for that. So I guess that means it's up to us."

Charlotte shook her head. This was the girl who thought everything was possible. Charlotte should definitely be interjecting some realism into the situation.

Natalie lowered her voice. "I'm thinking we'll need to sneak into the palace grounds as a starter. We're not going to be able to restrain her without more information on both her and those enchantments she's got locked up."

The protest died in Charlotte's throat. Go to the palace, to Henry? She felt no desire to talk Natalie out of that.

Natalie gave her a sly smile as if she knew exactly what Charlotte was thinking. Internally, Charlotte winced. Natalie had clearly been waiting for a partner in crime as reckless as herself, and a more sensible part of Charlotte knew she shouldn't encourage the other girl.

But it didn't matter what sensible thoughts Charlotte tried to think. Henry was in the palace right now. It had been too long since she'd seen him, and she couldn't bear to sit in Natalie's house waiting for someone else to figure out a way to rescue him. Easton could meet the rebels and make connections. Charlotte was going to do what she'd come to the mountain kingdom to do —she was going after her husband.

"So," Queen Celandine said in deceptively gentle tones, "you've returned."

She gazed down from her throne, meeting Gwen's eyes with an outward calm that met Gwen's own. It unnerved Gwen more than anger would have done. She knew her mother was furious with her. She had to be. And yet nothing in the queen's manner gave it away.

Celandine had always been the same—at least for all of Gwen's life. It was the reason Gwen had learned from an early age how to wear a composed mask in her mother's presence. Celandine didn't give way to emotion, and she didn't appreciate others who were unable to do likewise—even small children.

To Gwen it had always made the queen's cruelties more chilling since they were done without the heat of emotion behind them. Celandine didn't lash out in anger or pain, hurting people and then regretting it later. Everything she did was done with calm intention.

The queen rose from the throne in one smooth movement, and it took all Gwen's training not to flinch. Behind her gently upturned lips, she was clenching her teeth as her mother descended the steps toward her.

When the queen wrapped her arms lightly around Gwen and placed her cheek against Gwen's own, she waited for the poisonous words to be whispered in her ear.

They never came. And in the empty room, there was no need for the queen to hide her malice anyway. Anything she had to say she could have said from the throne.

Gwen frowned slightly, too confused to entirely hold herself in. She had never been as good at the skill as her mother.

"You have returned in excellent time," her mother almost purred, and for the first time Gwen wondered if her mother's relief at her reappearance was so great that it outweighed any anger.

A little of the heaviness inside her lifted. If Celandine was that relieved, then the state of the court must be even more fragile than Gwen had realized. Maybe they really could succeed at outwitting the queen.

"I'm sure you'll understand that your actions have destroyed my trust in you," Celandine said silkily. "I'm most disappointed. Naturally you will need to be closely watched."

Gwen's voluminous dress concealed several deep pockets, and she thrust her hand into one solely so she could clench her fingers into a fist. In the process, they brushed against something round and cool. For a second, Gwen forgot to focus on her mother, her mind scrambling to make sense of the object. Then memory returned in a rush.

The golden apple given to her by the godmother. She had forgotten she still had it in her pocket.

Unease gripped her. She should have left it with Easton or Charlotte. Bringing it into the presence of the queen had been foolhardy. Gwen had seen how much Celandine valued godmother objects. She wouldn't hesitate to claim it if she discovered what Gwen had in her possession.

Wrapping her hand around the cool sphere, she drew several calming breaths, trying to slow her racing heart before it gave her away. But the movement proved more distracting than settling.

The moment her fingers closed around the apple, her awareness shifted. She couldn't have said what sense she was using, but she was suddenly gripped by the knowledge that the queen also carried a godmother object in her pocket.

Although she had no memory of seeing it in the queen's display room, she could easily call up an image of it in her mind's eye. The plaited multi-strand length of cord was about six inches long and included several colors along its woven length. To outward appearance, it was a useless item, but Gwen hummed with the awareness of its power. It could—

She frowned. She could feel the awareness almost there, hovering on the edge of her mind, just out of reach.

She let go of the apple, and the awareness of the cord in the queen's pocket immediately vanished. Gwen tried to call its image to mind again, but it was hazy and indistinct.

She blinked, trying to focus on her mother's face and keep her own features steady. When she touched the apple for a second time, the calm façade was difficult to hold, almost overwhelmed as the awareness of her mother's object came flooding instantly back.

At least she had confirmed the new knowledge definitely came from the apple. Did that mean its purpose was to reveal the presence of other godmother objects? Gwen couldn't help a sinking disappointment. For one brief moment when she'd remembered the apple's existence, she had hoped it might turn the tide against the queen. But apparently it was better for little more than a parlor trick.

"Are you even listening to me?" the queen asked, her eyes tightening for the first time.

"Yes, Mother. Of course." The words slid out easily, the product of instinct, but the title left a burning aftertaste. Gwen had rejected Celandine's role in her life only the day before, but it wasn't so easy to reject her to her face.

"Of course," her mother repeated, but the tightness hadn't left her face.

For a moment, they both remained motionless, Gwen barely breathing as she waited to see her mother's next action. It seemed impossible that they weren't even going to mention Gwen's flight, and yet the queen seemed ready to sweep the whole thing under the rug. As if, by returning, Gwen had absolved herself of her past misconduct.

But it couldn't possibly be so easy.

The queen straightened, pulling something out of her pocket. The movement dislodged something else, sending it slipping to the ground.

For a second, Gwen's eyes caught on a multi-colored strand before Celandine swooped down and retrieved it, thrusting it quickly back out of sight. Gwen hadn't missed the shape of it, though. It was exactly like the object she had just seen in her mind. The apple's revelation had been real.

Gwen barely had time to feel the thrill of confirmation before her mother held up the item she had been retrieving from her pocket. A brass key.

Gwen's insides froze, her breath stuttering. She had been right. Her mother didn't mean to forgive her flight. She was going to punish her. She was going to lock her in the dark. She was going to—

"Come with me," the queen said commandingly, sweeping toward the doors of the throne room.

Gwen trailed obediently behind, her brain still circling around the key and her coming imprisonment. Was the queen leading her somewhere even smaller than the closet where she had spent the days after Easton's disappearance? Would she be confined for an even longer time?

Gwen reminded herself to breathe, only for her head to grow

dizzy. She had made the opposite mistake and was breathing much too fast. She would lose her sanity inside whatever tiny hole her mother intended to imprison her in. This time Easton would come for her, but it would be too late. The Gwen he knew would have dissolved.

Her mother stopped in front of a door, and Gwen's brows lowered. It looked...familiar? Her panicked brain took a moment to comprehend what she was seeing. They stood in front of her own room.

"This is..." She didn't finish the sentence before her mother used the key to open the door and then stood aside and gestured for her to enter.

Gwen walked inside without conscious thought, the familiar environment flooding her with relief and reassurance.

"There are matters I must attend to," Queen Celandine said from the doorway with her previous calm indifference. "I'm sure you'll understand why I would like you to await me here." She paused. "You might like to know that the lock has been changed. This is now the only key."

Gwen nodded, still riding high on relief. She was only being confined to her room—her room that had windows and light and more than enough space to move. Her room that had a comfortable bed. She could have thrown her arms around her mother's neck and hugged her.

With a small smile, the queen withdrew, leaving her daughter to stagger over to the window seat, still reeling as the key turned in the lock. The familiarity of the view calmed her, and for a long moment she sat there, absorbing the sunlight that streamed through the glass and enjoying its warmth.

She was safe after all. Her mother hadn't shut her inside the closet. She had only—

Locked her in her room.

Gwen frowned. Her mother had sent Gwen to her room as if

she was a rebellious child. She had even locked her in. And Gwen had been thanking her! She had been grateful to her!

A slow tide of fury rose inside Gwen, moving slowly like creeping lava but burning just as hot. The queen had manipulated her. She knew of Gwen's fears, and she had showed her the key purposely to make her think she was being punished. And then she had delivered her to her room instead. If her fear hadn't been overpowering Gwen's mind, she would have been incensed to be locked in her room. Instead, she was relieved and grateful. She had been grateful to her mother! She had even thought of her as her mother again.

Gwen shivered. Celandine wasn't overlooking her rebellion, but her methods were subtle, not overt. She was manipulating Gwen as easily as she had always done, tearing her down and then reassuring her in just the right balance. And Gwen had fallen straight back into her old patterns, just like she had feared she would.

She paced up and down the room, storming and raging silently to herself. She had to be more aware. She couldn't let herself be sucked into her old thought patterns just because she had returned to a familiar environment.

As the hours dragged on and exhaustion set in, Gwen realized her mistake. She had thought her old mask would serve her best, so she had gone along with her mother's pretense of amity between them. But in their old roles, the queen had all the advantages. Gwen was in the process of making herself into a new person, but the familiar environment made it too hard to resist the strength of her old habits. She couldn't stand in the same rooms and interact with her mother in the same way as before and trust that her self-control and determination were enough to carry her through. If Gwen was going to emerge from the palace intact, she had to break free from the rhythms of her past. She had to confront her mother.

The decision to let go of her protective mask felt so momentous that Gwen expected her mother to arrive at her door the moment she reached her conclusion. When the hours dragged on without any sign of the queen, however, Gwen began to grow concerned.

How long was the queen planning to keep her confined? If she intended to lock her up until the moment of the wedding ceremony, Gwen wasn't going to be much use to the rebels' cause.

A key in the lock made her jump to her feet. But the person who emerged through the narrow opening lacked the queen's commanding presence.

"Miriam!" Gwen flew across the room and flung her arms around the young woman.

Miriam startled, barely managing to rescue the tray she was carrying from Gwen's affectionate attack.

"Sorry!" Gwen drew back and took the tray from her, quickly shutting the door with both of them inside.

Miriam regarded the closed door warily.

"I can't believe she let you bring me food!" Gwen continued, not sure if she was marveling more at the food itself or the choice of delivery person. "She really doesn't suspect any of you, then?"

Miriam hesitated before shaking her head.

"Thank goodness." Gwen collapsed onto the nearest chair. "I was worried. I…" She drew a breath. If she wanted to change, she had to start by taking responsibility for her part in the past. "I'm sorry for just running off and abandoning you all. You helped me, and I rushed to save only myself."

Miriam regarded Gwen more steadily than the princess could ever remember the captive servant doing in the past. Eventually, she nodded.

"You did leave," she said, "but now you've come back."

She began unloading the dishes from the tray Gwen held, taking it back from Gwen once it was empty.

"That's all?" Gwen asked with a lightheaded laugh. "I'm forgiven just like that?"

Miriam shrugged. "We don't have so many allies that we can afford to throw them away so easily. And you did come back."

Gwen sobered at the pragmatic response. Sometimes Gwen had forgotten she was a princess and thought of the servants as just her friends. But she doubted they had ever forgotten they were captives. If their plan succeeded, Gwen intended to free the captives as her first act as queen. But at that point, they would likely return home to the valleys.

Some might choose to stay. They had been taken because they were found alone, and some might have no one to return to after so many years in the mountain kingdom. But even if some stayed, Gwen would be their queen. There would always be a barrier and a power imbalance between her and Miriam and Alma and the others.

Gwen owed both duty and affection toward them, but they owed her nothing. If they helped with the rebellion, it would be for the sake of their own freedom. But that was all right. They were allies as Miriam had said, and Gwen could use all the allies she could get.

I suppose this is what it means to be queen, Gwen thought. Gathering allies and weighing how the motivations of others could be used to Gwen's advantage. She wasn't sure how she felt about it. Wasn't it the kind of thing her mother would do?

Even as she thought it, she rejected the idea. Her mother manipulated the motivations of others in order to gain an advantage over them and use them. Allies sought the places where their motivations converged and worked for the good of both parties. Gwen could be an ally to the captive servants and still hold her head high.

She smiled at Miriam. "I would be honored to have you as allies. And in exchange, I guarantee that when I sit on the throne, you will not only be freed, but you will be released with fair compensation for both your captivity and your labor."

Miriam's eyes widened. "You really did come back to challenge the queen, then? You mean to take the throne?"

Gwen nodded. "And I'm not alone." She considered adding more, but caution held her back. Just as she hadn't mentioned the captives to Count Oswin, she wasn't sure if it was safe to mention Easton or the count to Miriam. While she didn't doubt Miriam or Alma, she didn't know all the captives equally well. There might be one willing to bargain with information in exchange for Celandine setting them alone free.

"I need to tell Alma," Miriam murmured. She hurried to the door only to hesitate. "Is there…is there something you want us to do?"

Gwen also hesitated, aware that Miriam's hesitancy reflected the danger she was in from the queen.

"I'll let you know when the time comes," Gwen said at last, hoping her words sounded confident instead of vague.

Miriam accepted them with something like relief, slipping out of the room and locking the door behind her. Was she on her way to return the key to the queen, or had Celandine handed it off to the servants with the intention of keeping Gwen locked away for a long time? With Miriam gone, Gwen kicked herself for not asking such basic questions.

She resolved to be more prepared when one of the servants returned to either collect the tray or deliver another meal. But when the key next turned in the lock, the door was thrust all the way open, and the queen strode in.

For a frozen moment, Gwen was sure she had misjudged Miriam and the servant had already reported Gwen to the queen. But Celandine's expression had a haughty disinterest that didn't fit with that theory, and Gwen's racing heart gradually slowed.

As the queen surveyed the room, Gwen's heart immediately picked up again, however, as she remembered her earlier resolution. The queen might not be angry now, but a defiant attitude from her daughter would likely change that.

Gwen knew she had to act quickly before she lost her nerve. But as soon as she opened her mouth, the queen spoke.

"Come. It is time for you to meet your husband-to-be."

Gwen snapped her mouth shut, her planned words forgotten. Her mother intended to take her to Henry? Charlotte's Henry! Gwen had promised her friend that she'd find him, and now her mother was planning to walk her straight there. Gwen could at least keep her mouth shut long enough to meet the prince and find out where he was being kept.

"Yes, Mother." Gwen bowed her head quickly in submission, hoping the queen hadn't seen the surge of excitement in her eyes at mention of Henry.

She expected to be led into the depths of the palace—possibly even to the closet that she had once been trapped in. But Celandine walked only three doors along the corridor before stopping again.

The rooms around Gwen's had been empty for as long as she could remember—silent reminders that her father's death had also taken away the chance of future siblings. Their silent emptiness was so ingrained in Gwen's thinking that it had never occurred to her that Henry might be housed in one of them.

For a horrifying moment, she feared her friend had been mistaken in her husband and that Henry was the queen's guest. Then Celandine withdrew a key, and Gwen's fears receded. Henry was a captive just as she had been.

Gwen of all people knew that a pretty cage was still a cage.

After turning the key in the lock, Celandine paused, stepping back slightly and gesturing for Gwen to open the door. Gwen frowned but couldn't think of any reason to refuse the task.

Cautiously she opened the door and stepped inside. A flash of movement made her startle and flinch away as a solid brass candlestick descended toward her head. By the time she sucked in the breath to cry out, however, the candlestick had veered, missing her by an inch and dropping to the carpet instead.

A tall young man stood staring at her, his chest rising and falling with either exertion or strong emotion. Had he prepared himself for a desperate escape attempt only to pull back when he saw her face? Why?

Gwen had the vague impression he was handsome, but the only feature she absorbed were his piercing blue eyes. They first tightened and then widened as he looked at her.

"You're the princess?" he asked, and then slowly, as if struggling to remember, "Gwen, is it?"

Gwen's heart contracted. Her mother would never have referred to her as Gwen to this foreign prince. To her mother she was Princess Gwendolyn. If Prince Henry knew her as Gwen, then he had heard her name from Charlotte. But how had he recognized her face?

"I see the castle did its job," Queen Celandine entered the room with a satisfied smile. "My daughter is just as beautiful as her portrait, is she not?"

Her portrait? Gwen stared from her mother to the prince in dismay. Like the portrait of Charlotte and Henry that was hidden in her mother's room? Charlotte's description of Henry's castle had sounded concerningly like a mirror for the mountain palace, but this news confirmed it. There had definitely been a link between the mountain queen and Charlotte's home. A link that must have been anchored in the paired portrait that gave her mother a glimpse of Henry and his bride.

Gwen stuffed her hands in her pocket to hide that they were both fisted and trembling. Her mother had no shame and no limits. But she was fooling herself if she thought Henry and Gwen would ever be married.

Her right hand brushed against the apple, reminding her again of its existence. Curious, she wrapped her hand around it and waited to see if the queen still had the plaited cords in her pocket.

Instantly, she was hit with the same awareness as before. The queen's object was still in the pocket where it had been before, still carried on her person. But if last time her awareness of it had been like meeting a new acquaintance, now it glowed with the warmth of an old friend.

If Gwen didn't know better, she would have said her golden apple felt fondly toward the plaited cord that changed someone's shape in order to bind them to the mountains. Gwen blinked. She had known the cord was a godmother object before, but the awareness of its purpose and ability was new.

Apparently her apple was more useful than she'd initially realized. If the queen had possessed it, she would have known the cord's full purpose, and she would never have tried to use it to bind her people to her. Gwen's hand tightened around the apple. If her mother saw it, she would want to possess it, just like she had collected those other objects in her display room.

"Gwendolyn," the queen said in a low warning voice, and Gwen shook herself. She couldn't afford to let her mind wander in front of her mother. She needed all her attention to try to match wits with the queen.

"I thought it was prudent for the two of you to meet before your wedding day," the queen continued, "and clearly I was correct. Hopefully now you will be more cooperative." She gave a satisfied smile, apparently having mistaken Henry's surprise at the sight of Gwen for admiration. "As you can see, I am not attempting to offer you a bad bargain. My daughter is young and beautiful and has been raised as a proper princess. She is a suitable bride for the Arcadian heir."

Henry's eyes narrowed as he looked at the queen. Everything about him was tense, even the surreptitious glances he kept flicking at Gwen. Gwen didn't make the same mistake as the queen, however. He wasn't admiring her, Gwen could tell that much. Instead, she had the distinct impression he was barely restraining himself from asking her something.

"I will not and cannot marry your daughter," Henry said in clear tones. "If you had stopped to listen to me previously, you would know it is impossible. I'm already married."

Celandine made a dismissive sound and gesture. "Any previous ties are inconsequential. Of course you will marry Princess Gwendolyn."

"Inconsequential?" Henry raised an eyebrow, not flinching in the face of the queen's disdain. "I've spent the time I've been gone on research. I know the mountain kingdom was once connected to the Four Kingdoms and made treaties with them. Many generations ago, one of your ancestors closed off the mountain passes, and your kingdom has been all but forgotten. But some of the ancient records still remain, and they were reproduced for me by your handy bell."

The queen's face twisted at his mention of the bell, and he smiled slightly.

"I know that each kingdom agreed to honor contracts and marriages made in the other kingdoms. A marriage in the Four Kingdoms is a legal marriage in the mountain kingdom as well. I am already married and cannot marry your daughter."

Gwen wanted to cheer, but to her dismay, a slow smile spread over the queen's face.

"Officially registered marriages, certainly," she said in sickly sweet tones. "But you were married in the valleys—you must have been since the confines of the enchantment prevented you from leaving the mountains' foothills. So tell me, with which royal family has your marriage been registered?"

Henry's face paled, and Gwen's stomach turned in response.

The queen continued, her smile growing broader. "I assure you I have also not been idle in gathering information, and my teams have been visiting the valleys for years now. From what I understand, the valley officials only make the trek into Rangmere's capital every couple of years. If you wish to play the game of law, I believe you'll find that if a marriage is officially registered in the mountain kingdom earlier than it is officially registered in Rangmere, it is the Rangmeran marriage that will be deemed invalid."

"It may not be on the Rangmeran registry yet," Henry said in a dangerous voice, "but I was married according to valley tradition, and our names were duly recorded. I am already married, and I will not cast my wife aside and enter into another marriage."

The queen's smile dropped from her face, replaced with a dangerous glitter in her eyes.

"Then it seems we must seek a simpler solution. The validity of your first union will become irrelevant when your bride is dead. As a widower, there will be no bar in any kingdom to prevent you marrying the princess."

Henry went still, not even breathing as he stared at the queen. His hands were fisted at his sides, and Gwen wondered how much control it was taking for him not to attack Celandine.

The silence stretched out until the queen smiled again. "I'm glad to hear you've finished your foolish protesting. We will now continue with our plans for the wedding."

The queen continued to talk about the practical plans she had made for the ceremony, but Gwen barely heard her. She had resolved to stand up to her mother, and now was surely the time. Henry had attempted it and been silenced, so it was Gwen's turn.

But her mind struggled to form the necessary words, her thoughts constantly derailed by the continued glances from Henry. He also didn't appear to be listening to the queen, his whole focus on sending her a silent message unseen by the queen.

Gwen felt foolish and sluggish, unable to grasp what he was so desperately trying to communicate. She needed a moment alone with him, and she certainly wouldn't get one if she picked that exact moment to enrage the queen.

Henry gave a soft sigh, and Gwen could sense her own frustration rolling off him. Before she could attempt her own silent communication, though, his demeanor abruptly changed.

He turned his eyes on Gwen again, but this time his look was open and direct—meant to be seen rather than overlooked. The apparent warmth in his gaze made her squirm given the false note that lay behind it. She stayed silent, however, willing to play along with whatever drama he was enacting for the queen.

"I cannot deny that your daughter is beautiful," he said, aiming his words at Celandine but keeping his eyes on Gwen. "But I don't know if I can bring myself to marry a complete stranger." He finally turned to look at the queen. "May we not have some time alone?"

The queen raised her brows. "I have brought her to you, haven't I? Or are you saying you cannot become acquainted in my company?"

Gwen tensed at the suspicion in her words, but Henry merely smirked.

"There are some types of…acquaintance…that are uncomfortable to achieve in the presence of others," he said smoothly, his eyes returning appreciatively to Gwen.

His words surprised a mirthless laugh from the queen. "I suppose I can allow you a few minutes." She held up a finger, her tone turning to warning. "But a few minutes only. I'm sure I need not remind you that the wedding has yet to take place."

She swept toward the door, pausing at Gwen's side and leaning close to murmur in her ear.

"Take note of this lesson, my dear. For all their protestations, all men are the same. Attempt whatever coyness you like, but allow him a kiss now, and you will yet manage to control him."

Gwen stared at her mother's retreating form in shock. They had suspected her mother was struggling to maintain control in her absence, but even so she had expected more resistance to her return. She hadn't expected her mother to treat it like it had never happened. Before her defiance and escape, one of her mother's last commands to her had been about preparing for her wedding. She hadn't been concerned about the clothes or the ceremony, but rather about Gwen's need to control and manipulate her future husband. And now she was speaking as if that conversation had merely been interrupted by a night's sleep.

Her mother must be more desperate than the count realized if she truly intended to ignore Gwen's rebellion and disappearance. It was like time had rolled back in her mother's mind. Gwen had returned, and it was therefore as if she had never left.

Gratitude filled Gwen that she hadn't spoken up sooner. If her mother truly intended to deny reality, Gwen could use that to her advantage. And she would need every advantage she could manage. A Celandine desperate enough to react in such a way was almost more terrifying than Celandine in her right mind, in full control of every situation. It made her unpredictable and dangerous.

As the door clicked shut, Henry stepped toward her. Grasping her shoulders, he spun her slightly so that his back was toward the door and his body blocked most of hers from view. Leaning close, he positioned his face beside hers.

"Apologies," he whispered, "but if she opens the door, it will look from that direction as if we're embracing."

Gwen nodded, not wanting to waste any of their precious time.

"My wife mentioned you," he said rapidly. "She knew your name. And you seemed to react when you saw me. Have you met her? I don't know how it could be possible, but do you know her somehow?" Fear tinged his voice. "Do you know where she is now? Have you seen her in the last few days? She isn't here in the mountain kingdom, is she?"

Gwen winced, and Henry's face turned ashen.

"No," he whispered hoarsely. "How is that possible?"

"I'm sorry," she murmured, her words falling over each other. "She insisted I bring her here. She's determined to find you. She wants to—"

"Free me," Henry said on a groan. He strode once up and down the room, running an agitated hand through his hair. "I can't protect her if she's here!"

"Then maybe you need to let her protect you," Gwen said firmly.

Henry halted and stared at her. But before she could expand on the topic, he glanced at the closed door and hurried back to position himself in front of her again.

"She isn't alone," Gwen said softly, unable to ignore the pain and worry on his face. "And it isn't just me, either. We have allies. And a plan. There isn't time to explain it all now, but you should just be ready when the moment comes. I'm not working with my mother, and I won't marry you, no matter what she says or does. But we have to play along with her for now. Even if it gets all the way to the ceremony, don't worry. Just be ready to move on my signal."

Henry looked like he was about to argue, but the door clicked behind them. For a half second, Henry leaned even closer to her before a footfall sounded and he started dramatically away.

The queen chuckled. "I'm glad to see the two of you getting along."

Gwen hoped the flush of fury in her cheeks would be mistaken for embarrassment. She kept her face averted from the queen, lest the look in her eyes give her away. Instead, she gazed out the window, waiting for her emotions to calm.

A flash of movement outside caught her eye, and her gaze focused abruptly. There was someone out there, and it wasn't a captive servant or a guard. She recognized the swish of the gown that had disappeared around the corner because it was one of her own—one she had loaned to Charlotte after finding her friend still dressed in her nightgown.

The flush surged back into Gwen's cheeks, this time fueled by a combination of fear and nervous anticipation. She leaned into it, looking from Henry to the queen and then back to Henry before covering her heated cheeks with her hands and fleeing the room.

The queen's laughter chased her out, and as Gwen dashed along the corridor, she caught the distant words as the queen excused her daughter's naivety. Gwen rolled her eyes even while she felt relieved her spontaneous subterfuge had worked. She didn't know how long she had before her mother came looking for her—or set the palace guards to the task—so she couldn't waste time finding Charlotte and sending her away. The last thing they needed was for Queen Celandine to capture her. From what Gwen had seen, Henry would go along with any plan the queen demanded if she had Charlotte under her power.

wen ran straight to the nearest exit into the garden, weaving through the paths as she rushed toward the spot she had seen her friend. She stayed close to hedges as much as possible, hoping she wouldn't be spotted from any of the palace's windows, and so she nearly missed the two slim figures huddled together in quiet conversation in one of the more secluded spots in the garden.

"Gwen!" Charlotte called, her cry muted, and Gwen swung around.

Racing through the archway in the tall hedge, Gwen came to a stop in front of her friend.

"What are you doing here?" she panted, struggling to catch her breath. "You can't be here. Seriously, I mean it. It's too dangerous."

A militant light came into Charlotte's eyes. "Henry is here." She raised her chin stubbornly. "I won't leave him in danger while I lurk behind in safety."

Gwen huffed in frustration, distantly noting that Natalie had slipped away. She was too focused on Charlotte to ask what harebrained scheme the two had concocted.

"Henry being here is exactly why you can't be!" she protested, struggling to keep her voice low. "The queen is already threatening you to manipulate him, and that will only get worse if she captures you as well."

Charlotte's eyes lit up. "You've seen him? Is he all right? The queen hasn't hurt him?"

"Not physically," Gwen said, unable to help reassuring her friend. "At least not that I can see. But he's desperately worried about you."

Charlotte smiled softly, a dreamy look in her eyes. "Of course he is. That's very Henry."

Gwen sighed in frustration. Were she and Easton this irritating?

Discomfort filled her as she remembered that she and Easton were far from the position of Charlotte and Henry. The other two were not only married, they had each declared their love already. Gwen still had no idea how she was going to find out Easton's true feelings.

"The best thing you can do for Henry is leave immediately," Gwen said, trying again.

Charlotte shook her head stubbornly. "I won't leave without seeing Henry. There has to be a way to see him. I'm not going to sit around and wait and hope for the best without doing anything."

Gwen frowned. "Don't you trust us?"

Charlotte sighed. "I'm not saying I don't trust the count, but Henry isn't his priority. He's focused on breaking the enchantment, saving your kingdom, and putting you and Easton on the throne. That makes sense, but now that he knows Henry isn't part of breaking the enchantment, Henry has become little more than an afterthought for him."

Gwen sank back and let out a slow breath. She couldn't deny her friend's words. And while she wanted to assure Charlotte that Gwen herself wouldn't forget about Henry's safety, could she really guarantee it? She couldn't even guarantee her own safety.

She sighed. She didn't have the words to convince Charlotte to go back to the city, and neither could she physically force her to do so. In fact, Charlotte would only be in more danger if Gwen didn't get moving soon. Gwen's best hope for helping her friend was to think of a way for Charlotte to safely see Henry. But with Henry locked up and the key with her mother, how could Charlotte possibly get in to see him secretly?

Gwen strode across the small garden and back again, wracking her brains for a solution. As she walked, the apple in her pocket bumped lightly against her leg, causing her mind to briefly wander. With the apple, they could discover the extent of her mother's power. They might even be able to find a weakness they could use to bring her down or an object they could use to restrain her during the wedding ceremony.

But the apple hadn't revealed much the first time it came into contact with the plaited cords. It was as if it needed to get to know the other object first. And that meant if Gwen broke into the queen's display room right now, the apple wouldn't do her any good at all.

She groaned in frustration. Did she really need to break in more than once? The impossibilities only seemed to be mounting. Why couldn't she find solutions instead of more problems?

"What is it?" Charlotte asked, watching her pacing with concern. "Is it Henry? Is there something you're not telling me?"

"It's not that..." Gwen's voice trailed off as something occurred to her. What if there was one solution to multiple problems?

She turned to Charlotte. "I have an idea."

Charlotte rushed forward to take her hands. "What is it?"

"I've been trying to think how you can get in to see Henry without the queen knowing, but what if you don't try to avoid the queen?"

Charlotte frowned, letting Gwen's hands drop. "I thought you said I had to avoid getting captured at all costs?"

"I'm not saying it's not without risks, but your being here is already a risk. My preference would be for you to agree to leave now…" She looked at Charlotte inquiringly, but Charlotte shook her head, so Gwen continued.

"This is the solution." She drew the apple out of her pocket, extending it on her palm so the late afternoon light caught on the gold.

Charlotte sucked in a breath. "What is that?" she whispered.

"I got it from my godmother, which means it's the bait we can use for the queen. If there's one thing she's obsessed with, it's accumulating godmother objects. They're the basis for her power. If she sees this, she'll want it."

Charlotte frowned. "I don't understand."

"Offer it to her in exchange for seeing Henry," Gwen said simply.

Charlotte stared at her blankly. "Why would she agree to that? Surely she'd just arrest me and steal it?"

"That's the beauty of using this." Gwen smiled triumphantly. "All you have to do is tell her it's one of the objects that stops working completely if it's taken by force. It will only work if given willingly."

Charlotte's mouth dropped open. "That's actually brilliant!" she exclaimed. "Lots of godmother objects do work like that, so she'll likely believe it."

"As long as you make a deal that includes you being free to leave after seeing Henry, she'll have to keep to the terms of the bargain, or she'll lose the power of the object," Gwen added.

Charlotte reached eagerly for the apple, only for her face to darken and her hand to drop. "But I can't take this. It's yours. Your godmother gave it to you. I should use mine." She pulled out a smooth golden ball. "I was given something on the way here as well. If we have to give her a godmother object in exchange for my seeing Henry, it should be mine."

Gwen looked at the ball curiously, but their time was running out. She didn't have the luxury of idle curiosity. She wasn't her mother—she didn't need to own every powerful object she encountered.

"No, it has to be the apple." She pressed it on Charlotte. "I want the queen to have it, and this is a way to get it to her without her suspecting an ulterior motive."

Charlotte put away her ball and slowly accepted Gwen's apple. "Why would you want her to have it?" she asked. "What does it do?"

"It tells the person holding it about the power of other objects," Gwen said, watching Charlotte's face.

Her friend gasped, her eyes flying to Gwen. "I can sense my ball! It's like I can see it in my pocket. Well, not see it. More like I can taste it." She laughed. "No, that's not right. I don't know what sense I'm using, but it's there. And I can feel the golden halter you entrusted to me too." She frowned. "But I can't tell anything about either one's purpose, just their presence."

Gwen nodded, glad to have her experience confirmed. "That's why we need to get it into the queen's hands. She'll put it in her display room with all her other objects and that's what we need. It seems to need time around another object before it will reveal that object's purpose. We have to give it a chance to warm up to all the objects in that room, so that when we break in there, it's ready to tell us what they each do."

Charlotte shook her head. "Two birds with one stone," she murmured.

Gwen grinned slowly. "Exactly. I'm ready to start solving problems instead of amassing new ones."

Charlotte grimaced. "I know I'm one of those problems. But I can't just walk away from Henry knowing he's right there."

Gwen nodded. For all her initial frustration, she understood.

If there had been a way for her to get to Easton anytime in the last ten years, she would have done anything to reach him.

"Don't worry," Charlotte said, determined. "I'll explain everything to Henry and make sure he goes along with the plan."

"Unless you can find a way to get him out immediately?" Gwen challenged, a brow raised.

Charlotte hesitated, her bottom lip gripped between her teeth. "No," she finally said on a sigh. "I won't try that. I know you need the queen to continue planning this wedding." She looked sharply at Gwen. "That is what's happening? She hasn't hurt you?"

Gwen nodded. "She's fully focused on the wedding. Henry will be safe until then. As long as he doesn't do anything foolish himself."

She didn't say aloud the rest of her thought. Helping Charlotte to make direct contact with Henry was as much about ensuring his compliance as anything else. From his level of agitation earlier, now that he knew Charlotte was in the mountain kingdom—and under open threat from its queen—Gwen didn't put it past him to make some foolhardy attempt at escape before the wedding. But even if he wouldn't listen to Gwen, surely he would listen to Charlotte.

Gwen froze, her ears pricking. Footsteps on gravel sounded from more than one direction, and from the measured cadence, it wasn't courtiers out for a casual stroll.

"Hide!" she hissed, giving Charlotte a light push. "Get out of sight somewhere while I distract them. And then get somewhere close to the palace walls, on the south side. Get the apple out and just throw it around a bit, like you're playing. I guarantee my mother will see you."

Charlotte hesitated for only a moment before nodding decisively and diving into a nearby clump of bushes. Gwen smiled for a fraction of a second at her friend's enthusiastic and literal interpretation of her instructions before she hurried back through the arch.

No guards were in sight yet, but from the sound of the footsteps, she would see them soon. She considered hurrying in the other direction, but after only a moment of indecision, she sank onto the closest bench. As far as the queen knew, Gwen had been overcome with embarrassment and rushed out to cool down. The last thing she wanted was to create the impression she had been attempting to run away.

Slumping down, she leaned her forehead against one hand, breathing slowly.

The footsteps drew closer.

"Your Highness!" The gruff voice made her look up, disappointment rising when she didn't recognize the speaker or his companion. She shouldn't have been surprised, though. Of course her mother would send her most loyal guards to retrieve her recalcitrant daughter.

Gwen stood up slowly, trying to look unaffected.

"Is my mother looking for me?" she asked, careful not to look toward the arch leading into the garden where Charlotte was concealed.

"She merely wants to assure herself of your safety," the guard said, exchanging a quick look with his partner.

Gwen nodded as if that was understandable and started back toward the palace. The guards fell into step, one on either side of her. When the second pair appeared, a silent communication passed between all four guards, and the newcomers fell in behind the existing two.

Gwen expected them to lead her to her mother, but they merely kept pace as she chose her own course. Unsure what else to do, Gwen traced the familiar route back to her room, pausing for a moment in the corridor and gazing down toward Henry's door.

Shaking her head at herself, she pushed open her own door and paused to give the guards a firm look. None of them protested when she shut the door in their faces, and she breathed a sigh of relief. As much as she wanted to go and test Henry's door, she couldn't risk it. Charlotte might already be on her way to the part of the garden closest to Celandine's wing, and Gwen had to give her friend a chance to get to Henry before Gwen disrupted anything else.

She only wished she was as close to being back in Easton's arms again.

CHARLOTTE

Charlotte's heart pounded as she wove her way through the gardens, her ears straining for the sound of footsteps. She wanted Celandine to be the one to find her, not a random pair of guards. They might throw her out of the grounds —or worse, into a cell—without ever giving her the chance to propose a trade with the queen.

She saw no sign of Natalie as she moved. Had the other girl hidden nearby to hear Gwen's plan? Charlotte hoped she had. At least that way the rebels would know what had become of her if everything went wrong. But it was just as possible Natalie had headed out to pursue their original mission—finding more information about the queen's movements.

Charlotte slipped her hand back in her pocket and curled it around the apple. She no longer felt the presence of the golden ball since she had left it buried beneath the bush where she had hidden herself along with the golden halter. She didn't want to risk carrying either one into Celandine's presence. They were already handing over one object to her. There was no need to make it three.

In the garden with Gwen, the plan had seemed solid, but the

closer she got to the castle, the faster Charlotte's heart beat. What if the queen didn't see her? Or what if she wouldn't agree to the trade? If she had no interest in the apple, or decided to take her chances and seize it by force, Charlotte would be left helpless and with nothing to use to buy her freedom.

Charlotte shook her head, focusing her thoughts on Henry instead. It would all be worth it if she could see him. And she didn't intend to be tricked into giving Gwen's object away for a mere few minutes either. If Celandine would be bound by their agreement, Charlotte intended to bargain well.

When she reached the south side of the building, she approached close, peering into the windows she passed. The largest showed an expansive room furnished as a study and lined with bookshelves. An elegant woman wearing a glittering circlet sat at the large desk, her head bent over a stack of papers.

Charlotte immediately pulled back, her heart pounding. She had found the right place, but she needed to stage herself better if she was going to outwit the queen.

Strolling casually in front of the window, she didn't glance toward the glass. Instead, she gazed out at the city, which stretched below the palace, choosing a place to sit on the grass and angling her body so she could keep her apparent focus on the view while giving the queen a clear line of sight to Charlotte's profile.

As soon as she was seated, she pulled out the apple and threw it into the air. Tracking its flight, she smiled at the way the lowering sun caught on the gold, making it shine. Perfect.

It landed in her palm with a dull thunk, the weight of it nearly catching her off guard. She quickly flicked it up again, watching its rise and then descent. It was taking all her self-control not to look toward the window, but she didn't want the queen to know she was aware of her presence, and if their eyes locked…

It flew up again and then a fourth time. When she fumbled the catch, the apple dropped to the grass and rolled a short way.

Charlotte retrieved it with her best approximation of a carefree laugh. It barely squeezed through her throat, though, the semblance of calm difficult. She wasn't sure if she was more terrified of the coming confrontation with the queen or more elated at the prospect of being reunited with Henry. Within minutes, she might be at his side, held in his arms. Waiting was both painful and never-ending. Minutes had never moved so slowly.

She'd lost track of the number of times she'd thrown the apple when a shadow fell across her. Shielding her eyes with one hand, she gazed up at the queen.

Gasping theatrically, she scrambled to her feet and dropped into an instant curtsy.

"Your Majesty," she said, glad her voice trembled only a little. "I apologize for disturbing you. I didn't know..."

The queen's eyes were trained on the apple, her expression hinting at the greedy desire Gwen had been sure she would feel. But at Charlotte's words, she tore her gaze away and looked at Charlotte's face.

Her eyes widened, a crease appearing between her brows, and Charlotte remembered Gwen had once mentioned a portrait.

"What are *you* doing here?" the queen breathed. "*How* are you here?"

Charlotte stayed silent, reminding herself that it didn't matter if the queen recognized her. She would have realized the connection as soon as Charlotte suggested her bargain anyway. But she needed to choose her words carefully.

"There's nothing I wouldn't do to be reunited with my husband," she said. "Nothing I wouldn't give."

"Even in my youth I wasn't so foolish," the queen said, but she looked pleased. "However, if that is truly your heart's desire, maybe I can help you."

Charlotte didn't have to feign her eagerness as she looked up, meeting the queen's eyes. "You know where Henry is? You can take me to him?"

The queen cocked her head. "Give me that apple, and I will do so."

Charlotte looked down at it, drawing it back against her body, as if uncertain about the trade.

The queen's eyes followed the object. "You said you would give anything. Surely you would not begrudge such a bauble."

Charlotte drew herself up, pretending to gather her courage. "If one such as Your Majesty desires it, it must have value."

The queen's eyes narrowed. "You know who I am. With a word I can have you arrested and take everything you possess."

Charlotte held her ground. "The old woman who gave it to me said it won't reveal itself if taken by force. She said it can only be used by someone who has received it as a gift, freely given."

Celandine let out a sharp breath, and Charlotte had to suppress a smile. Their gamble had worked. The queen believed it.

For all I know, it might actually be true, Charlotte thought.

"If I give it to you," Charlotte continued, "I want more than to just be taken to Henry."

The queen's brows rose, but Charlotte thought she detected amused respect beneath the disbelief. Celandine thought she had the unassailable upper hand, so she was willing to play along with Charlotte's game. Now Charlotte had to turn that to her advantage.

She'd spent her time waiting on working out a strategy, so the words came easily. "It's nearly sunset. In exchange for this object, I want to spend the whole night with Henry. Just the two of us alone."

Another smile flickered across the queen's mouth. "Just one night?" she asked, the words almost mocking. But Charlotte knew she had to walk a fine balance. If she asked for too much, the queen might decide to risk taking the apple.

"One night undisturbed with Henry." She lifted her chin. "And in the morning, you let me walk away from the palace and its grounds alone and unharmed."

The queen let out a laugh. "You're a bold one. Are you sure he's worth it?" The amusement danced in her eyes, inviting Charlotte to doubt her husband. But she met the queen's gaze unflinching. She wouldn't fall into the same trap again. She trusted him.

"That's my bargain," Charlotte said. "I get tonight with Henry, and in the morning I walk away. If the conditions aren't met, the object will cease to work and become an ordinary apple. Assuming we can believe the old woman's words."

She could see the sour note in Celandine's gaze. She didn't want to give authority to the godmother, but she also understood the futility of trying to deny it. She had a whole room full of their objects, so she couldn't deny the High King's power.

Charlotte gave a final small toss of the apple, letting it wink in the fading light.

"Well?" she asked.

The queen glanced at the approaching sunset, her jaw setting. Then something shifted in her eyes, and she looked back at Charlotte and laughed.

"If you will willingly walk into the spider's lair, who am I to deny you?" she mocked. "It's a bargain."

Charlotte moved the apple to her left hand and thrust out her right. After only the smallest pause, the queen took it and shook, her face twisting. But Charlotte didn't care. Her heart was singing. She was about to be reunited with Henry.

The queen pulled her hand free of Charlotte's as soon as possible and held it out, palm upward. Charlotte dropped the apple into it, glad she had thought to bury the other objects.

Celandine gazed down at her new treasure, her expression gloating. But before long she looked up again, glancing once more at where the sun hung low in the sky.

"Come," she said, her tone cold and commanding.

Charlotte hurried behind her, barely able to keep up with the queen's long strides. Everything had gone as Gwen had predicted, but it was hard not to feel a shadow of dread as she stepped inside the palace. If Gwen had miscalculated or Charlotte had misread the queen, everything could be about to go terribly wrong.

The queen opened a door and ushered Charlotte inside. She hurried in, full of excitement, only for her heart to plummet as soon as she saw the empty space.

"Where—" she cried, turning back to the queen.

"It is not yet night," Celandine said curtly, cutting her off. "Your bargain was to spend the night with your prince. You will be guided to him after sundown."

Charlotte tried to protest, but Celandine had already left, closing the door firmly behind her and turning a key in the lock. Charlotte blew out a long breath. It wasn't what she had been hoping for, and after the heady expectation of only moments before, it was bitter to find herself still parted from Henry. But the situation hadn't exploded yet. She had always expected the queen to do as little as the bargain would allow—it was why she had tried to word it carefully. She only needed a little more patience and she would be with Henry again.

At least the room she was confined in had a small window, allowing her to watch the sunset. The sun had never descended so slowly, but finally—finally—the last of it slipped beneath the horizon and the sky darkened.

She ran to the door and banged on it. When no one answered, she tried the handle, aware of the futility of the attempt. To her surprise it twisted beneath her hand. When had it been unlocked?

She pulled the door open tentatively, peering at the corridor outside. A large white bear filled her view, startling a screech out of her. But the bear made no aggressive moves, and after a moment she calmed, embarrassed at her outburst. She had seen

Gwen and the count change the night before, and she had spent months' worth of days with Henry in his bear form. She even knew the palace was full of bears at night. She shouldn't have been so startled.

The bear didn't respond to her outburst, waiting patiently for her to exit the room. She did so cautiously, examining the bear for any sign of its human identity.

The only thing she could tell, however, was that it wasn't Henry. His bear form was familiar to her, but she didn't know how to distinguish anyone else. For all she knew, it could be Queen Celandine herself.

Charlotte doubted it, though. Something about the bear's air didn't match the queen's commanding arrogance. Charlotte wasn't going to risk making assumptions, however.

"Where's Henry?" she asked, keeping her words to a minimum.

"Follow me," the bear said in a deep, gravelly voice.

Charlotte nodded and waited for the bear to start down the corridor. Trailing behind, she felt the earlier anticipation sparkling through her veins again. It didn't matter who was leading the way—she was going to Henry.

They crossed several corridors before the bear stopped in front of a wooden door. He remained silent, indicating it with his head.

Charlotte brushed past him, her breath catching as she saw the key sticking out of the keyhole. It was really happening. Her husband was waiting on the other side of that door.

Forgetting all about the bear, she turned the lock and slipped through into the luxurious bedchamber on the other side. She forced herself to shut the door behind her and lock it from the inside before turning to scan the room for Henry.

"Henry?" she called, her voice quavering.

There was no response. Frowning, she stepped further into the room, her eyes drawn to the large four-poster bed. It was strangely early for him to be asleep, but a human form was visible beneath the blankets, a riot of dark hair on the pillow catching her eye.

She ran to the bed, her steps faltering as she took in the features of her husband. Comfortable familiarity laced through with love washed over her. She had only seen his human face for a few brief minutes, but his appearance was burned into her mind.

"Henry," she said again, tears escaping her eyes and tracking down her cheeks. "I came for you, just like I said I would."

He didn't stir, and the first tendrils of concern unfurled in her mind.

"Henry!" she said again, louder, but he still didn't stir. Leaning forward, she shook him by the shoulder, her movement growing more and more rough as he didn't respond.

It made no difference. Her husband lay in the bed like one dead.

CHARLOTTE

Fear rolled through Charlotte, hot and slow and then swift and overwhelming. Something was wrong with Henry.

She held her breath as she leaned over him, placing her cheek in front of his lips. When she felt his soft breath against her skin, her knees nearly collapsed. She grasped the bedcovers to keep herself upright, sucking in sharp gasps of relief. He was alive.

She cupped the warm skin of his face in her hands, calling him softly to wake. She shook his shoulders so hard that his body rolled from side to side in the bed. She even shouted, her fear and anger growing as she commanded him to wake up.

The more vigorous efforts made him groan and roll away from her, but nothing made his eyes open. Henry was deeply, impossibly asleep.

Charlotte dashed away the tears on her cheeks, her anger burning hot. The queen had betrayed their agreement. But even as she thought it, Charlotte was kicking herself. She had thought to demand the whole night and to specify they had to be alone, but she had made a mistake. It had never occurred to her to

97

require him to be conscious. The queen had stolen her night with Henry, and now she had Gwen's apple.

Charlotte squeezed her hands into fists, feeling her nails dig into her palms. She forced herself to relax her muscles, releasing her fingers and holding for a moment before squeezing them back into fists again. She completed the exercise over and over until her mind calmed.

It wasn't a total disaster. Gwen had wanted the queen to have the apple, so at least Charlotte had delivered it in a way that allowed the queen to believe herself the victor.

The calm, rational thoughts were hard to maintain, though. It felt to Charlotte too like the queen was the victor, and defeat was a bitter taste in her mouth.

At least I've seen him, she told herself. *At least I can see he's physically unharmed—apart from the sleeping, that is.*

The day before, she would have given much for a mere glimpse of him, but it no longer felt like enough. Perhaps there was still hope, though. Whatever enchantment the queen had used on him might run out before morning. He might wake up at any moment, and they still had hours before them. Charlotte would keep watch, ready for the first sign of his waking.

But sitting by the bed, so close and yet so far from him, was unbearable. She climbed in beside him, slipping beneath the covers and curling at his side where she could feel the reassuring warmth and solidity of him. She would still stay awake and keep watch, she would just do it from the bed.

But staying awake became harder and harder as the night hours wore on. The pillow was soft and the mattress comfortably firm, and more importantly, Henry's breaths were steady and reassuring, setting the rhythm of Charlotte's own breathing. She had lain beside him for so many nights, reassured by his presence, and her body remembered those nights despite her mind's efforts to stay alert.

Eventually she couldn't resist any longer, and she slipped into the welcoming embrace of sleep—the deepest since she had lost Henry.

She woke to spears of sunlight and turned her head sideways. For the first time ever, she had a morning view of her husband still in bed beside her. A rush of joy filled her, only to immediately be doused by the memory of where they were. They weren't in their castle in the forest. They were in the mountain kingdom, and Henry was a prisoner under an unnatural sleep. She flung off the covers, crawling over to shake him again.

She had slept the night away, and now morning had already arrived. She had to wake him before it was too late. The queen's guards could burst in at any moment—she was surprised they hadn't already arrived.

"Henry! Henry!" she cried, fresh tears streaming down her cheeks.

He stirred in response, groaning and running a hand over his face, his eyes shut.

"No," he grumbled, his voice rough with sleep. "I want to stay in this dream. Lottie's here."

Charlotte's tears fell more thickly, blurring her vision. "Wake up, wake up!" she cried. "I'm really here, but we only have a moment. Wake up!"

His eyes sprang open, and for a silent second she stared down into the piercing blue eyes that had haunted her every moment since he'd disappeared. Then he surged into a sitting position, his arms sweeping around her and bundling her onto his lap where he held her tightly against his chest.

"Lottie," he said thickly. "Lottie."

Pressed against his strong chest, safe within the circle of his arms, her tears turned into full sobs. She knew she needed to regain control—that they had important words to exchange—but she couldn't do anything but revel in the moment.

He was the one to recover first, pulling back slightly to look down at her.

"Wait," he said, his clarity returning by the second. "What are you doing here? You can't be here, Lottie!"

She wiped at her cheeks, trying to remember what she needed to say.

"I'm so happy to see you again," she managed instead. "I missed you so much."

His arms tightened again, his eyes piercing into hers, devouring her face.

"It seems impossible." He cupped her face gently in his large hands, his eyes slipping down to her mouth. "I didn't think I'd ever see you again."

Charlotte angled her face up invitingly just as he pressed his lips down, meeting hers in a fervent kiss. She sank into it, absorbing all his longing and relief and desire and returning it in equal measure.

The door banged open, startling them apart. Awareness rushed back to Charlotte, and she gasped. She had been given two precious minutes, and she had spent them crying and kissing him.

"Wait," she cried as the queen swept into the room, a line of guards behind her.

She tightened her grip around Henry's neck, leaning forward to murmur in his ear. "I only bargained for the night. I'll be safe, but only if I leave now. You have to play along and do what Gwen says."

His head moved as he looked toward the queen, and Charlotte could feel the horror in every line of his body.

A guard seized her from behind, prying her away from Henry. When she didn't let go, another guard came forward to help.

The second she ripped free, Henry leaped from the bed, fists raised, fury on his face.

"No!" Charlotte lunged forward, surprising the guards enough that they momentarily lost hold of her.

She placed both hands on Henry's chest in a restraining

gesture. "You can't fight them." She captured his eyes with hers, holding them with determination. "You have to let me go. I told you I have to leave now. I said I'll be safe."

The guards leaped forward again and took hold of her, dragging her away from Henry. He swayed toward her, his hands still fisted, and she shook her head frantically. Reluctantly, he looked at the massed guards and then the queen and remained in place.

"And the other thing!" Charlotte cried as she was dragged backward from the room. "Promise me, Henry. Promise me!"

She caught the moment of acceptance and begrudging acquiescence in his eyes just before she was pulled out into the corridor. As soon as they stepped sideways away from the door, the guards stopped, holding Charlotte in position, just out of sight of those in the room.

She looked toward the door, presuming they were waiting for the queen, but Celandine didn't appear. Instead, Charlotte heard Henry's voice, the angry rumble too low for her to catch the specific words, and then the queen's response, colder and higher, easy to decipher.

"I told you before," she said, "and I'll tell you again. There is an easy solution to any legal dispute. And as you can see, such an action is well within my power. If you want that girl to live, then you will cease any useless attempts at defiance."

Charlotte went cold all over. It was just like Gwen had said. Celandine was using Charlotte to control Henry.

She wanted to scream and fight, to run back in there and tell him to ignore the queen's words. But she knew it would do no good. She would never convince him not to protect her over himself. She had thought she was so clever, tricking the queen, but she was the one who had been tricked. Everything had played right into Celandine's hands.

Even the few extra moments past dawn that had been granted them had been done with a purpose. She was taunting them, reminding them who was in control, and making sure that Henry saw for himself that Charlotte was there, within the queen's reach.

Charlotte wanted to kick and punch at the guards around her, just for the satisfaction of unleashing the rage inside her. But she couldn't give way to it. She couldn't give them any excuse to violate the rest of the bargain.

The queen stepped out of the room, making a show of shutting and locking the door behind her. At her appearance, Charlotte shook off the guards' hold. They let her do so, stepping back.

Charlotte met the queen's eyes, barely reining in her anger to speak calmly.

"Call off your guards," she said. "The bargain was that I walk out of here unharmed and alone."

The queen gestured down the corridor. "By all means. No one is stopping you."

Charlotte narrowed her eyes, disliking the slight smile that hovered around the queen's eyes and mouth. But there was nothing left for her to do except take the offered chance to escape. A direct confrontation with the queen wouldn't achieve anything good. Not yet, anyway.

She held her head high as she spun on her heel and walked down the corridor. She wanted to sprint as fast as she could run, but she had specified that she be allowed to walk out of the palace, and she wouldn't risk changing a single aspect of the bargain in case it provided the queen with a loophole.

At walking pace, it seemed to take an eternity to find a door that opened to the outside, but she finally stepped out into the morning air. The gravel paths of the gardens stretched before her, and she picked up her pace slightly. Every time she glanced over her shoulder, there was no one in sight, and by the time she was halfway through the grounds, she concluded she wasn't being followed. It seemed impossible that the queen was just going to let her walk away, but apparently the pull of the godmother object was as strong as Gwen had claimed.

She still jumped at every minor sound, flinching away from every moving shadow. She wouldn't be safe until she'd made it back to Natalie's family.

She had been too distracted by Henry all night to spare a thought for the younger girl, but she remembered her guiltily as she traversed the gardens. Surely Natalie had returned home before dark rather than risk being caught in the streets at night.

Charlotte's hand moved to her arm where thin bandages still lay beneath her sleeve. The salve had worked wonders already, but Charlotte could feel the ache of it whenever her mind quieted.

The outer edge of the garden approached, and Charlotte's attention shifted to the streets beyond. As predicted by Natalie back in the basement, there was a steady trickle of traffic on every street within view, although the ones nearest the palace moved about their business quickly, their eyes averted from the looming structure.

Charlotte's family had traveled through Rangmeros when they moved from Northhelm to the valleys. It was her only visit to a capital city, so she still remembered it vividly. She had been nervous because the other kingdoms considered Rangmere to be a cold, hard place, but the city had bustled with life, and she hadn't sensed any of the fear that radiated from the mountain people.

Charlotte's shoulders hunched, her senses on high alert. Everything about this place put her on edge.

She stepped onto the cobblestones of the closest street, taut with tension. Her heart lay behind her in the palace, and her mind was leaping ahead to her destination, but a prickle in the back of her neck placed her firmly in the moment.

Her eyes darted to various side streets, her mind instinctively looking for routes she could take to escape nonexistent pursuers.

Her measured steps took her further into the street as she remembered she didn't have to walk anymore. She could run all the way back to Easton and Natalie if she wanted.

No sooner had the thought occurred to her than doors opened in several directions. Guards poured out of the surrounding buildings, streaming toward her from every direction she had just scoped.

Charlotte froze, spinning to look behind her. Guards had even appeared from the gardens, closing off her retreat.

"Nonononononono." The syllables poured out of her in a constant stream as her eyes and brain scrambled to find a solution. She couldn't allow herself to be captured and used against Henry.

The guards closed in, not bothering to run given they had her surrounded. She backed toward one of the few buildings that hadn't disgorged guards.

"Here!" a high voice called, dragging her attention upward.

A hand was hanging down from the portico above the front door, gesturing for her to approach.

"Hurry!" the voice said again, and Charlotte thought she recognized it.

Leaping the rest of the way to the house, Charlotte jumped onto the rim of one of the large clay pots that flanked the door with decorative flowers. Taking the hand held out to her, she gripped the other person's wrist while they did the same to hers, securing the firmest hold they could manage.

The person above hauled upward while Charlotte jumped and caught the edge of the portico with her free hand. Her legs waved helplessly for a moment while the person above her grunted and pulled. Then she was high enough to get the forearm of her other arm over the edge of the roof, allowing her proper purchase.

Shouts from behind made her redouble her efforts, grunting as she scrambled inelegantly onto the small stretch of roof that jutted out over the door. As soon as she had her knees under her, she looked up and met Natalie's eyes.

"Totally predictable," the other girl said with rolled eyes. "You need to learn to word your bargains better. You're lucky I was hiding nearby to hear what happened and could easily see how it would all end." As she talked, she climbed onto a protruding window ledge above them and from there up to the two-story roof of the house, using a vine that wound down the stone for purchase.

Charlotte winced and tried to hurry after her. The guards were already on the ground below them, attempting to climb up without assistance from above. It wouldn't take them long to manage it.

She scrambled from the bottom of the window ledge to the thin lip above the window, wobbling dangerously as she clutched at the ivy around her. The greenery began to tear away from the building, and she screamed as her body swayed backward away from the wall.

Before she could topple far enough to lose her foothold completely, however, Natalie's slim, firm hand grabbed the shoulder of her dress. A seam somewhere in the material tore, but the dress itself stayed in place, and Natalie's intervention steadied Charlotte.

With a helping hand, she managed to pull herself all the way onto the roof. Once she had both feet under her, she breathed a sigh of relief, careful not to look toward the edge.

"Come on," Natalie said shortly, sprinting off across the sloped surface.

Charlotte's face paled, but she followed at a slower pace. She didn't want to escape the queen's guards only to fall and break her neck.

When they reached the edge of the house, Natalie didn't slow. Taking a running leap, she flew across the narrow gap between the house they were on and the one behind it.

Charlotte gulped, eyeing the narrow alley that lay between the houses. But she couldn't stop. The angry cries behind her had already reached roof level.

Backing up a couple of steps, she ran forward, pushing off against the edge of the roof and sending her body flying into the air. For a heart stopping moment, she soared, certain she was going to slip when she hit the other side and bounce her way to the ground below.

She landed on her feet, falling to her knees but remaining firmly on the new roof.

"See, it's not that hard," Natalie said from where she had paused to check Charlotte's progress.

A chuckle burst out of Charlotte. "It was actually sort of fun." A glance over her shoulder quickly sobered her. "But please don't tell me we have to do a lot more of those before we get to your house. And I definitely can't jump over the width of a full street."

"We'll never make it to my house via rooftop," Natalie said undaunted. "But we don't need to stay up here much longer anyway. We just needed to get you out of that trap."

She took off running sideways, skipping across a row of connected houses. Charlotte followed, finally finding her gait on the rooftops as she got the hang of how to keep purchase on their surface.

The last house in the row stood on a corner of two minor streets, and a balcony wrapped around the front and side of the building. Natalie slid down the roof, dropping onto the balcony below. Charlotte followed her, feeling the rush of free falling, her heart soaring into her throat. Despite their situation, she landed with a smile on her face.

Natalie had already disappeared, so she hurried to follow her down the trellis that stood against one end of the balcony. After their route so far, the trellis seemed as secure and simple as a staircase, and both girls reached the ground in less than a minute.

"And now," Natalie said, tucking her head down, "we run."

Charlotte didn't have time to catch her breath before they were both off. Pumping her legs as hard as she had ever done in her life, Charlotte flew down the street behind Natalie. They wove in and out of foot traffic, carts, and carriages as they crossed the city's streets.

When a small dog turned unexpectedly, putting itself in her path, she didn't even break stride. Leaping over it in one smooth motion, she immediately had to duck beneath a giant crate being carried by a man two steps further down the street.

"In here," Natalie panted, turning into yet another narrow alley.

Charlotte followed, acutely aware that their pursuers were in human form this time. A narrow alley wasn't going to foil them.

But the guards had fallen behind, slowed by the need to clamber up and down roofs to follow where the girls had gone. So when they darted out of the alley into another street, there was no one visible behind them.

Natalie looked over her shoulder, checking the street behind them was clear before she swerved suddenly into yet another alley. Charlotte followed, nearly colliding with her three steps in.

Instead of the usual hodgepodge of walls and doors that lined most of the alleys, this one contained one smooth, unbroken wall as if the whole length bordered a single property.

"What—?" she asked, but Natalie was already moving again.

Climbing onto a crate, she strained upward, just managing to reach the top of the wall. "Give me a boost!" she whispered, and Charlotte rushed forward, offering her laced hands as a foothold.

Natalie stepped into her fingers, pushing off and hauling herself over the edge of the wall. Charlotte stepped toward the crate, ready to follow her—or at least attempt to do so—but Natalie's head was still poking over the wall, now on the other side.

"Go further down," she hissed. "I'll meet you there."

Charlotte hesitated, struck with the irrational anxiety that

Natalie meant to abandon her. But the girl had been the one to lie in wait for her with a plan for their escape. Charlotte would trust she knew what she was doing.

Running down the alley, she heard footsteps keeping pace on the other side of the wall, reassuring her that Natalie was still with her. As she reached a small door in the stretch of wall, it swung open. Charlotte slid to a stop, panting.

Grabbing at the edge of the wood, she pulled herself through and slammed it closed behind her. Her breaths rasped in and out as she stared at Natalie, the two girls now safely on the other side of the wall together. Laughter bubbled up inside her, pushing its way out, and she doubled over, giggling.

Natalie stared at her doubtfully before giving in and laughing along with her.

"L…Latch it," Charlotte managed to force out, and Natalie leaped into action, securing the door behind them.

They both quieted down, the emotional release giving way to labored breathing that slowly calmed.

Charlotte looked around. "Where are we?"

They stood at the end of a stretch of greenery that was denser and less sculpted than the palace gardens. Some distance away, a large house rose above the green, its crisply painted walls shining in the morning light. Charlotte didn't remember many details of Natalie's family home, but it definitely wasn't this mansion.

"I told you," Natalie said. "My house is too far. This is Count Oswin's city home."

Charlotte whistled softly. "He really is important!" She glanced around, uneasy. "But will he be angry that we turned up like this? What if we led the guards to his house?"

Natalie shrugged. "I checked before we dashed in here. There wasn't anyone in sight."

Charlotte frowned, not quite satisfied. "They might ask around. Someone might have seen us."

"The people of the city won't help Celandine's guards,"

Natalie said dismissively. "I'm not saying they'd risk their hides to help us, but not getting involved is the safest option anyway, so they'll all say they didn't see anything and get away from the guards as quickly as possible."

Charlotte sighed, having to accept Natalie's greater understanding of the city and its people. She still didn't like involving so many other people in her own folly, though.

She didn't regret the time with Henry, and at least she'd sent Gwen's apple where it needed to go. But in every other regard… She sighed again.

"There's no need for the count to know anything about it, anyway," Natalie said carelessly. "We can just wait here in the garden until the guards give up and go back to the palace and then slip out again."

"No." Charlotte shook her head decisively. "We're here now, and we should go in and find the count. He said everyone in his household is trustworthy, so we don't have to worry about being seen."

Natalie gave her a doubtful look, but Charlotte held firm.

"Thinking I could foresee and control all the variables is what got me into this trouble," she said. "I'm not making the same mistake again. We need to tell him what happened and the danger that someone might trace us here."

"I suppose—if you insist," Natalie said a little sourly. But she made no further protest, leading the way through the garden to the back door of the mansion.

When she went to open it, Charlotte leaned around her with a warning look and knocked on the wooden panel instead. Natalie rolled her eyes but stepped back, crossing her arms and waiting silently.

It didn't take long for footsteps to sound from inside. When the door swung open, the footman on the other side regarded them both with raised brows.

"We don't usually get visitors to the back door," he said.

Charlotte smiled as sweetly as she could manage. "I'm guessing most of your visitors don't come over your back wall."

The footman's brows drew together.

"We're here to see Count Oswin," she hurried to add. "He's not expecting us, but he'll know who we are. You can tell him Charlotte and Natalie are—"

An instant change came over the footman's face when he heard the names. Leaning out, he pulled them both inside and shut the door behind them.

"They'll be glad to see you," he said with an easy grin that took her by surprise. "Come on, I'll show you the way."

GWEN

Waiting for sunset in her room, wondering what was happening to Charlotte, was torturous. But she couldn't go out with the sun so low on the horizon. Being seen around the palace in her bear form would not only enrage her mother but also damage the plans of the rebels.

Gwen had escaped the mountain kingdom and then ridden the wind back to save it, but both sides still wanted her to play a false role as the pure princess—someone whose apparent virtue seemed to involve sitting around waiting and doing nothing at all.

She paced up and down, her thoughts alternating between Charlotte—was she with Henry now?—and Easton—was he thinking of her as much as she was thinking of him? Every now and then she stopped and looked around her room in wonder. It should look different. After all the changes in her, it should look different.

But everything was exactly the same as she'd left it. This was the danger she had recognized earlier. Trapped in the same environment, the new Gwen wavered before the old one.

Walking slowly over to her bureau, Gwen stared down at the

various jars, bottles, brushes, and handheld mirrors arranged on its top in an orderly fashion. Half in a dream, she reached out one arm and swept it all off with enough force to send some of the smaller items hurtling into the wall.

They fell with various crashes, bangs, and tinkles as glass smashed and liquid sloshed onto the carpet. The cacophony drove back the dreamlike feeling, and a burst of energy took its place.

She stared at herself in the mirror, a smile growing on her face as she reached up and tugged at the mirror's edges. For a second it resisted before pulling sharply free and crashing against the surface of the bureau. Buzzing, Gwen moved to the wardrobe, ripping its doors open so violently that one of them pulled free of its lower hinge.

She seized the contents in large armfuls, tossing the garments over her shoulder and seizing more until the wardrobe was empty. But it wasn't enough. Bracing one shoulder against the side of the robe, she shoved with all her strength. At first it resisted, but she gritted her teeth and shoved harder. It wobbled once and then crashed over with a muffled thud.

She swept on, upending the bedside cabinet and pulling out all its drawers, tipping over the table and chair where she had eaten countless meals. Gripping the curtains of the bed in both hands, she pulled, reveling in the feeling of them ripping free and collapsing to the ground around her.

As she looked around for something else to overturn, she felt the now familiar itchy tingling, followed by the tearing sensation. She squeezed her eyes shut, waiting for the change to finish. When she opened them again, she looked down at enormous paws and sharp claws and her smile returned.

Turning on the bed, she unleashed her bear strength, ripping through the pillows until feathers floated through the room in all directions. She tore at the bedspread and even the mattress underneath, leaving them in ribbons.

The curtains on the windows came next, and the upholstery on the chairs. Then she turned her claws against the walls themselves, ripping long gouges down the wallpaper.

It felt good to be reckless and even better to use the full strength of this new form. In the days since she had stopped taking the drugged drink each night, she had been so careful and so restrained whenever she was a bear. But now she felt her muscles stretching and straining, and it felt good.

Part of her worried guiltily about destroying items that still had use in them. Some had even been beautiful. But at the same time, she knew she could never sleep in that bed again or sit in one of those chairs. She had been obediently doing so for twenty years, and now they represented nothing but captivity of both her body and mind.

She sat back on her haunches and surveyed the destroyed room with satisfaction. Princess Gwendolyn would never have dared do anything so dramatic and defiant. This was no longer Princess Gwendolyn's room, and Gwen was no longer surrounded by a familiarity she didn't want. Everything about this scene was sharp and uncomfortable and confronting.

She had been ready to endure an uncomfortable night amid the ruin of her room, but her bear self was as comfortable on the carpeted floor as she had been in the forest of Charlotte's valley. She curled up, surrounded by feathers and torn material, and slept as easily as she had under the stars.

Gwen woke, sore and disoriented. It took her a moment to make sense of the ruin around her, memory returning slowly. Morning had arrived some time ago, and her human body was much less comfortable on the floor than her bear one.

She rose slowly, rubbing at the shoulder that ached from pushing against the wardrobe the evening before. She didn't regret anything, though. It would have been much more terrible to wake in her bed, thinking for those first bleary moments that she was back in her old life as Princess Gwendolyn.

Looking at the window, she realized again that the first hours of the morning were already past. She needed to find out what had happened to Charlotte.

Choosing simple clothes from a bureau drawer that had survived the night's rampage, she dressed and tried her bedroom door. To her relief, it opened. More than anything, that freedom confirmed her mother's retreat into the past—an option Celandine apparently preferred to facing a reality that no longer conformed with her plans.

Gwen's stomach rumbled as she hurried down the courtyard, and her steps turned instinctively for the kitchen. She didn't correct them. If she needed information about any dramatic events in the palace, the captive servants were the best place to start.

Pausing on the threshold, Gwen breathed in the delicious smell of roasting food and baked treats. She admired the bustle of activity, wishing she didn't have to disrupt it. She had always loved the kitchen as a child, going there often with Easton. But she had been restrained to only the most occasional visit in the past ten years—a rule enforced by Alma. Since Alma sought to protect the captives from the queen's wrath, Gwen couldn't argue with her strictures. It had been yet another loss, though.

Thinking of the risk if she was seen by a courtier, Gwen stepped all the way inside, out of clear sight from the corridor. The movement attracted attention, and a ripple spread through the servants as they looked in her direction and whispered among themselves.

Gwen cleared her throat. "I missed breakfast."

A cook offered her a seat at the well-scrubbed wooden table that ran down the center of the room. As she sat, a young man slipped out the kitchen door, taking off at a run.

Sure enough, she had barely started on the food laid before her when Alma appeared, puffing slightly. Her brows rose when she saw the princess, but she took a moment to catch her breath before speaking, giving time for multiple other servants to slip in behind her, mingling with the crowd already in the kitchen.

"So you really are here," Alma said at last. "I suppose I shouldn't be surprised."

A rush of affection filled Gwen at sight of the older woman. She hadn't realized how much she needed a friendly face. But she also didn't want to forget the realization she had come to with Miriam.

She put down the piece of bread in her hand. "I'm sorry. I didn't mean to cause trouble by coming here, I just—"

"No." Alma said the word firmly. "Miriam told us everything. You came back for us, Your Highness, and we can brave more than this. This is our chance." Her face darkened. "Some of us have been waiting a very long time for any sort of chance."

Gwen hoped she didn't look as terrified as she felt. So many people were relying on her, unaware that Gwen had very little idea what she was doing.

"I came to find out if there was any news of Charlotte," she said.

Alma frowned and glanced around the kitchen. She was met only with blank stares and shrugs.

"Is that someone from the city?" she asked. "I don't think there's a courtier named—"

"No, she came with me from the valleys," Gwen said. "She's the lowlander prince's wife."

Another murmur swept through the room at that. The captives might not have heard of Charlotte, but they knew something about Henry.

"Have you been taking him food?" she guessed.

Alma hesitated. "We've been preparing it, but the queen delivers it herself." She paused. "We've heard rumors that he's cursed."

It was clear from the captives' faces that they didn't know what to make of that suggestion. Gwen almost told them it was the opposite—he was the only one to have freed himself—when it hit her like a bolt.

The captives were as ignorant as she had once been. They knew something happened in the mountain kingdom at night but not what. They didn't know about the transformations.

Gwen didn't hesitate. If they were going to join the rebels, they had to know what they faced.

"Actually," she said, "it's not the prince who's cursed, it's me." A gasp of surprise swept around the room. "Me, and my mother, and all the courtiers and guards. We are tied to these mountains because at night we turn into large, white bears."

"You—what?" Alma asked in a dazed voice.

"At sundown I turn into a bear," Gwen repeated calmly. "And at sunrise I turn back again. I'm still myself in my head the whole time, though. We don't turn wild or anything."

"I…" Alma collapsed into a nearby seat. "We've come up with lots of theories over the years, but I can't say anyone came up with that. Every one of us was drugged for the journey across the mountains, so we never saw…"

"It does explain it, though," the cook said. "We wondered how they made it across."

"And some of the messes we've had to clean up make more sense too," a younger woman muttered. "Remember those gouges high up on the wall of the green sitting room? None of us could work out what could have made them."

Gwen thought guiltily of her room. "If any of you have the job of cleaning my room, please skip it today. And tomorrow. And— actually, you can forget about it all together."

Alma raised an eyebrow. "Do I want to know what you've done?"

Gwen smiled. "I'm going with no."

"I thought *you* were going to marry that prince." The cook regarded Gwen skeptically. "We've all been worked off our feet preparing for it. So how can he have a wife?"

Gwen grimaced. "My mother isn't used to having her plans foiled. She's determined to go through with it, and for now at least, we're playing along." Her voice turned firm. "I will not be marrying Prince Henry, however."

Yet another stir ran through the crowd.

"But please continue with your preparations in line with the queen's commands," she said hurriedly. "We'd rather not tip our hand yet."

Facing only Miriam, it had seemed sensible to say nothing. But with the captives massed before her, she couldn't bring herself to treat them with suspicion. They had been stolen from their homes and turned into slaves for the mountain queen— some for almost ten years. The queen had no allies in this room.

"So this Charlotte is part of your plans?" Alma asked shrewdly. "But she's crossed the queen somehow?"

Gwen grimaced. It was a little more complicated than that, but the sentiment was close enough to the truth.

Alma exchanged a look with the cook, waiting for him to nod before turning back to Gwen. "We haven't heard anything about an unknown girl," she said briskly, "but the orders for the prince's food changed late yesterday. We were instructed to deliver a drugged drink, just as we used to do for you."

She gave Gwen an apologetic look as she said it, but Gwen had long forgiven the captives' role in her previous life. They hadn't done any of it by choice.

"He was drugged all night?" she asked, heart sinking. That must mean Charlotte had succeeded in bargaining for a night with Henry. And the queen had found a way around the bargain's terms. Did that mean she'd also found a way around the terms intended to protect Charlotte?

"There definitely hasn't been any talk of preparing food for another captive?" she asked.

The cook and Alma both shook their heads. Did that mean

Charlotte had succeeded in getting out of the palace or just that she hadn't been fed yet?

Sighing, Gwen rose. She was going to have to find her mother after all.

Before leaving, she faced Alma and the cook. "Miriam asked what you could do."

They both tensed.

"Please let me know if the queen ever asks you to drug any food or drink again," she finished, and they relaxed. It wasn't a huge request, but it might prevent a future calamity like Charlotte's attempted night with Henry.

Gwen left the room, heading for her mother's study as she considered how to get access to Henry again. If he hadn't spoken to Charlotte, then it was up to Gwen to give him further reassurance and stop him from doing anything foolish.

She arrived at the door of the study only to hear the tromp of boots behind her. Glancing back, she saw a weary-looking squad of guards heading in her direction. She stepped to the side, allowing the two in the lead to enter the study ahead of her. They were both rigid and tense, apparently too distracted to even notice her.

The rest of the guards remained behind in the corridor, at least half of them openly gawking at her. But they didn't make any move to restrain her or question her presence.

"You what?" the queen cried from inside the room, and Gwen flinched instinctively.

The guards flinched even more, however, and Gwen made up her mind, slipping into the room. No one noticed her entrance.

"One girl," the queen said in lower but equally threatening tones. "You only had to detain one girl. Exactly how many men did you take with you?"

Both guards shifted nervously.

"There was another girl waiting for her," one said. "She helped—"

"A single other girl?" the queen demanded. "Is that supposed to be an excuse?"

"Without our bear senses," the other one tried, "we couldn't follow."

"I see." The queen's voice was ice. "So you have allowed your nightly forms to become a crutch and an excuse. Clearly it is time for the royal guards to get in shape. I want every guard not on active duty to report to the training yards. Sunup to sundown. And you will train there every day until I deem you are no longer a disgrace to me."

The men's eyes widened, but neither protested.

"Yes, Your Majesty." The first one bowed low, and the other quickly followed.

Gwen kept her face impassive but inside she was crowing. Not only had Charlotte managed to escape—with Natalie's help from the sound of it—but the queen's reaction had played even further into their hands. An exhausted, distracted guard force could only help the rebel efforts.

The elation died as she finally noticed the man standing to one side and slightly behind her mother's desk. He was half in shadow, barely noticeable beside the commanding presence of the queen. But he had noticed her.

Gwen shivered at his gaze. What was Lord Rafferty doing here where she might once have expected to find Count Oswin? Before her escape, he had leveraged a moment of surveillance of Gwen into inclusion with her mother's inner circle of courtiers. Apparently, in the weeks since he had made fast use of that opportunity.

The feel of his eyes made her want to flee. But her mother had finally spotted her.

"My daughter," Celandine said smoothly, her manner changing completely.

Both the guards threw Gwen an alarmed look before bowing

again toward the queen, a third time to Gwen, and hurrying out of the room.

"Where have you been?" Celandine asked, although she sounded distracted.

"In my room, of course," Gwen replied. "Resting."

The queen relaxed a little at her answer. "You should get all the rest you can now. After the wedding, matters will proceed quickly."

"Matters?" Gwen asked, her eyes flicking to Lord Rafferty.

"The matters we spoke of previously," the queen said in a voice that shut down any further conversation. "But that is not something you need to think of. I will manage the situation."

"Yes, Mother," Gwen said meekly, a little relieved her mother hadn't expanded on her words. Did that mean Lord Rafferty wasn't yet included in all her plans?

If the queen was edging out Count Oswin and replacing him with someone of Lord Rafferty's ilk, then they couldn't make their move fast enough. The queen had enough ambition of her own without listening to someone who obviously had just as much as her.

CHARLOTTE

*E*xchanging surprised looks, Charlotte and Natalie both followed the count's footman without comment, allowing him to usher them into a brightly lit sitting room filled with people. Charlotte faltered on the threshold, trying to make sense of the gathering.

"Natalie!" Patti rushed to her daughter's side, throwing her arms around her neck.

"Really, Mother!" Natalie sounded disgusted, but Charlotte caught the pleased light in her eyes. She was at that age where she still wanted her mother's affection but wasn't willing to admit it.

"Charlotte! What a relief." Easton crossed more calmly to Charlotte's side, his parents trailing behind him.

"Well, this is good timing," the count said, not sounding altogether pleased. "I was about to head to the palace to see if I could get any word of you."

"How could you leave without telling us?" Patti scolded Natalie. Dane stood at her side, giving his daughter equally disappointed looks.

"We were going to be back by sundown," Natalie replied, seeming unaffected by their disapproval. "But then Charlotte got herself into trouble. Since she came with Princess Gwen and is supposedly married to that lowlander prince at the palace, I figured you wouldn't want me to abandon her to be captured by the queen." She shrugged.

"It's true," Charlotte rushed to say. "Natalie appeared in the nick of time and saved me. I owe her a debt of gratitude."

A soft snort in the background drew her eyes to Natalie's brother.

"Always has to be the hero," Baden muttered, earning himself a fiery look from Natalie.

"I suppose in that case…" Patti seemed torn between indignation at her daughter's behavior and pride at her success.

"Were your meetings with the rebels a success?" Charlotte asked Easton softly while Patti and Dane continued to affectionately chide their daughter.

"I'm afraid the reality of me and my last ten years doesn't quite live up to their imaginings," he said with a self-deprecating grin.

"Nonsense!" Lydia said firmly, her gaze bright as she watched her son. "They loved you."

Jett cleared his throat. "Perhaps not quite that. But they were more than pleased that the time has finally come to move against the queen. And some of them were quite enthusiastic at the prospect of Easton as king. After ten years, they see our family as belonging to the city more than the court, so they're pleased to think of one of their own on the throne."

Easton ran a hand through his hair, and Charlotte could easily recognize the concern on his face because it was the same concern she felt whenever she thought about Henry's true role. Most of the time it was easy to focus on the crisis in front of them, but every now and then she remembered what would happen if they succeeded, and she wanted to run and hide. She had no qualifications to become Crown Princess Charlotte.

Easton lowered his voice, angling himself toward Charlotte. "Did you see Gwen?"

Her lips twitched as she looked at him. "You are aware that everyone here already knows the two of you are in love, right? Our entire plan is literally built around it. You don't have to whisper."

Easton flushed, and she regretted teasing him. The poor man's entire life had been overturned without warning. It was no wonder it took a bit of getting used to.

"I did see her," she said softly. "And she looked well. Unharmed, anyway. And plotting how to work against her mother. She had an object from her godmother." She proceeded to explain about the apple and what she had exchanged it for.

At some point in the story, the rest of the group drifted over, listening as she outlined her failed night with Henry and their escape across the rooftops.

The count shook his head. "That was a very foolish risk."

"I know," Charlotte said quietly. "I'm sorry."

"There's no use trying to tamp down the fervor of youth, Oswin." Jett clapped him on the back. "We'll never succeed at that, so we'll have to content ourselves with channeling it in useful directions."

"I had a chance to speak to him briefly, at least," Charlotte said. "And he promised he'd play along and assist Gwen. So hopefully that was enough…" She trailed off, wishing she'd had time to tell him more of their plans. It would take strong nerves for him to play along all the way to the middle of the wedding ceremony.

"We're relying on the princess, then," Oswin said. "Hopefully she's managing to hold firm against her stepmother."

Charlotte's thoughts snagged on his final word. "Her what?"

The count gave her an odd look. "Queen Celandine, of course."

"No, I know who you mean," Charlotte said. "I just thought…

are you saying she isn't Gwen's birth mother? She isn't any blood relation at all?"

Easton also gave her an odd look. "No, she isn't. But she doesn't let anyone talk about it at court and especially not anywhere around Gwen. I didn't even know myself until I was thirteen and overheard my parents mention it. They hadn't told me because they were worried I would tell the princess." His mouth twisted. "I was so incensed that everyone was lying to her that I flew straight off to confront the queen, setting off this whole situation."

"None of it is your fault," his mother murmured, but Easton ignored her, still focused on Charlotte.

"But I'm surprised Gwen didn't mention it to you," he said. "It's the reason she finally defied her mother and escaped."

Charlotte's frown deepened. "I don't think so. It was finding out about being drugged every night and being a bear that pushed her to escape. She's always talked as if Celandine is her..." She trailed off as she reviewed their conversations, skimming over them in her mind, her certainty growing. "Gwen thinks Celandine is the woman who gave birth to her," she said with confidence.

"No, that can't be right," Easton cried. "I'm sure she said..." He too trailed off into thought, and when he spoke again, he sounded uncomfortable. "Or did I just assume she'd found out the same thing I did?"

"What are you both talking about?" the count asked. "I heard her say it with my own ears. Back in that basement hideout, she plainly said Celandine isn't her mother."

"She did say that." Charlotte drew out the words. "But I interpreted it to mean she was rejecting Celandine's role in her life. Don't you remember how nervous she was to say it? Like she was anxious over the rejection." Charlotte's feelings about her own parents had seesawed often enough for her to have recognized the high emotion of the moment.

"You're right." Easton sounded horrified. "She could easily have meant that. And the rest of us just assumed…"

"How is that possible, though?" Charlotte asked. "Why is Celandine queen if she's only a stepmother, and how could it possibly have been kept a secret from Gwen? What has been going on in this kingdom?"

"What hasn't been going on?" Baden muttered, and for once Natalie nodded in agreement.

"I suppose you don't know anything about our history or laws, do you?" Lydia asked.

Charlotte winced apologetically. "In the Four Kingdoms, the mountain kingdom is seen as a myth, if it's thought of at all. I didn't even know it was a real place until Gwen said she came from here."

"Our succession laws are a little complicated," Lydia said. "The oldest child of the previous monarch inherits the throne, but if they marry, they rule jointly with their spouse."

"So if they die, their spouse just becomes the monarch on their own?" Charlotte asked doubtfully.

"Not exactly." Lydia sighed. "If the next heir in line is an adult, the throne passes immediately to them. But if they're a child, then the spouse continues to rule as before until the child comes of age and is able to take the throne themselves."

"Like a regent?" Charlotte asked.

Jett nodded. "But without the limitations of a regency."

"Celandine must have married Gwen's father when Gwen was very young if she doesn't remember anything about it," Charlotte said, trying to puzzle it all out.

"Sadly, Gwen's mother died in childbirth," Lydia said. "Gwen never had the chance to know her. And when Gwen was three, King Isander became ill. The royal doctors could do nothing to prevent his decline, and the king—who loved his daughter very much—decided to take her to spend some time away from court before the end."

"I thought you were all trapped in the mountains?" Charlotte queried.

"They didn't go far," Jett clarified. "Just to a lodge belonging to the royal family that's on the very edge of our valley. In the past, it was used frequently by the royal family as a retreat where they could spend time together without the pressures of court. But it's fallen into disuse since Celandine took the throne. She said too many bad memories resided there for her to take the princess back." He fell silent, and his wife continued the story.

"While they were at the lodge, King Isander's health deteriorated faster than expected, and he died there. The princess was brought back to the castle by Celandine, who claimed to be her stepmother and the queen."

"What?" Charlotte cried, startled. Whatever she had been expecting, it wasn't that. "But everyone at the palace knew her, right? She'd gone down there with them?"

Lydia shook her head. "She met the king during his final weeks at the lodge. He sensed his death was coming sooner than anticipated and proposed marriage so his daughter wouldn't be left alone without a parent. He wanted her to have a proper monarch to take the pressure from her shoulders during her childhood and youth. She had the marriage certificate and the proper seals, and the servants and guards who returned from the lodge all corroborated her story."

Lydia shrugged. "I was busy with a young son at the time, but it seemed just like Isander not to want to abandon his daughter to so many years in a regency. I only wish he had made a better choice for his new wife. He had no idea what misery he was condemning the poor princess to."

"So Celandine turned up, claimed the throne, and then made everyone pretend she was Gwen's real mother?" Charlotte gaped at them. "How is that possible?"

"The loyal guard force she brought with her were persuasive," the count said dryly. "And those of us closest to the king scrutinized the documents closely. There was nothing out of order." He sighed. "If we'd known how it would go, we might have fought harder, but she was charming and persuasive back then, before she'd consolidated her power. And King Isander had consistently refused to name a regent. It had all of us worried, concerned about what would happen in the case of a sudden decline. It made sense to us that he had held off because he had another plan in mind, and none of us relished the power struggle that would eventuate if we had to choose a regent instead. We let it happen, and by the time Celandine made a move—evicting those members of the court most loyal to Isander and replacing them with her own people, her hold had become far too strong to be challenged."

"But someone did eventually challenge it," Jett said ruefully. "A thirteen-year-old boy. And she responded by binding the court to her with an enchantment. No one knew what we were facing twenty years ago."

"That is one massive loophole she exploited," Charlotte breathed. "But Gwen's been an adult for years. Why is Celandine still queen?"

The count sighed. "Celandine has always ruled with the expectation that she would eventually hand over to Gwendolyn. That was part of the reason she was initially accepted. But she has played the enchantment to her advantage, always coming up with a plausible excuse for why Gwendolyn isn't ready to take the throne. Marriage to a prince, along with the destruction of the enchantment, was supposed to be an end to any possible excuses. She'll have to step down. Or at least, she should be forced into it. Knowing her, though, I'm sure she has some further plan to delay the handover of power."

"Something Gwen said gave me the impression she did mean for Gwen to take the throne after her wedding," Charlotte said thoughtfully. "She meant to install her as a puppet queen. I guess she had to make sure Gwen was sufficiently beaten down before taking that risk."

Easton winced, his face lined with pain. He had been gone for the past ten years, but he must have seen enough in the ten years before that to know what Charlotte was talking about.

"And we just sent her back there," he murmured under his breath. "Alone. And now it turns out she doesn't even know the truth. Celandine has never acted as a true mother to her, and she didn't birth her either. Gwen has no ties to her and owes her no loyalty. But Gwen is the only one who doesn't know that."

He blew out a breath, straightening. "I have to go to her."

"No!" his mother cried. "It's too risky! What if the queen sees you?"

"I don't care," he said, his voice granite. "I'm not abandoning her to that place for a second time. Not knowing the truth makes her vulnerable. I should have gone to her and told her the truth immediately after I found it out. I've spent ten years regretting that, and I'm not going to regret making the same mistake again. I have to find her and make sure she knows everything."

He scanned the room. "If none of you will help me, at least don't try to stop me."

"I'll help you," Charlotte said quietly.

Gwen had helped her get to Henry, and now she would help Gwen's beloved find his way to her.

GWEN

This time, Gwen didn't return straight to her room. She couldn't bear to be shut up in there for endless more hours, just waiting. But neither did she want to endanger the servants by seeking them out. Which left her once again alone, walking the corridors she had roamed so often.

But these weren't just halls she had once walked alone. They were also the play spaces where she had run with Easton, and she chose to think of him as she walked instead of dwelling on the painful, solitary years. Without him and Nanny, her life would have been only one long stretch of bleak darkness. The two of them had saved her, and now she was choosing to return to the Gwen they had helped form. The Gwen she wanted to be.

When her steps finally circled back to her room, she slipped inside with a soft sigh. She couldn't avoid the mess she'd made forever.

The chaos assaulted her vision, distracting her enough that she missed the flash of motion from one side. A hand clamped over her mouth, stifling her scream, and a strong arm circled her shoulders, pulling her firmly back against a solid chest.

She thrashed, trying to maneuver her teeth for a bite until the words in her ear permeated her brain.

"Gwen! Gwen! It's me. It's Easton."

She stilled instantly. Easton? Was it possible? She had spent half the day dreaming of him, so was it possible she was dreaming this too?

But she could feel the solid warmth of him, goosebumps rising where his breath brushed behind her ear. He was real. He was there.

She slumped in the circle of his arm, her eyes welling with tears. Easton immediately dropped his arm, instead taking her shoulders and spinning her so he could see her face.

"Gwen?" His voice was rough and his face drawn. "What is it? What's wrong? Are you hurt?"

She managed a tremulous smile, drinking in the sight of him. His face was somehow afraid, angry, and achingly beautiful all at the same time. She had never seen such a welcome sight.

"I'm sorry," she managed to choke out. "I'm fine. Really. Just glad to see you."

Easton glanced around the room, his eyes coming back to hers. "I didn't dare wander the palace looking for you, but when I saw what had happened here..." He shuddered. "I've been going out of my mind waiting in this room!" He pointed at one of the walls. "Those are claw marks, Gwen! Don't try to claim they aren't."

Gwen bit her lip guiltily. "That was me. In a fit of...defiance? Rejection of my past? It wasn't exactly rage, but..." She shrugged.

Easton finally let go of her shoulders, falling back a step and laughing. "It was you? You did this?" He looked at the mess with new eyes, his lips twitching. "I approve. I just wish I'd been here to join in. I always hated this room. I hated the thought of you stuck in here all the time."

Gwen smiled. "But it brought you to me today. You knew

where to find me." Her smile fell away as reality intruded. "But what are you doing here? You shouldn't be here!"

Easton swallowed, the light dimming from his eyes. "I had to see you. There's something I have to tell you."

Gwen's heart seized. Was he here to tell her that being king was a burden too heavy for him to accept? Was he going to say he was pulling out of the plan?

He stepped forward and took both her hands in a gentle grip. She wanted to prod him to hurry up and say what he was going to say, while at the same time she wanted to beg him not to say it.

When he hesitated, she nearly pulled her hands away, unable to bear the tension. But he gave her fingers a squeeze, and her heart calmed. Easton of all people wouldn't desert her. Somehow they would find their way through this—whatever it was.

"Ten years ago, I made a horrible mistake," he said. "I learned something about the queen—about you—and I went to her to confront her instead of coming to you. I've regretted it ever since."

"You said that back in Ranost," Gwen said, frowning. "Surely you don't think I blame you for that?"

He let one of her hands go, raking his fingers through his hair. "When I said that in Ranost I thought—I assumed—you'd discovered the same truth I discovered ten years ago. But I just learned from Charlotte that you probably don't know it after all." He swallowed. "I couldn't leave you here believing a lie. After everything that woman has done to you, I couldn't leave you even the tiniest bit more vulnerable to her."

Gwen frowned, utterly lost. "What are you talking about? What did you find out ten years ago?"

"She isn't your mother." Easton spat out the bald words. "Celandine is your stepmother, not your birth mother. It's just another one of the secrets she forced the court to keep from you."

Gwen's mouth dropped open. "What are you talking about? Are you saying I'm not really the princess?"

"What? No!" He groaned. "I'm fumbling this. Your parents were king and queen when you were born, but your mother died in childbirth. Celandine was King Isander's second wife."

"I…" Gwen's head spun. "I don't…"

She staggered and Easton rushed to right a toppled chair for her. Its upholstery was torn, but Gwen sank onto it anyway, raising a hand to her head.

"Celandine is my stepmother." She said the words slowly, like she was trying to absorb them. "My father's second wife." She looked up at Easton, lost. "Why would she lie about something like that?"

He shrugged uneasily. "To ensure your loyalty maybe? She's obsessed with loyalty."

"Is that why she didn't come with us to the lodge?" she muttered. "Did my father leave her back at the castle because she wasn't my real mother?"

"What?" Easton frowned at her.

It was her turn to shrug. "It's a little thing, really, but I always wondered. I don't have any memories of my father before his final illness—I was too young. I don't remember anything from before that at all. My earliest memories are of that trip to the lodge, so I've thought of it often since. I remember his death so clearly. I guess it's the sort of thing that sticks with you." She shivered.

Easton didn't say anything, his expression turned soft and compassionate, so she kept talking. "I was so excited to be by myself with him, but at the same time I was terrified because I somehow knew he was going to leave me. I don't think anyone had told me directly, but I knew. When he died, I cried and cried. I thought I was going to be left all alone in the world. I can still remember the relief when Celandine walked into the room and picked me up."

She scrubbed a hand over her eyes. "She used to get so angry when I tried to bring up that time and those memories, so I quickly stopped talking about it altogether. But I always thought it was a little strange. I remember the relief of her arrival so vividly, but it wasn't attached to any feelings of love. I wasn't glad to see her specifically, I was just glad someone was there." Her voice dropped. "I thought there must be something broken inside me because what sort of small child doesn't love their mother? I tried so hard to find memories of her from before the lodge trip, sure I would feel the love in those, but I could never recall anything from before. And all the time, I wondered why she wasn't on the trip with us. If she had been, I would have remembered her, and that meant so much to me—to remember my mother from before."

She sighed. "I have this memory of Count Oswin—a much younger version of him—telling me how much my father wanted to spend time just with me. It made me feel so guilty. I was the reason my mother missed out on my father's final weeks. And I always wondered if maybe I'd been the one to insist she didn't come—because I didn't love her the way I loved my father. Maybe that's why she's always been so cold toward me ever since."

"I remember how hard you tried to love her when you were a child." Easton stared at her. "I couldn't understand it given the way she treated you. Is that why?"

Gwen nodded. "But this information changes those memories completely. The love wasn't there because I didn't even know Celandine. She wasn't my mother, she was almost a stranger!" Her brow creased. "But when did she marry my father? They must have been newlyweds. How could he have left her behind?"

"Your memories must be mixed up," Easton said. "Celandine was there at the lodge—that's where you both met her. They were married at the lodge only a week or so before King Isander's death."

Gwen stared at him, fresh shock washing through her. "Are you saying she wasn't part of the court?"

"Apparently not. My parents said they'd never heard of her before she appeared after the king's death with you in tow."

Gwen swallowed, her mind whirring. "She appeared at court and claimed to have married my father on his deathbed and *everyone just believed her?*" Her voice rose at the final words, and concern sprang into Easton's eyes.

Gwen leaped to her feet. She was shaking again, but she no longer felt weak. Instead, she blazed with fury.

"She had their marriage certificate and all the relevant papers," Easton said uneasily. "And while there were minimal servants and guards at the lodge—that's its purpose—the ones who were there all backed up her story. The count said…" He trailed off, brows lowering further and further as he watched her face.

"I told you I have no memories of court from before my father's death," Gwen said slowly and carefully, "but I clearly remember the weeks at the lodge. I've gone over and over those memories a thousand times in the years since. My father was desperate to spend every minute with me. He had a little bed set up by the window of his room so we never had to be parted. I was with him every moment, except when his manservant was helping him wash. *And I never saw Celandine until she walked into the room after his death.*" She enunciated each word of her final sentence carefully and clearly.

"Are you saying…" Easton began, and Gwen finished for him.

"If Celandine didn't marry my father *before* we went to the lodge, she never married him at all."

Easton fell back several steps, his face paling. "So it's…all a lie? The whole thing? Not just being your birth mother but being the queen? Everything!"

Fresh fury ripped through Gwen. "No wonder she wouldn't

let me talk about my father's final weeks and refused to ever take us back to the lodge! And no wonder she had everyone lie to me. She must have been terrified about what I might say. She must have either bought off the servants and guards at the lodge or used an object to enchant them, but I was the one witness she couldn't buy."

"So instead she tried to undermine, silence, and manipulate you." Easton's fury now matched her own. "If only we'd had this conversation ten years ago. We could have confronted her together in front of the court and—"

Gwen suddenly deflated, the righteous anger draining out of her. "And what? You said she has papers and witnesses and what do I have? I have no proof."

"But still! How could she—"

Gwen took his hands, silencing him. "Thank you," she said simply. "Thank you for coming here. Thank you for understanding how important the truth would be to me. You don't know how much it means to me that you came despite the risks. That woman has never been a nurturer to me, and so I've been trying to cut the remaining ties in my mind, trying not to think of her as my mother, but..." She sighed. "It's been hard. I'm fighting so many years of ingrained habits. But now I know it's not only her treatment of me that disqualifies her. She's not my birth mother either, and nor is she even my stepmother. She's literally just a usurper who has spent twenty years stealing the people, relationships, and position that should have been mine."

"Gwen..." Easton looked down into her face, his eyes growing warm. "I—"

Gwen's hand flew to his mouth, silencing him as her eyes grew wide.

"Did you hear that?" she whispered, glancing around frantically for somewhere to hide. "There was a step!"

The door handle rattled, and her heart stopped. Pushing

Easton violently to the floor, she scooped up a long, torn curtain and flung it over him. She had just pulled the corner over his left boot when the door was pushed open.

She straightened and spun toward the new arrival, hoping it was Alma or Miriam.

It wasn't.

GWEN

Queen Celandine—the usurper—strode into the room and faltered. Her eyes widened as she surveyed the chaos. Gratitude flooded Gwen that she had so effectively destroyed her room. She could never have hidden Easton in time otherwise.

And the physical evidence of her defiance no longer mattered. Given what she had just learned, there was no way she could have faked her old self and called Celandine mother. She could barely even look at her.

"What happened here?" Celandine stared from the mess to Gwen.

Gwen shrugged. "I did some redecorating."

"*Redecorating?*" Celandine's eyes narrowed. "Are you trying to tell me something, Gwendolyn?" she hissed.

Gwen met her eyes steadily. "I suppose I am. I'm telling you I don't want any of this from you. All I want is my throne."

Celandine's nostrils flared, but for once she didn't have a ready quip.

"I'll go ahead with this wedding you have planned," Gwen continued, "and then I'll take the throne that is owed me." She paused and smiled sweetly. "Unless you think the wedding isn't such a good idea after all?"

Celandine let out a heavy breath. "Is that what this is about? You think if you throw a tantrum, I'll cancel the wedding? Do you really have so little ambition? Arcadia could soon be yours, and the rest of the Four Kingdoms after it."

"Don't you mean yours?" Gwen asked. "The Four Kingdoms will be yours. Why would I want that?"

Celandine threw her eyes toward the ceiling. "You'll be the one sitting on the throne with every luxury you can ask for! Don't talk as if I'm planning to lock you in a dungeon."

She looked ready to do just that, so Gwen moderated her tone, aware that she was not only walking a fine line, but that Easton was one wrong step away from discovery. She needed to get Celandine out of her room.

"And why should I believe that?" Gwen asked. "I'm twenty-three, and so far you've done nothing but talk about me sitting on the throne one day."

Celandine relaxed the slightest bit, and Gwen felt a surge of satisfaction from knowing she had said the right thing.

"This time is different, my dear," the queen said. "I held off in the past only because I was waiting for the perfect moment. And that perfect moment has now arrived. You will free our people and then lead them to their glorious future. No one will dare challenge us then."

Her eyes lit with fervor, and Gwen felt an unfamiliar pang of sympathy for her. Celandine was broken in ways Gwen hadn't been able to recognize as a child. And although they had lived side by side for twenty years, Gwen would probably never know what pain from her past had broken her.

But that new awareness changed nothing. Celandine had destroyed countless lives, and there was no place for her in the mountain kingdom. A deep weariness gripped Gwen. She wished it could have been different—that Celandine could have broken the cycle of pain instead of inflicting it on Gwen. But all Gwen could do was resolve that she would be the one to forge a different future. If she was blessed with children one day, she would make sure they knew every day that they were loved and valued.

"Fine," she said, injecting the word with the youthful petulance she had never dared show in her younger years. "But if you're not true to your word this time, you won't like the results."

Celandine looked like she was barely refraining from rolling her eyes as she assured Gwen of the glorious future before her.

"I'm tired," Gwen muttered, staring pointedly at the door.

Celandine's eyes narrowed, but she seemed to think better of whatever rebuke hovered on her tongue. Instead, she swept silently out of the room.

Gwen watched her go in astonishment. She had always been the one restraining herself in her mother's presence. It was surreal to see that reversed.

When the door closed behind the queen, she waited a breath and then two and three. But the door didn't swing back open, the footsteps retreating away down the corridor.

"You can come out," she said on a long exhale.

Easton burst up from the floor, sucking in gulps of air. "I was afraid to even breathe in case she saw the curtain moving. I've been doing a delightful experiment on just how shallow you can make your breaths without passing out."

Gwen winced. "Sorry. I'm just glad we managed to hide you in time. That was way too close."

"Do you have a key for your door?" He eyed the lock dubiously.

"Sadly, no. I used to, but she changed the lock while I was gone."

Easton surveyed the room as if looking for a more comfortable hiding place. Unfortunately Gwen's destruction of the room had removed most of the options.

"Wait!" she said. "How could I forget?" Walking across to the wall, she pressed on a spot at hand height, revealing a hidden latch.

Easton's eyebrows rose. "How did I never notice that door? It's just like all the storage cupboards around the palace corridors—designed to blend in with the wall but not so well disguised as to classify as a hidden room. But why would the princess have a storage cupboard in her bedchamber?"

Gwen smiled wistfully. "We used to love playing spies in those cupboards. This room isn't for storage, though. It's the sleeping space for a servant. When I was a child, Nanny slept in here so I was never alone." She stepped involuntarily back as she remembered what it had been used for after Nanny's death.

Easton stepped into the small space, peering around. When Nanny had been alive, Gwen had loved to sneak in there and burrow into Nanny's bed, insisting she read her stories or brush her hair. But after Nanny died, the queen had used the space for Gwen's punishments, and she hadn't voluntarily stepped inside for years. Once she had become so compliant the punishments had stopped, she had managed to push the memory of the room almost completely from her mind.

"It's not much bigger than those storage cupboards," Easton noted, and Gwen felt a rush of guilt. "There's barely room for a cot in here."

As a child it had merely seemed cozy, and she'd never questioned why she had such an excessively large room while Nanny had a tiny one. It was only after the woman was gone, when Gwen was older, that she started asking questions like that.

Easton smiled and held out a hand to her. "We can talk in here. That way if anyone comes, you only have to dash out and close the door on me."

Gwen reluctantly stepped inside, waiting for the panic to overtake her. But it didn't come. With the door open and Easton at her side, the space had transformed back into the cozy haven of her young childhood. She breathed a sigh of relief.

"I still miss Nanny sometimes," Easton said with a sigh. "She was always as kind to me as she was to you."

Gwen swallowed against the looming tears. "I miss her all the time. But I'm also glad she wasn't around to see what happened with my mo—Celandine. She would have been heartbroken at the way she treated me. And if she had spoken up in my defense and Celandine punished her, I would have been beside myself."

"I always felt that way when she punished you," Easton said, his voice soft and warm and laced with regret. "I used to dream of racing in to rescue you, but…"

"You did rescue me." Gwen took his hand, raising it to her cheek. "You were everything to me."

His cheeks warmed beneath her touch, his eyes riveted on her face. "You were the beautiful princess from a fairy story and also my best friend. It never felt quite real to me," he whispered. "There isn't a day that's gone by since we were parted when I haven't thought of you."

"Me either," she whispered back.

"Gwen." The word sounded torn from him.

It hit her heart with a shot of pain. For her, being back in his presence was nothing short of beautiful and miraculous. Every moment felt precious.

But he sounded broken and unsure. If he truly didn't want the life here, she couldn't tie him to it because of his feelings for her. If she let him do that, he would come to resent her and that would be the worst thing of all.

So how could she be sure of his true feelings? He would never want to hurt her, and neither would he abandon an entire kingdom—his kingdom.

He wouldn't lie to you, a voice said inside, and she recognized it instantly as the truth. If she wanted to know how he truly felt, she only had to ask. But that required the courage to hear the answer.

She drew a breath, willing herself to say the words, but his eyes were no longer on hers. They had dropped to her lips, and Gwen could no longer remember the sentence she was trying to form in her mind. All she could think about was their close proximity, the warmth of his hand against her cheek, and the way his eyes darkened as they looked at her.

Here in this private, close space, it felt like the rest of the world had disappeared. Like their problems no longer existed, and there was only the two of them and the vast ocean of love and belonging that tied them together.

"Gwen," he murmured again, his voice even more ragged, although this time it was a different sort of torment in his voice.

"Easton," she breathed back, angling her face up toward him.

He sucked in a breath and bent to press his lips to hers, his free hand circling her waist while his other one continued to cup her face.

Their first kiss had burned bright and hot, the culmination of years of separation and longing. It had shaken Gwen's carefully guarded heart apart. This second one filled her, mending the lost and lonely corners inside her. With Easton, she was never alone. With Easton she belonged.

She wanted it to go on forever, but he broke it off, his chest heaving with sharp breaths as he leaned his forehead against hers.

"Gwen," he whispered for a third time, and this time it was warm and loving. She wanted to hear him say her name like that every day for the rest of her life.

Awareness rushed back in as she remembered the unsettled matters between them, the unspoken topics that needed to be discussed. She had already known Easton felt enduring affection for her and also desire. But she needed to know if that was enough for a future. She didn't have the luxury of choosing her career, and neither would her husband. They would both be chained to a demanding role that they could never put down, never rest from.

Gwen gently pushed him away, knowing she needed distance if she was going to manage the conversation that had to happen. Easton's brows drew together, his expression bereft. He reached for her, but she shook her head.

"Easton, I have to know," she said. "And I'm trusting that you won't lie to me."

His jaw flexed. "I would never lie to you," he replied, and she believed him.

"I know. I trust that." She drew a deep breath. "And that's why you have to tell me the truth—even if you think it will hurt me. Even if you think others might suffer for it."

"Gwen, you're scaring me." He tried to step toward her again.

She shook her head, and he froze, watching her with concern.

"I know you care about me, Easton." She hated the wobble in her voice. "But that doesn't mean you should be forced into marrying me—forced into becoming king—before you've even had a chance to properly consider the matter. We hadn't been reunited for even a full day before you were being asked to commit to me for life. That's too much! I know it's too much. And I'm afraid you'll say yes because you know how much it matters to the kingdom. But I can't bear to see you tied to me because of that."

"That's what's been bothering you?" He laughed, relief and something less certain in the sound. "Gwen, I knew I wanted to grow up and marry you when we were thirteen. I just didn't think anyone would let me, given you were the princess. I've spent ten years wishing there was a way to come home to my family—home to you. You are home to me, Gwen, and I care about that far more than I care about what I do or what role I fill. If you needed me to build a house for you and bring home wood every day for our fire, I would do it without a second thought.

And if you need me to put on a crown for you, I'll do that with equal gladness. One thing the years in Ranost taught me is that I can find experiences to enjoy and fulfilling tasks anywhere and in any job. But without the people I love, they'll always feel a little empty."

He gave a low laugh. "You're asking me to become royalty, Gwen! It might be a burden, but it's not a hardship. I love this kingdom, and I would gladly serve it even if it wasn't you asking it of me."

A weight lifted off Gwen, and she felt so light she wondered at the fact she didn't float straight out of the door and bob around on the ceiling of her bedchamber.

"It's you I'm worried about," he said in a low voice, bringing her back to the ground. "You answered the count so quickly, so certain of your feelings for me, and I can't help but wonder…"

He hesitated, and she waited, having no idea what he could be concerned about. Her feelings for Easton had never wavered.

"You loved me when we were children, but you barely know me as a man! The queen kept you so isolated that it's no wonder you clung to the memory of our friendship. How do you know your feelings aren't just childish leftovers that will wither and die under the pressure of daily life?"

Gwen wanted to instantly protest, but she forced herself to consider the question. It was a valid one.

"You're right that we missed a lot of years," she said softly. "And there are so many things to relearn about each other—things I want to know about your life in those missing years. But even one day was enough to see that you were still you. And I never loved you just because you were the only boy I knew. Back then you were honest and loyal, and you still are. You're still brave and outspoken—but you won't hesitate to apologize when you know you're in the wrong. I've watched the court for enough years to know what a rare combination that is. You're confident without pushing yourself forward, and you're always thinking of me." She gave a cheeky smile. "I'm only human. I can't help but find that attractive."

Easton laughed, the sound freer than it had been before. "If you keep going with that list, you're going to make me blush."

"How about you kiss me instead?" Gwen suggested, her eyes sparkling. "Because as far as I'm concerned, this is the true moment of our engagement."

Easton wrapped both arms around her waist, but he continued to lean back, gazing down at her face.

"You're really sure, Gwen? It still feels a little hard to believe. You really want me?"

She nodded, emotions rising up to clog her throat.

"In that case," he murmured, "will you marry me, most beautiful of princesses?"

"Of course," she said on a shaky laugh.

"There," he said with satisfaction. "*Now* we're truly engaged."

She wrapped her hands around the back of his head, standing on her tiptoes and dragging his lips down to hers. He came without protest, and for a long time they stayed lost in each other.

But when the warm light on the floor of her chamber crept all the way to the door of their hidden room, she reluctantly stepped back from his arms.

"It's getting late," she said. "And you need to leave."

"Gwen," he sounded dazed and reluctant, and she understood his distaste at the idea of parting. But she wouldn't put him in danger.

"It's too dangerous for you to stay here," she said firmly. "And you can't travel through the city at night. You need to go now while you can still creep out safely. Once everyone turns into bears, someone might smell you."

He grimaced but didn't protest again. And at least she was able to accompany him through the corridors, checking around each corner for him and guiding him to the nearest door. He told her not to come outside, though, pointing out that he could more easily creep unseen through the gardens alone.

She had been the one to insist he leave, but it was still painful to watch him go. Words to call him back kept rising to her tongue, nearly escaping. But she bit down on them and held them inside. They were in a desperate fight for their future and their happiness, and she couldn't let a moment's weakness ruin everything.

CHARLOTTE

They had returned to Natalie's house, but Natalie herself had disappeared somewhere. As Patti plied them all with endless cups of tea, Charlotte tried not to worry about what trouble the girl was getting into.

Charlotte felt out of place, aware that she was being treated more frostily since she had returned from the palace without Easton. But her diversionary efforts had only been required to help get him into the building. He had assured her that once inside, he knew every corridor, cranny, and hiding place. That didn't mean she would breathe easily until he returned safely, however—preferably with good news about Gwen. She didn't even blame his parents for assigning her some of the blame for his foolhardy decision to breach the palace. They had only just been reunited, and now he had placed himself straight into danger again.

She had positioned herself in a corner, as out of the way as possible, while she watched Patti and Lydia work together seamlessly, ferrying hot drinks and preparing the evening meal. Lydia in particular fascinated her. Lydia had once been a courtier, but she seemed to have adjusted to life as an ordinary citizen. Could

Charlotte do the same in reverse? Would she one day be as comfortable in a palace—on a throne—as Lydia was in a kitchen?

The sound of the front door banging open made her sit up, half-hopeful, half-scared. But the sounds that emerged from the front hall were welcoming, and she sank back against the sofa.

Easton appeared in the sitting room doorway, still slightly out of breath, as if he'd run through half the city to get to them before sunset. He endured exclamations, hugs, and scoldings from both Lydia and Patti before he noticed Charlotte sitting quietly in the corner. He gave her a meaningful nod, his face serious but his eyes bright, and a further knot of tension released inside her. He wouldn't look like that unless Gwen was all right.

His safe return changed the tone in the whole house. No one sent her looks of recrimination anymore, and further new arrivals—including Count Oswin, his son, and numerous rebels Charlotte didn't recognize—only increased the buzz in the atmosphere. And best of all, Charlotte even saw Natalie slip in, unnoticed in the chaos except by Charlotte and Baden.

"Thank goodness," Baden muttered to his sister. "Mother was starting to talk about sending me out to look for you."

Natalie rolled her eyes. "As if you would have been able to find me."

"That's what I tried to tell her," he replied, unoffended by her response.

Patti finally noticed her daughter's arrival, pulling her in to help with the evening meal, and Charlotte went with them. In the kitchen, surrounded by women who worked around and over each other, their voices and hands overlapping as they prepared a last-minute feed for a crowd, she could almost pretend she was back home in the valleys. The mountain people might be the stuff of fairy tales, but they gathered together and shared meals to mark significant occasions just as the valley folk did. She only wished Henry was there with her. As it was, she kept looking over her shoulder, half-expecting to see him. Without him present, something essential was missing.

When the count and his son transformed into bears, there was only a small ripple of unease among the rebels present which spoke of how much the two of them were trusted. And when everyone had eaten their fill, they gathered back in the sitting room, faces turning serious. There weren't enough seats for everyone—especially with the count and his son in their bear forms—so Charlotte wedged herself into a corner, content to sit on the floor. This had been their fight long before it was hers, and while they were allies, they had different final goals.

As quiet finally settled on the room, everyone having found a place, Charlotte noticed the way everyone's attention turned to Easton. He was a recent arrival just like her, but he belonged here in a way she didn't. Already the rebels were looking to him as much as Count Oswin as their leader. Clearly they had accepted the idea of him as future king.

"I spoke to the princess," he said, his voice grave. "And I learned something important." He paused and everyone stayed silent, attentive. "Celandine's reign is illegitimate. She never married King Isander. She was never truly queen."

Murmurs and exclamations swept the group. Charlotte felt no great surprise, though. She had only heard the story of the king's marriage earlier that day, and unfettered by years of accepting it as truth—especially knowing what they did now of Celandine— the whole tale had sounded implausible to her.

"Does the princess have proof?" asked a rebel Charlotte didn't know.

Easton shook his head, his expression grim. "Unfortunately not. She only pieced it all together today after finally discovering Celandine isn't her mother. She knows the story isn't true because she remembers their visit to the lodge. She was with her father the whole time, and Celandine wasn't there like she claimed she was. But twenty-year-old memories aren't proof."

"They're proof enough for me," someone muttered, and several people called out agreement.

"It's enough for me, too," Easton said. "But it isn't enough to march into the palace right now and remove her from the throne. I hope we can use the information, though. It's another tool to sway the court when we make our move."

Heads nodded in all directions.

"I also got confirmation that the wedding is planned for the day after tomorrow," he said. "Which means we need to start planning how we get ourselves into the palace. From what I've learned, we won't want to leave it until the last minute. At the moment, the queen is busy punishing her guards for failing to catch Charlotte."

Heads briefly turned in her direction, and she managed an awkward smile.

"She has them training from sunup to sundown," Easton continued, "which means there are only the standard patrols in the gardens, and they're tired and making sloppy mistakes. But it will be different on the wedding day itself. Every guard will be on duty, watching the perimeter of the gardens and the palace. And they'll all be on high alert since they'll be released from the extra training if the wedding goes smoothly."

"So we need to get in the day before," Jett said, leaning forward. "Tomorrow. We need our whole force concealed in the palace before sundown the day before the wedding."

"Is that even possible?" Dane asked doubtfully.

Count Oswin exchanged a look with his son. "I think I can help with that. It can be done."

"Wait." Jett held up his hand. "Don't say any more details now. I trust you know what you're doing, and the less we all know ahead of time the better."

He cast a look around the group, and Charlotte expected to hear protests or at least looks of discontent at the implication they weren't trustworthy. But all she saw were grim nods of approval. Apparently after twenty years, the rebels were past personal affront, their focus only on the success of their mission.

They discussed who would be present and how large a force they would need, the conversation washing over Charlotte since she recognized none of the names. The rebels who lived nearby started leaving, willing to brave the city at night if they lived in the neighboring streets.

As each one left, Easton and the count took them aside, murmuring at what time and from which direction they should enter the palace grounds the next day. From the occasional overheard whisper, Charlotte gathered they would be trickling in forces all day rather than risk a larger group attracting attention.

Others—those who lived in different parts of the city—were staying the night. They still gave their farewells and received their information, however, departing for the beds prepared for them on the upper story.

Eventually, Charlotte was once again alone with the original core group.

"Is it really that simple?" she asked.

The count sighed. "I imagine the reality will be anything but simple, but there's only so much we can prepare in advance."

"Talking about preparing in advance..." Patti hauled herself to her feet. "We'd better do some preparations for the morning meal now." She gave her husband a significant look before seizing an arm of each of her children. "You can all help me."

Both Natalie and Baden protested, but she swept them firmly from the room, her husband trailing behind. Charlotte threw a confused look at Easton, but it was the count who explained.

"They're going to stay behind tomorrow," he said. "If something goes wrong, we need someone left who can coordinate whatever rebel forces remain."

"Jett and I want to be with our son," Lydia said softly, "but Natalie is only fourteen, and Rebecca is even younger. Patti and

Dane want to keep their children here safe, and we understand that."

"And we're needed more than they are, anyway," Easton said. "None of the city rebels know the palace like me and my parents do. We'll be the ones to meet each incoming pair and lead them to the hiding place." He looked at the count. "Which means we need to know where it is."

"My son's apartment," the count said immediately. "It's large enough to fit everyone."

"And it won't be suspected?" Easton asked skeptically.

"You wouldn't be aware since you haven't been here," the count said, "but this is the first time my son has been at any rebel meeting. He's been part of our cause from the beginning, but the queen has been starting to grow suspicious of me—something I have long feared was coming. In preparation for such an eventuality, my son and I have cultivated the appearance that we've fallen out and barely tolerate each other. Most of the court believe we only maintain any contact because of Emmett. Everyone knows I wouldn't do anything to risk losing contact with my grandson. As a result, while Celandine has started excluding me where possible in the last weeks, my son still holds his position of respect as the leader of the trading groups that cross the mountains."

Charlotte turned a disapproving look on the younger man who had been almost silent the entire evening. She didn't appreciate working with someone responsible for snatching innocent valley folk to become slaves for the queen. Easton was regarding him with the same cold look and visible shame washed over the nobleman.

"I'm not unaware of my own wrongdoing," he said in a low voice. "In the early days, I thought..." He sighed. "It doesn't matter what I thought. But I came to realize my mistake and—" He turned to Easton. "Ask your princess. She can confirm there haven't been any new captives for a long time."

"Except for Henry," Charlotte said, ice in her voice.

The count's son—whose name she didn't even know, she realized—looked at her guiltily.

"That's different," he said. "He wasn't intended as a long-term captive. We thought he would break the enchantment and allow us to free everyone—the mountain people and the valley captives—from the queen. We didn't know—" He glanced at Easton and grimaced.

"We've done the best we can," the count said firmly. "And, more importantly, we're doing our best now to fix our mistakes. If you want to insist on retribution anyway, we all might suffer."

Charlotte deflated, her cheeks flushing. She was the last person who should be raking someone over the coals for past mistakes. The pressure of Henry's arms around her and the feel of his lips on hers filled her mind. When he had woken to find her with him in the palace, there had been no lingering trace of judgment in his eyes for her own colossal mistake.

Easton nodded. "If the mountain kingdom is going to have a new future, we can't begin with a pointless game of assigning blame. Celandine is the problem, and we all need to be focused on removing her and her loyal guards from power."

"What about the remaining loyal members of court?" the count's son asked, his voice tentative. Charlotte wondered how many of them were his friends.

"The newest piece of information about the illegitimacy of Celandine's reign should help in their case," Easton said. "I believe that when they realize they were tricked, it will be enough to sway them into accepting the reality of the change of power."

Both Count Oswin and his son relaxed. Had they been worrying about a bloodbath after Gwen took the throne? If so, they didn't know her very well. Charlotte herself had only known Gwen for a short time, but she knew such vengeful violence wasn't in her nature. Gwen had cared for Charlotte from the moment they met, even when they were virtual strangers.

"What about the queen?" Jett asked. "Do we have a way to restrain her during the change in the ceremony? Because without that…"

"Actually, Gwen has a plan for that," Charlotte said, thinking of the apple. "She's found a way to make use of her stash of godmother objects."

"Excellent," the count said briskly. "In that case, we'll find a way to make contact with the princess once everyone is safely hidden in the palace. We would have needed to do that anyway."

"There's one last matter," Jett said. "We didn't want to mention it with the broader group in case anyone became over-enthusiastic and started spreading hints too early. But it would be best if we can include the people of the city in the changeover of power—and not just the prominent citizens invited to the wedding. I'm picturing a crowd who could burst into the palace in support of Queen Gwendolyn at the optimal moment."

The count and his son exchanged a look, brows knit. Rousing the inhabitants of the city was outside their area of influence.

"We can help with that!" Natalie burst into the room, dragging Baden with her.

The rest of the adults gave her disapproving looks, but Charlotte just grinned. Of course Natalie had been lurking in the corridor, listening. Was there anything surprising in that? The girl didn't believe in limits.

"And how could you help?" Lydia asked, somehow making the words sound kind rather than dismissive.

"We'll send out word for the youth to gather. Since we gather whenever the boredom gets overwhelming, it won't raise any suspicion. And no one would betray us to the adults." She wrinkled her nose, as if such an act was unthinkable. "Once everyone is there—right when the wedding is happening—we'll let them know why they're really there and send them home to rouse their families."

Easton looked thoughtful. "That might actually work."

"Of course it will work," Natalie said.

Charlotte suppressed another laugh. Natalie had an impressive ability to be both infuriating and likable.

"In that case, we have our plans." The count rose. "And now these old bones need to get to a bed. Once upon a time, I could function on little to no sleep, but those days are long behind me, regardless of my form."

Lydia led him and his son out, and Charlotte was left to wonder if there was any chance everything would go as they'd planned.

The night had passed easily despite Gwen's fears. She was still worried for Easton, but after their conversation, she felt a warm glow whenever she thought of him. And it was easy to drift asleep to the memory of his arms around her.

When she woke, her focus turned to one thing. There had been more than enough time for the apple to warm up to every object in Celandine's collection. Now Gwen needed to find a way to sneak in there and steal whichever of them would let the rebels restrain the queen for the length of the wedding ceremony.

Timing was crucial. If she did it too early, the queen might discover the theft. But if she left it too late, Gwen might be swept up in wedding preparations and be unable to get away. Unless it would be better to assign the task to someone else? But who could get all the way into the queen's bedchamber other than her supposed daughter?

Gwen's mind went round in circles, and she still hadn't finalized a plan when a team of seamstresses descended on her in a whirl of material, scissors, and tape measures. They took one look at the mess in her room and bore her off to an empty meeting room to complete the final fittings and measurements for her wedding gown.

Knowing she would be wearing the outfit when she married Easton, not Henry, Gwen couldn't help taking an interest in the elegant concoction of ivory satin with a gossamer layer over the top. Looking at herself in the full-length mirror held up by one of the women, Gwen felt for the first time that she could be both a princess and herself. Princess Gwendolyn had been a mask, but perhaps it was possible for Queen Gwendolyn to be her true self.

When she finally made it back to her room, it was long past time for the midday meal. She was rewarded with the sight of a tray—the food cold but still edible. She consumed it ravenously and was still finishing the last bites when her door opened, the movement too tentative to herald Celandine's arrival.

Gwen gulped down the final mouthful and stood to face Miriam. The captive's face lifted when she saw Gwen.

"Oh thank goodness! Officially I'm here for the tray, but I've been checking every half hour, wondering when you'd return. I was starting to worry about someone seeing me popping in and out of here like a jack-in-the-box."

Gwen's lingering good humor from the gown and her full stomach instantly evaporated.

"What?" she asked. "What is it?"

"We've received another order from the queen." Miriam gathered up the dishes as she talked, placing them back on the tray. "We're supposed to drug Prince Henry's evening meal again, just like last time."

Gwen sucked in a breath. "Charlotte must have used her ball to make a second deal! She should have told me!"

"Maybe she's relying on you to handle it even without a conversation," Miriam suggested, and Gwen felt warm at the suggestion of confidence in her abilities.

She nodded decisively. "And I will handle it. You'll need to serve the drink, of course. We don't want the blame coming back to any of you. But I'll find a way to talk to Henry and warn him not to drink it."

Miriam looked relieved, although whether at Henry's potential escape or their own lack of involvement, Gwen wasn't sure. Either way, she thanked the princess and hurried out of the room.

Gwen sighed and sank into the single upright chair. Plans to break into her mother's collection of objects would have to be put on hold. It was more urgent to find a way to talk to Henry.

If only she could burrow straight through the walls. She wouldn't have to break through very many before she reached the room holding Henry. Unfortunately, even in her bear form, solid stone walls presented a problem.

It would be easier to walk straight through his door. But Celandine was the only one with a key.

Or was she? Gwen sat up straighter. Her mother had specifically told her that she had changed Gwen's lock while Gwen was gone. But surely she hadn't changed every lock in the palace. Henry's door could probably be opened with a master key, and Gwen knew from experience that copies of that could be obtained if you had the right access.

She stood. The guards were all busy doing exercises all day, leaving their barracks deserted. She smiled. Perfect.

Both the head housekeeper and the captain of the guard had a copy of the master key, and both had a healthy fear of doing anything that might bring them negative attention from Queen Celandine. They had long ago made an arrangement to keep a spare copy of the key hidden in case either of them ever lost theirs and needed to replace it quickly. Easton had been the one to discover this fact and steal the spare fourteen years ago. The captain had assumed the housekeeper had needed it and promptly had it replaced. There was every likelihood the replacement—or another subsequent version—was still in the same place.

She walked through the palace as if she belonged there, aware that hurrying would only attract attention. And she had walked the corridors aimlessly so many times that no one she encountered spared her a second look.

Her heart was still pounding when she reached the barracks, however. They were connected to the main palace by a single door, and once she had passed it, she would have no excuse for her presence.

Lingering would only increase the risk, though, so she pushed inside. Her gaze darted around the room, and she expelled her held breath. It was empty just as she'd hoped.

She hurried through the communal room and past doors leading to smaller bunk rooms, only stopping when she reached the captain's office. Standing on tiptoes, she sighed with relief when she found the key to the room still hidden above the doorframe. The encircling mountains that trapped them away from the other kingdoms also protected them from serious threats, making it difficult for the guard force to remain vigilant for decades on end.

She let herself in and raced to his desk, her fingers fumbling as she used the same key to unlock the third drawer on the right. She pushed aside some papers and finally caught sight of it. The key.

She stuffed it in her pocket, pushing the door closed and running out again, moving even more quickly than on her way in. She flew past the bunks and out again into the main palace. She didn't stop until she was several corridors away, the key seeming to burn in her pocket.

Gwen stopped and rested her back on the cool stone wall, sucking in lungfuls of air. The key wasn't really hot, and it didn't blaze with light to attract the attention of anyone who saw her. There was nothing to indicate its presence in her pocket.

Even so, she didn't have the nerves for any more waiting. She would go straight to Henry.

She retraced her steps, seeming to reach Henry's door much more quickly than she had managed the route in the other direction. She almost missed the lock on her first try, but eventually the key slid in and turned with a satisfying clunk.

She didn't make the mistake of rushing straight in, though. Opening the door only a crack, she put her mouth against it and whispered into the room, "It's Gwen! Don't attack!"

Only then did she push the door the rest of the way open and step warily inside, looking for candlesticks despite her warning.

Henry stood several steps away, his arms crossed and his shoulders tense. At least he made no move to attack her.

"Don't worry," he said. "I wouldn't dare attack anyone. Not when the queen might have Charlotte in her clutches."

Gwen shut the door behind her, her eyes softening. "Don't worry," she said hurriedly. "She got away. If you've seen guards running laps outside or sparring endlessly all day, that's punishment for letting her slip past them."

Henry staggered back, sinking into a chair and covering his face. "Oh, thank goodness," he murmured.

"I'm sorry I didn't manage to come to you sooner," Gwen said. "It was a risk, so I didn't…But I should have…"

Henry looked up, the momentary weakness of his relief already passed. "So why are you here now if not to reassure me? Has something happened? Do you need me to do something? Charlotte made me promise to listen to whatever you said and help you."

Gwen felt another surge of gratitude for her friend's trust.

"I think Charlotte must be coming back," she said, making Henry's eyes brighten and then dim again.

"She shouldn't risk that," he said harshly.

Gwen grimaced. "I'm afraid she didn't discuss it with me, so I didn't have an opportunity to talk her out of it. But the queen had you drugged last time Charlotte made a deal to spend the night with you, and now she's given the order for you to be drugged again."

"Drugged?" Henry's eyes narrowed. "Is that what happened? I woke up to Charlotte at my side, but we didn't have time for her to explain anything. I've been utterly confused as to what happened."

"She was with you all night," Gwen said softly. "But you were drugged so she couldn't have woken you."

Gwen turned away from the expression on Henry's face, feeling as if she were intruding on his private emotions.

"She lay at my side all night?"

She turned back at the soft smile in his voice.

"The sleeping draft will be in the drink," she said. "You have to pretend to drink it and then pretend to fall asleep. The servants won't say anything about taking away a full glass, but if you can find a way to drain it somehow that would be even better."

He was nodding as she spoke, his face creased in concentration.

"If you can avoid being drugged, you'll have the whole night together," Gwen continued. "And Charlotte will know more about the rebel plans than I do. She can tell you everything that's going to happen and what they need you to do."

The more she thought about it, the more she thought that must be the reason Charlotte had made a second bargain. There must be important information the rebels needed to pass to Henry. She just wished there was a way for her to talk to her friend and get more information herself.

"So all I have to do—" Henry started only to break off as the door was thrust violently open.

Gwen flinched, but there was no time to attempt to hide. By the time she'd even processed what was happening, Celandine was standing in the doorway, looking between them.

"Well, well, well," she said. "I'd like to say I'm surprised, but that wouldn't be true."

Gwen's mind raced, trying to think of an excuse for her presence, but her thoughts kept tripping over each other as she wondered how long the queen had been out there. How much had she overheard?

"So you came to warn the prince not to drink his drugged drink tonight," Celandine said coolly. Her eyes narrowed. "I'm disappointed in you, Gwendolyn. I gave you a second chance, despite my better judgment, and this is how you repay me?"

"How—" Gwen gaped at the queen, despair filling her as she realized she had no way to fix the situation.

Henry stepped forward, his attitude menacing now he knew Charlotte wasn't in the palace. But the queen glanced at him with such dismissal Gwen felt sick.

"Oh, stand down, brave boy," she drawled. "Your precious Charlotte may have slipped through my hands last time, but I'll have her soon enough."

Henry froze, his muscles stiffening.

Celandine's eyes went back to Gwen. "That's right. I know all about the rebels' plans. There are still some people left in this city who know where their best interests lie."

Gwen's heart sank. A traitor among the rebels? She forgot all about Charlotte for a moment, her mind full of Easton. If only she had some way to warn him!

"What I didn't know," the queen continued, "was whether my servants were part of the conspiracy. And so I set up this little test."

Gwen gaped at her. It had all been a test? The servants had warned her about the queen's command because Gwen had asked them to. She had kept them a secret from the count and his rebels only to betray them directly to the queen.

Tears burned her eyes, her breath catching. Whatever happened to them now was her fault.

"Your mistake, Gwendolyn," the queen said with venom in her

voice, "was looking to anyone other than me. You will only let others down and betray them. It's in your nature."

Gwen sunk in on herself, her mind shrinking inward as the queen's words reverberated in her head. But deep inside, she found something different.

There were other voices inside now. Easton's words of love and confidence. Charlotte's words of friendship and trust. Even the count's as he declared he had been waiting for her because she was the queen they needed. When there had been no voice but Celandine's, Gwen had been unable to push her words out, no matter how hard she tried. But now there were other words filling those spaces instead. The hollow inside Gwen was no longer empty, and it had no room for Celandine's lies.

She raised her eyes, her shoulders straightening.

"No," she said firmly, the word complete and final in itself.

The queen's eyes widened, and a flash of fury crossed her face, the emotion seeming to catch Celandine off guard as much as it did Gwen.

She stepped forward and grabbed Gwen's ear, twisting it until Gwen cried out. When she pulled, Gwen had to follow, the pain forcing her limbs to comply.

Henry tried to intervene, but Celandine had Gwen out of the door too fast, shutting it in the prince's face and turning the key in the lock.

Tears leaked from Gwen's eyes as Celandine dragged her down the corridor.

"I will deal with the servants soon enough," she hissed. "But first I'm going to deal with you."

CHARLOTTE

*E*aston had suggested Charlotte could stay behind with Patti and Dane, but he didn't argue when she refused. He must have already known the attempt was futile. There was no way Charlotte was remaining in the city while the false queen attempted to marry Henry to Gwen. And if everything went wrong, she would be the only one thinking of Henry first.

The count had commanded them to wait until the end—the last of the rebels to arrive in the palace grounds. Easton had protested that, reminding them he was supposed to help guide the other arrivals. But the count insisted Jett and Lydia could manage the task, pointing out that Easton was the most important of all of them. As the man Gwen loved, he was the only one who could free the mountain court from their enchantment.

Easton had reluctantly agreed, and Charlotte had been assigned as his companion. The two of them would creep in together, and they wouldn't need a guide. But as soon as everyone else had departed, they made a slight adjustment to their plan. Instead of going straight to join the other rebels, they would find Gwen first. They were both desperate to see her for their own reasons, so neither needed much convincing.

They wore cloaks pulled up high over their heads as they strode through the streets in the waning light, keeping to shadows wherever possible. The afternoon was already wearing down, and the city's people had started dispersing to their homes. If they'd left their departure much later, they would have stood out on the nearly deserted streets.

It wasn't their first time making the same trek together, but Charlotte had never felt so tense as they crept into the palace gardens. Last time, when they saw a patrol in the distance, Charlotte had made enough noise to draw their attention before fleeing back into the city before they could see her identity.

This time they both needed to make it inside. But Easton must have been right about the guard numbers. They didn't even encounter a patrol as they wound a circuitous route through the gardens, staying out of sight of the palace windows. Charlotte even grew bold enough to stop and dig up her golden ball and Gwen's harness. Who knew what need they might have for the objects before the next sunset.

Inside the building, Easton took the lead. But as they walked the corridors, something nagged at Charlotte. The route felt strangely familiar. A door came into view, and she instinctively slowed, half a beat before Easton did.

When he also slowed, stopping at the door, Charlotte's eyes widened. The gardens and furnishings were so different that she had nearly forgotten the palace was the original version of her and Henry's castle. And Gwen had the same room she and Henry had shared in the other version.

Chasing away a shiver, Charlotte slipped into the room behind Easton. As soon as he stepped aside, she gasped.

Someone had torn the room to pieces, leaving shredded stuffing, loose feathers, and torn material everywhere she looked. In one corner smashed glass and broken bottles lay shattered across the floor, and even the wardrobe had been toppled.

Her hand flew to her mouth. "What happened to Gwen?" she cried.

"What?" Easton whirled, his pale face fixing on her. But a moment later he relaxed. "Oh, you mean the room? She did it herself."

Charlotte's brows rose. "Wow. She really…" She shook her head. But part of her felt proud of her friend. Had it felt as cathartic as it looked? "That's all right, then," she added. "I thought someone must have attacked her."

"I thought that at first too. But where is she now?" Easton looked around uneasily. "The state of the room doesn't mean anything, but she's not here. I thought she'd be here this late. Her bear form is supposed to be a secret."

Charlotte shrugged, trying to chase away the tendrils of panic that stirred on the edges of her own mind. "We knew it wasn't a guarantee we'd find her here. It isn't quite sunset yet. And we can't go blundering around the palace looking for her. That would be asking to be caught."

Easton reluctantly nodded, but his body didn't relax, the lines of his muscles remaining tense.

Turning abruptly, he strode to one of the walls and fumbled with something out of Charlotte's view.

"It's locked," he said, clearly frustrated. Banging his fist on the wall, he raised his voice. "Gwen? Gwen? Are you in there?"

"Shhh!" Charlotte hissed. "What are you doing? Do you want someone to hear us?"

Easton slumped. "It didn't used to be locked."

"Is that a door?" Charlotte said, able to see the lines of it now she was paying attention. It wasn't entirely hidden, but it had been designed to blend in with the wall. "I'm sure if she's in there, she would call out and let us know."

"We both wanted to speak to her," Charlotte continued, "but it's not essential to the plan. We should get to the others so they know we're safe, and then we'll come back at night when we know for sure she'll be here. The count said we had to make contact with her."

She could still read the reluctance on his face, and she suspected she knew the reason. The count wanted a rebel to make contact with Gwen, but it didn't have to be Easton. Once they joined the others, it was unlikely Easton would be allowed out again until the crucial moment. But his importance was the reason they couldn't put off going to the specified apartment any longer. If the rebels thought something had happened to Easton, they would risk going out into the palace to look for him.

Easton knew the realities as well as she did, and he finally sighed and nodded. "Let's go, then."

Charlotte winced sympathetically, staying quiet since she knew any words of hers would be meaningless. She felt the same tension in her own belly, urging her to run off and find Henry. But she had already done that once with nearly disastrous results. This time she was going to follow the plan.

Easton's pace had slowed, but he still led them steadily down corridors and around corners, presumably making for the apartment of the count's son.

"It's just up ahead," he murmured at last, gesturing to the nearest corner.

But before they rounded it, they both pulled up short, exchanging looks. The tramp of boots sounded in the distance. Not the measured tread of a routine guard patrol or the casual stroll of a courtier—multiple people in heavy boots were running full pace in their direction.

Charlotte had only had time to panic when the running feet stopped. She didn't even finish her breath of relief before the fear returned, however. The sound of an aggressive fist pounding on wood reached them.

"Open in the name of the queen!" a man called.

Charlotte and Easton exchanged horrified looks, both still frozen in place.

The fist banged again and then the creak of the door opening.

"What is the meaning—" the voice of the count's son started in cold tones, but the first voice cut him off.

"Don't bother, traitor," he snapped. "You're surrounded."

Instant chaos broke out just out of sight, shouts, cries, screams, and pounding feet. It sounded like furniture was being overturned, and Charlotte could barely breathe, let alone move.

Easton sprang into action, however. Dragging Charlotte with him, he pulled open a narrow door that was almost hidden in the paneling of the wall, just as the one in Gwen's room had been. He shoved her inside. Following behind, he pulled the door closed.

Enough light came in around the door for Charlotte to identify their location as a storage cupboard. Easton bent down at an awkward angle and pressed one eye against the wall. Charlotte stared at him in confusion until he pulled back and gestured impatiently for her to go to the other side of the door.

There was just enough room for her to fit, so she obeyed, eyeing him as he bent over again. From the new angle, she could see he was pressing his eyes against a tiny circle of light. A peephole!

Searching the wall in front of her, she found another point of light and bent toward it. She didn't know how long she could maintain such an uncomfortable position, and she couldn't imagine why anyone would put peepholes at such a level. Charlotte was short, so if it was uncomfortable for her, it wouldn't suit anyone but a child.

Understanding dawned. Of course. Easton and Gwen had spent their childhood roaming these halls. Apparently spying from storage cupboards had been part of their childish adventures. No wonder Easton had known just where to go.

She positioned herself so she could see out into the corridor beyond. It was empty, but the distant sounds of a scuffle were dying down now, replaced with barked orders and the occasional muffled cry. They didn't have to wait long before a line of people came into view.

The rebels had their hands on their heads, their expressions ranging from terrified to resigned. A line of guards marched on either side of them, swords gripped in their hands and faces stern.

Charlotte had to clap her hand over her mouth to keep from crying out when she saw Jett and Lydia marched past, and Easton went rigid beside her. But the worst was the very end of the line. The final figure was much too short, his movement out of step with the others due to the crutches beneath his arms.

Behind him, two guards hauled a man who wasn't marching but instead struggling with his captors. When his face flashed in their direction, Charlotte recognized the count's son—Emmett's father.

"My son is not part of this," he said in heated tones. "I don't even know why he was home. He's only seven!"

Emmett flinched, and it was easy to guess he and his mother had been sent away for safety but he had snuck back. The clack of his clutches didn't falter, though, his head high as he followed in the line of prisoners.

The guards at the back were all turned toward the struggling nobleman, but he twisted in the direction of the storage cupboard, facing directly toward their hiding place.

Easton straightened, and before Charlotte knew what was happening, the door had flashed partially open before immediately closing again.

The count's son went slack at the brief glimpse of Easton, his eyes fixed on the now closed door. Several of the guards also turned that way, following the direction of his gaze. There was nothing left to see, however, thanks to Easton's quick movement, and the count's son quickly resumed his struggles, distracting them.

"What was that?" Charlotte hissed at Easton, as quietly as she could.

He shrugged. "I saw an opportunity, and I took it. At least now they know we're still free. And that we know what happened to them."

"But how do we know they're not all being marched off to be executed?" Charlotte whispered as the sound of their marching line faded from her hearing. Tears of panic and horror pricked at her eyes, and she could only imagine how much worse it had to be for Easton.

Easton slid slowly down to sit on the floor, his hands fisted and eyes blazing but the lines of his body broken and weary.

"We can't know for sure, but I doubt it. That isn't the queen's style. She won't want to just eliminate her enemies. She'll want to make sure no one else tries the same thing. She's making a grand spectacle of this wedding—even some of the more prominent people from the city have been invited—so I don't think she'll miss the chance to make a show of this as well. Whatever she intends to do to them, it will happen tomorrow, in front of the wedding guests."

"Tomorrow," Charlotte said slowly. It was only a small reprieve, but it was better than thinking of all those people already dead.

"And surely she wouldn't execute Emmett in front of a crowd," she murmured. "That would hardly garner sympathy."

"We can only hope so," Easton said roughly, and Charlotte guessed he was thinking of his parents.

"She isn't going to execute anyone," she said in a bracing voice. "We're still free, and we'll find a way to rescue them."

Easton gave a bark of humorless laughter. "How are we going to do that?"

Charlotte straightened. "We're not. I am."

Easton frowned.

"I know you don't want to hear this," she said firmly. "But the count already told you how important you are. Your role is to appear in the middle of the wedding. No matter what else happens, we can't let that fail. And that means you need to stay right here in this cupboard."

"You want me to just sit here while—"

"Yes," she said, cutting him off ruthlessly. "I know I'm asking the hardest possible thing. I know it's the last thing you want to do. But this is what is needed from you, Easton."

"How can you save them on your own?" Easton shook his head. "Alone, and a stranger here no less."

Charlotte drew herself up. "I won't be alone. There's someone else who knows this palace almost as well as you do."

Easton scrambled to his feet. "We don't even know where Gwen is. And if it's too dangerous for me to get involved, it's several times more dangerous for her." He groaned and scrubbed a hand over his face. "If the queen somehow knows our plans, she must already know Gwen is involved as well. Who knows what she's done to her."

"Stop!" Charlotte commanded. "Stop thinking like that, or you'll drive yourself mad. Believe me. I have reason to know."

Easton subsided, apparently remembering how long the queen had been holding Charlotte's husband a prisoner.

"There's someone else who knows these corridors and rooms," Charlotte said more softly. "Or at least, a copy of them. Henry. Just give us a chance."

Easton hesitated for a moment before he groaned and sank back to the floor. "Who has more experience at waiting than me?" he asked bitterly.

"I'm sorry." Charlotte hesitated, but the best reassurance she could offer was to succeed at rescuing the other rebels. "I'll come back for you as soon as I can. Promise you'll still be here?"

He nodded, not looking at her, and she had to accept it.

Stooping to check the peephole, she confirmed the corridor outside was still empty before leaving the cupboard. She scanned the corridor, locking each distinguishing feature in her mind so she could find the place again.

Drawing the golden ball out of her pocket, she stared down at it. The godmother who had given it to her had said it would help her find her true love. She still didn't know how it was supposed to work, but it was all she had.

She placed it gently on the ground and, feeling foolish, whispered, "Please take me to Henry."

Nothing happened, and her sense of foolishness grew until suddenly, without visible impetus, the ball began to move. It rolled down the corridor, following after the departed prisoners, and she hurried in its wake. She was relieved the ball was leading her in the opposite direction to the apartment used by the rebels. It seemed likely there would be guards stationed there still, waiting in case she and Easton appeared.

But soon she didn't have thoughts for anything except the task of following the ball. It moved at pace, and she worried about losing it every time it rounded a corner—almost as much as she worried about it leading her straight into a squad of guards or a group of courtiers.

But almost as if it knew, the ball led her only down deserted corridors, or through empty rooms. When it finally rolled to a stop, it bumped gently against a concealed door that looked almost identical to the one on the storage cupboard half a palace away.

She frowned at the ball. Henry was concealed inside a storage cupboard now? Tentatively she tried the door, and it opened without resistance. Peering inside, she saw only similar supplies to those that had filled the last cupboard, although these appeared to be finer in quality, the pillows and blankets soft and luxurious.

She went to shut the door, but the ball rolled inside. Confused, Charlotte followed. When she bent to retrieve it, it zipped away from her, rolling just out of reach. She stepped closer to try again, and it did the same thing.

Throwing her hands up, Charlotte cried, "Fine!"

Closing the door behind her, she crossed her arms. "I'll stay in here if that's what you want."

The ball immediately rolled forward and bumped gently against her boots.

Charlotte retrieved it without trouble this time, considering what she should do. She could leave now that she had the ball secured, but where would she go?

Spotting the circle of light from a peephole, she bent to peer through it. Maybe it was worth watching for a while to see what happened.

CHARLOTTE

The minutes stretched long, and Charlotte began to regret her plan, her back spasming from the awkward position. She was about to give up and straighten when a sound caught her ear. Pressing her eye closer, she forgot the discomfort.

A door almost directly opposite her opened, and a subdued pair of women emerged. For a moment, disappointment speared her until she spotted what was in the hands of the woman in the lead. Draped over her arm was an unfinished but elaborate outfit—the kind that might be worn by a male at a wedding or similar celebration.

She sucked in a breath as the woman turned to her younger companion. "Those measurements should have been done two weeks ago. We'll be lucky to have this done on time, even with the whole team working all night. You lock up and return the key, and I'll get this straight to the others."

The younger woman didn't look happy with the arrangement, but the other was already hurrying away. With a slight tremble in her hand, the remaining seamstress fit the key in the lock and turned it.

Charlotte could barely breathe at the opportunity before her.

"Good ball," she whispered, stroking it as if it was a sentient creature. "Good ball!"

She waited until the woman turned to go and then flung open the door. Barreling out into the corridor, she clutched the woman from behind, one hand over her mouth. The seamstress hadn't even had time to scream.

As she had expected from her earlier demeanor, the woman immediately went limp, shaking all over.

"Please don't hurt me," she sobbed against Charlotte's hand.

Charlotte winced, but she couldn't falter. Using the hand that wasn't covering the woman's mouth, she wrested the key from her slack fingers.

Looking around, she found a door with a keyhole and pushed the woman toward it. The seamstress stumbled forward on faltering feet, still not putting up any significant fight. Did she think Charlotte had a weapon?

Opening the door, Charlotte glanced inside at the untouched bedchamber. It was too pristine to be in regular use, so she released the woman and gave her a hard shove from behind. The seamstress staggered into the room, dropping to her knees.

Before she could turn around, Charlotte whisked the door closed, sighing with relief as she turned the key in the lock. As she'd hoped, she was now in possession of the master key Gwen had mentioned.

"Sorry!" she called through the door, feeling another spurt of guilt at the muffled sobs from the other side.

But she had the key in her hand! She ran to the door the woman had closed, thrusting the key into the lock and turning it. Bursting into the room, she closed the door behind her.

"Forget to measure the length of one of my fingers?" a sardonic voice asked from the window, its owner not turning to look at her.

"Henry," she said, half sob, half word.

He whirled, his blue eyes finding her instantly, his whole face transforming.

"Charlotte!" He ran to her, and she ran to him, the two of them colliding in the middle of the room.

"I found you! I found you!" she cried, tears running down her cheeks.

"Oh, my love," he murmured, wiping them away and gazing at her in wonder. "How can you be here? The queen…"

Charlotte sniffed, trying to pull herself together. "She captured the rest of them. Or almost all of them. Do you know where Gwen is?"

Henry's face twisted. "She came to warn me about something, but it turned out it was a test the queen had set up. Celandine dragged her away."

"Oh no!" Charlotte stared at him in dismay. "Everything really has gone wrong."

"It's hard to believe that when you're standing here with me," he said.

"Oh Henry! I keep messing everything up, but this time I need to save everyone. We need to save everyone."

"Slow down," he said. "I've been locked in here the whole time with only the occasional, confusing snippet of news. What's been going on out there?"

Charlotte's whole body buzzed with energy, and she would have paced the room if she could have brought herself to leave Henry's arms. But he had wound one arm around her middle, and she wouldn't have pried herself away for anything.

Speaking as slowly as she could manage, she explained everything that had happened so far, sticking only to the necessary facts.

"So the queen is still progressing with this wedding," he said when she finished. "And that's a good thing—but only as long as we can make the swap in the middle."

Charlotte nodded, her hands creeping up to grasp the front of his shirt. "I'm not letting her marry you off to Gwen or anyone. You're already mine."

He smiled affectionately down at her. "Do you think I would marry anyone else? I already have a wife. A delightful—if occasionally exasperating—one."

She giggled and hiccupped at the same time, a final tear leaking out.

"Henry, I'm so, so sorry," she said. "If I'd just trusted you and waited…"

He bent to kiss the tear off her cheek. "Charlotte, you made a mistake, but it was an understandable one. I forgave you immediately. And look what you've managed since! I never thought you could actually find a way to come here. But you're not only here, you have the whole kingdom in open rebellion."

Charlotte gave a watery chuckle. "I definitely can't take credit for that."

Henry smiled down at her. "Maybe not, but it does seem like we can be of some help. So maybe we're right where we're supposed to be?" He sighed, his arm around her tightening. "I'm the one who never properly apologized for involving you in all this to begin with. I married you without telling you the truth, knowing I was caught up in an enchantment worked by a dangerous woman. You were wronged by me more than I ever was by you."

Charlotte shook her head stubbornly. "Now that I know everything, if I had my choice again, I would still marry you in a heartbeat. You are worth every moment of pain."

"I had no idea how well my heart picked when I saw you in the woods," he murmured before lowering his mouth to hers.

Charlotte returned the kiss eagerly. Her husband felt utterly familiar—home in a way no place had ever been—but this part was still new. Feeling his arms around her, his chest firm against hers, his mouth moving on hers was exquisite and wondrous and almost too much.

When he pulled back, she made a soft sound of protest, and he groaned and almost pulled her close again. But he stopped with his mouth a whisper from hers.

"Don't we have some people to save?" he whispered.

Charlotte squeaked, memory rushing back as her cheeks flushed.

"One day soon," Henry said with a grin, "I'm going to find a castle in the woods where the two of us can be alone together without any bears. But for now, I think we have a kingdom to help save."

"I'd like to find Gwen, if we can," Charlotte said. "But the queen will have to bring her to the ceremony, at least. She's too important to Celandine's plans for her to do anything too drastic. So it's probably more important for us to find the rebels before she decides to start executing people."

"Do you have any idea where they're being kept?" he asked, stepping away from her, all business.

She sighed softly at the cold air between them before turning her mind to the job ahead.

"Unfortunately, no," she said. "But this palace is just like your castle. You spent much more time roaming around it than I did—all those days as a bear before I arrived. Were you able to tell just from the layout and position of the rooms what they were supposed to be for? Could you guess where a large group of people might be kept?"

Henry frowned. "I could guess, but that wouldn't mean I was right."

"At this point, an educated guess is better than wandering around blindly and hoping we trip over them."

Henry winced. "There's really no one else who could help them?"

"That would lead us back to finding Gwen first. Do you have any idea where she's being kept?"

"Unfortunately, I don't know that either. They might even be together."

Charlotte tried not to let panic overwhelm her. She had been so certain that if she could just find Henry, the solution would be simple. Now she wondered how much of it had been her own emotions talking.

Henry instantly picked up on her mood. "Don't worry," he said sounding more confident than he could possibly feel. "We'll find them. The two of us together can manage anything."

Even though she knew the words were only meant to bolster her confidence, somehow they worked.

"What about a guard hall or…or barracks or something? Do you remember anywhere that looked like it could have been that?"

His eyes brightened. "Actually, yes! There was a small wing joined to the rest of the building by only a single door. I noticed that some of the rooms had brackets in the walls that looked like they were intended for bunks."

"We should start there," Charlotte suggested, grateful to have somewhere to begin. "Even if they're not there, we might manage to overhear something or follow some guards to their prisoners."

She didn't mention the difficulty of getting into the guards' barracks without being seen. The job already felt overwhelming, so they should tackle one thing at a time.

Henry nodded and took her hand, winding his fingers through hers as he led her toward the door. She looked down at their joined hands, a smile stealing up her face despite the circumstances. Another thing they couldn't do before.

When Henry stepped out into the corridor, he drew a deep breath as if the air was fresh and clear instead of just like the air inside his chamber. How many hours had he spent staring at that door, wishing he could walk through it?

He pulled her to their left, but she froze, pulling back against him. Tugging her hand free, she whispered, "Wait," and dashed back to the door.

Pulling the key out of her pocket, she locked the door behind them. Henry watched her, confused.

"What's the point of that?"

She put a finger to her lips, and he fell silent. Hurrying back to the room where she had left the seamstress, she slid the key beneath the door.

A gasp on the other side told her the woman had been sitting watching the door.

"His door has been locked again," Charlotte called through.

"Thank you," came the wobbly reply.

Dashing back to Henry, she seized his hand and took off running, pulling him with her. As soon as he'd recovered from his initial surprise, he easily kept pace, quickly outstripping her and tugging her along behind.

Once they were several corridors over, she stopped, bending over to catch her breath. Henry stopped as well, gazing down at her with a quizzical expression, barely out of breath himself.

"What was that?" he asked.

"One of the seamstresses," Charlotte explained. "Now she can return the key like nothing happened. And when someone comes in the morning to bring you food, they'll find the door locked and you mysteriously vanished. No one will be able to say exactly when in the night it happened or that it had anything to do with the poor seamstresses."

"Was that wise?" Henry's brows furrowed. "She might go straight to check if I'm in there and then run to the queen."

Charlotte shrugged. "I suppose it's possible, but you didn't see her. She might be a lovely person, but she is not what you'd call courageous. I'd be willing to bet a lot that she goes straight on as if nothing happened, hoping the whole time that no one ever connects her to any of it." Her mouth twisted. "I'm sorry, Henry, but she was just so terrified. I couldn't abandon her to take all the blame."

He smiled down at her, his face softening. "I wouldn't expect anything else from your soft heart."

She made a face at him.

"It's too late to worry about it anyway," he added. "The best we can do is get moving quickly."

She nodded agreement, and they began moving again, although this time at a more sustainable pace.

"Does it seem normal to you that the corridors are so empty?" she asked after several more turns without anyone coming into view.

Henry grimaced. "I'm afraid the servants were implicated in the rebels' plans. I suspect the queen has confined them all somewhere. And the guards must be busy rounding up and guarding the rebels. As for the courtiers…"

"Even the ones uninvolved must have worked out something is going on," Charlotte agreed. "If it was me, and I lived in Celandine's castle, I'd be lying low, too."

Henry glanced at the darkness out of a window they passed. Charlotte couldn't remember when night had arrived, but even the traces of sunset were gone.

"There's something else to consider," he said. "Anyone we encounter at this point won't be…human."

"They won't have a human body," Charlotte said reprovingly. "They're still people underneath."

Henry smiled lovingly at her. "It always amazed me how easily you saw me for me, even when I wore a bear's body. But in this instance, I'm more worried about their teeth and claws. And size."

"I think it's actually their ears and noses we should be most concerned about." Charlotte put her hand on her arm where she still wore a slim bandage beneath her sleeve.

Henry's eyes followed the movement, and he frowned. "What is it? Were you hurt somehow? Did one of the bears—"

His voice rose, and she shushed him urgently. "Do you hear something?"

He froze instantly, his head cocked as if listening. His eyes grew wide.

"Yes," he hissed. "Run!"

Grabbing her hand again, he sprinted, pulling her behind him almost too fast for her to keep her feet under her. She found a rhythm and tried to pull her hand free, but he held on tight. She stopped fighting and focused on running, her breath sawing in and out of her lungs.

Pounding steps sounded behind them accompanied by heavy breathing that didn't sound human. They ran harder.

They reached a strangely shaped intersection, two corridors branching off. Henry pulled her in one direction, but a bear appeared in the distance. It stopped, its head coming up in alert at the sight of them.

Charlotte backtracked, dragging Henry with her as she took the other direction. He seemed almost reluctant, though, his eyes frantically darting all around them.

They careened around a corner, and Charlotte discovered the source of his reluctance. They had reached a dead end.

She barely managed to stop herself from running headlong into the smooth stone wall.

"A window?" she rasped out, struggling to catch her breath.

A low growl rumbled down the corridor, building as two voices overlapped. She spun around, her knees nearly giving out at the sight of two enormous white bears prowling toward them.

Her arm throbbed in memory, and she whimpered. Henry stepped in front of her, his face determined, and it galvanized her into action, strengthening her knees. She looked around, but the windows here had crossed panes. She didn't think she could smash them if she tried.

"We surrender!" she called quickly, raising both hands.

The bears didn't pause, continuing to pace toward them. Henry had never lost his human side, and Gwen had claimed to be the same. But these bears looked like predators to her, their eyes dark and fixed on their prey. Were they lost in the hunt?

Henry backed up, pushing her behind him, but all too soon, her back hit the wall and his hit her. They both stopped.

"If only I was still a bear myself!" Henry muttered, and for the first time Charlotte wished his bear form back. Without it, it looked like they were about to die.

GWEN

Celandine dragged Gwen along the corridor, but they didn't go far. When she reached Gwen's room, she pushed her inside, finally releasing her ear. Gwen staggered, rubbing at it.

As soon as she regained her balance, she lunged for the door, but the queen moved quicker. Grabbing one of Gwen's arms, she twisted it behind her, immobilizing her.

Gwen panted, desperation fighting with her desire not to give Celandine the satisfaction of seeing her break.

"I thought you had finally learned your lesson," Celandine snarled. "Learned that you're nothing without me. Why else would you come crawling back?"

"I came back because someone had to stand up to you," Gwen snapped. "You've plagued this kingdom long enough!"

Celandine snarled again and thrust Gwen toward the wall. Too late Gwen realized what she was doing. She must have prepared because the door to the servant room was propped open, the small space inside a looming darkness.

Gwen cried out, grabbing with her free hand at the edge of the doorframe. But Celandine twisted her other arm, angling

Gwen so that her precarious hold slipped free, and she stumbled into the room. Again she turned and lunged for the door, and again Celandine moved too quickly for her, this time slamming the door in her face. Gwen collided with the solid surface, slamming her nose against it.

She fell back, her eyes stinging with more than pain. It couldn't be happening. Not all over again.

Distantly, she heard a key turn in the lock. Holding herself together by the barest thread, she stumbled over and tried the handle anyway. It had to open. It had to open.

It didn't open. She slumped to the floor, a sob tearing from her throat. She had come so far. She had finally found her strength and defied Celandine to her face, and yet here she was back where she had begun.

The darkness pressed on her like a physical force, and with the barest whimper, Gwen's senses slipped away from her. She could see nothing, hear nothing, feel nothing except the presence of her panic, sliding down her throat and up her middle and coating her hands. She buried her head in her hands, trying to drown it out, to hide from it.

A scream burned up her throat, but it came out like a whimper, her chest unable to expand enough for any volume.

Dark. Dark. Dark. Dark. Dark. Alone. Alone. Alone. Alone. Alone.

The words echoed in her mind until they had no meaning. She was going to die here. She would grow hungry and thirsty—so thirsty—until the pain stopped gnawing at her and consumed her whole.

She would never even see the light again. She had thought Celandine had already stolen everything from her, but now she had even stolen the sun. Gwen would die in darkness.

She curled in on herself, time losing all meaning.

At one point, something echoed distantly. Some outside sound or presence. Her brain reached for it, but it was too far away to properly grasp. A pounding perhaps. Or even her name?

Gradually, too gradually, it permeated into her brain, pushing back the darkness. Had she only imagined it, or was someone there?

She staggered to her feet, her muscles contracting strangely, as if they'd forgotten how to work. Someone was there, and they would rescue her.

"Please!" she called, pounding on her side of the door. "Please! Is there someone there?"

She was greeted only with silence. She had taken too long to respond, and whoever had been there must have left.

Tears dripped unheeded down her cheeks, and shame filled her. She was a grown woman, and all that was needed to reduce her to this was to be locked in a small space. It made no logical sense. She knew that. But she couldn't fight the sheer terror that had her in its grip, her younger self rising to swallow the new her.

She pounded again and again until her hands hurt, but no one responded. She was alone once again.

She slid down to sitting again, but she had regained some measure of calm. It was dark in here but not nearly as small as that dreaded closet where she had been confined for days after Easton's banishment. She could move and stretch out. Even lie down when she got tired.

It was surprising the queen had put her in such a large space, even if it was conveniently close.

Remembering the sequence of events that had led her here wasn't pleasant, but it helped her cling to the grip of her sanity. She had endured worse. She could endure this too. She could endure until someone came to rescue her. This time Easton would come for her.

And then the tingling started. Gwen fell forward, her mind seizing as the tearing sensation began. She was growing bigger, so much bigger, and the space was growing smaller. The walls really were closing in on her. And they wouldn't stop. They would keep going until Gwen was squeezed to death, her bones and muscles sandwiched flat, and her life extinguished. There would be no need to wait for the hunger and the dehydration.

The scream fought its way out, coming out as a terrifying baying, howling growl that sounded horrifyingly inhuman. She would never be herself again, never be held by Easton again. She was alone. It was dark, and she was alone.

She thrashed around, no longer conscious of what she was doing, just desperate for an escape from the darkness around her and her own mind. Coherent thought had fled, and she had only wordless impressions and fear, fear, fear. So much fear.

Gwen had no idea how much time passed in that state. She had no more sense of its passage than she had rational thought. But eventually, a single image intruded.

Easton. His face appeared in her mind's eye, driving back the darkness. He was coming to the palace to face the queen, and if Gwen stayed stuck here, he would face her alone. Another face appeared. Alma, followed by Miriam. What was her mother doing to them while Gwen remained trapped here?

Other faces crowded in. Charlotte. Natalie. Easton's mother, who had always been kind to Gwen and now apparently lived in the city. Even Count Oswin.

The queen had tormented Gwen for years, but she had also tormented these people. If Gwen gave in completely to her panic, Celandine won. And yet...And yet...

Gwen put her head in her hands, only to find she was reaching up with paws instead of fingers. She froze, closing her eyes against the terrifying, encroaching black around her, and thought of nothing but her body. She could feel its unfamiliar shape, the pulsing strength of her muscles, and the sharp points of her claws and teeth.

Her mother thought Gwen was a victim. She shut her away thinking she would buckle and collapse. And Gwen had nearly done exactly that. But Gwen was finished being a victim. She hated the dark, and she would never like small places, but this room wasn't her tomb. She had strength still. And it was time to use it.

With a growl that built in volume and strength, she turned to where she knew the door was. Rearing back on her hind legs, she fell forward with her full force against the wood, claws extended. It cracked. She reared back again and fell forward, paws swiping as she descended. The door splintered, one of her paws breaking through, and light burst in.

She blinked, her eyes stinging at the sudden illumination. Shutting them, she lowered her head and rammed the shards of the door. It teetered and collapsed outward, sections of the wood snapping completely.

Gwen staggered through the opening into the untouched chaos of her bedchamber. The room had never looked so beautiful to her.

She collapsed, sucking in long, sweet breaths as her eyes adjusted to the light. Then she lumbered to her feet, shaking herself. While she would always avoid small, dark places if possible, they would never have the same hold on her again—not now she had fought her way free.

She breathed in, sucking the air through her nose, and froze. Easton and Charlotte. She easily picked their scents from everything else—fresh but not immediately so. Someone had been there! It was his voice she'd heard!

But where were they now? She tensed, the lingering fear still bubbling through her veins, convincing her they must be in trouble.

The door to her room was ajar, allowing her to easily push through. *I'm coming,* she thought silently, lifting her snout to sniff the air.

Easton's scent was fainter out here, harder to pinpoint. But Charlotte's seemed fresh. Gwen followed it to the door of a random, unused bedchamber on the opposite side of the corridor. She frowned. What could Charlotte have been doing there?

She didn't seem to have gone inside, though. Her scent continued down the corridor toward Henry's room instead, which made far more sense. Gwen followed, the physical activity driving out the remaining trembling and weakness in her limbs.

She stopped outside Henry's room. Should she try to open the door? But Charlotte's scent lingered in the corridor, and it was joined by a new one. Gwen frowned, considering. Unlike Charlotte and Easton, she had never smelled Henry while in her bear form. But something about the new scent felt vaguely familiar. If she had to guess, she thought it was him.

Intrigued, Gwen hurried faster, following the scent of the two of them. It wasn't part of the plan for Charlotte to free Henry at this point. What had been happening in her absence?

A third scent appeared, triggering a low growl. The new one was unfamiliar, but it screamed of a threat. Here in the palace, an unknown bear could only mean one thing. Charlotte and Henry were being pursued.

Gwen broke into a lumbering run, bumping against walls as she rounded corners, her ears picking up the distant sound of overlapping growls. She pushed herself still faster.

She reached a familiar intersection, the sounds and smells coming from the dead end on the left. She didn't hesitate as she raced around the final corner.

Several things reached her consciousness at once.

Charlotte and Henry were trapped against the wall, and Charlotte's arms were raised in surrender. The two bears weren't stopping, however. They advanced on the two smaller figures, their growls threatening.

Had they lost their minds? Or had the queen ordered that Charlotte was to be killed if found? Henry was likely to die attempting to protect her if so.

Fury ripped through Gwen. A growl she didn't know she

could produce thundered down the corridor, and she leaped forward, claws flashing.

She raked the rump of the bear on the left. He whined, falling sideways away from her. She leaped again, flying through the opening he had created and stopping just short of her friends' astonished faces.

Spinning, she lowered her head, her ears pinned back as she growled a warning.

The other two bears responded in kind, but their eyes showed confusion. They had no idea who she was.

The uninjured one tried to lunge forward, and Gwen slashed at him, her movement so quick her eyes couldn't follow. A trail of red down his arm was left in her wake. He pulled back, his gaze growing even more wary.

Gwen peeled her lips back and growled in satisfaction. The guards liked using their bear forms to terrorize the city, but they weren't used to facing another bear.

"Don't touch them!" she said in a low, threatening voice.

"Gwen!" Charlotte cried in recognition. "Oh, thank goodness."

The two guards froze, exchanging looks. Their confusion had overtaken whatever bloodlust or order had driven them. Like the rest of the palace and city, they had no idea their princess turned into a bear at night just like them.

"Yes, that's right," she said, her words clear despite her gravelly bear voice. "I'm your princess, and I order you to stand down. Now!" She roared the last word, and they both fell back, looking terrified.

Gwen smiled, feeling a different kind of strength coursing through her. She was not only finished being a victim, she was finished being the pure princess who hid in her room and earned her supposed virtue through inaction. She was done cowering and hiding. No matter what her form, Queen Gwendolyn would stand in the breach for the weaker members of her kingdom every time it was needed.

"A…apologies," the guard with the injured rump stammered, clearly not knowing what to do with her.

She wasn't their queen, but they did think she was their queen's daughter, and they knew she would soon sit on the throne. It was no surprise when they both turned tail and ran.

"Gwen!" Charlotte ran forward, tears in her eyes, and flung her arms around Gwen's neck.

"Thank you, Your Highness," Henry said more carefully. "You arrived at just the right moment."

Gwen leaned into Charlotte's hug for a moment, catching her breath.

"We should get moving," she said. "I don't know who those guards are going to report to, but word will get back to Celandine soon that we're here."

Henry grimaced. "We were hoping to keep my escape secret for longer."

"Never mind that," Charlotte said. "We need to take Gwen to Easton. He's worried sick."

"Easton?" Gwen's eyes lit up. "You know where he is?"

Charlotte nodded. "The queen caught all the other rebels, but Easton and I had gone looking for you, so we weren't there yet. I made him hide, and he promised he'd stay there." She smiled brightly. "And now he's about to be rewarded for his superhuman forbearance."

"Wait, Celandine caught the others?" Gwen cried, dismayed. "All of them?"

Charlotte winced. "I'm afraid so. Even Emmett."

"What?" Gwen stared at her, her mind racing. What was going to happen to the plan now?

"Come on," Charlotte said. "I might need the two of you to help me find the way. I'm fairly sure I remember the place, but…" She smiled, the expression not quite reaching her eyes. "We can work out what to do once all four of us are together."

Thankfully, Gwen was able to lead the way to the section of the palace that contained the apartments of the count and his adult children. Once in that more familiar environment, Charlotte was confident in bypassing the dangerous apartment and leading the others straight to the storage cupboard.

She opened the door with a flourish, more relieved than she wanted to admit when Easton blinked up at her from a seated position on the floor. He raised his hand against the light, and Charlotte beamed at him.

"You're welcome," she said, standing back and gesturing toward Henry and the bear in the corridor.

Easton leaped to his feet. "Gwen!" He rushed to her side, relief lighting up his face. "You're here! Charlotte found you!"

"As promised," Charlotte said smugly before her face twisted a little. "I haven't found the others, though. At least not yet," she added hastily.

"We'll find them together." Gwen leaned her head against Easton's side.

He put an arm around her head, and she looked like she could have started purring with satisfaction. Charlotte hid a smile. Henry used to look like that sometimes in the library in their old castle when she scratched behind his ears or in other hard to reach spots.

"We should find somewhere less open," Henry said tensely. "We're not all going to fit in that cupboard."

Gwen shivered, and Charlotte was glad she had Easton at her side. Whatever had happened to Gwen after she got dragged away by the queen, she clearly hadn't fully recovered from it.

"This way." Gwen led them to a door one corridor over.

Easton turned the handle for her and stepped into a deserted sitting room.

"No one comes here during the day, let alone at night," Gwen said.

"What about our scent?" Charlotte asked. "Couldn't they track us?"

"Actually, I think I can do something about that," Henry offered.

Charlotte raised her eyebrows. She only hoped they weren't going to have to slop through any water troughs.

"Give me a minute."

He was gone for far longer than a minute, and when he returned, Charlotte wrinkled her nose in disgust. A highly unpleasant aroma clung to him.

Gwen, on the other hand, gagged, turning away with disgust.

"What do you think?" He directed his question at Gwen.

"Real bears probably think that smell is normal, right?" she asked. "Unfortunately my bear senses and human mind are working together in a terrifying alliance. It's like the most awful stench you've ever smelled amplified ten times."

Henry nodded with satisfaction. "I got rid of it all before I came in, so this is only a minor version of how it smells out there and all down the surrounding corridors."

"Is that horse manure?" Easton asked tentatively.

Henry smiled with satisfaction. "From the stables. I'm just glad I won't be responsible for cleaning your palace when this is all finished, Your Majesties."

Easton made a choked sound, his eyes bulging, and Gwen gagged again. Charlotte laughed, however. "Brilliant!"

"Hopefully this buys us some time," Henry said. "I'm not convinced we want to do anything too hastily."

Everyone shared what had happened to them in the last few hours, Easton drawing even closer to Gwen when she gave an emotionless recitation of her time in the small room.

"We were right there!" Easton cried in a tortured voice. "If we'd just stayed a little longer, or if I'd called for you a little louder..."

"It's my fault," Charlotte said, misery washing over her. "I told you to lower your voice and said we had to leave. I didn't think you were actually in there, Gwen."

"No!" Gwen's voice came out unexpectedly strong. "You were doing what you thought would be best for me. I understand that. And I'm actually glad you didn't find me. I needed to break free myself."

"You're always so gracious," Charlotte sighed, wondering if she would be the same after years of being a princess. Was it something you learned by being a royal?

Gwen drew a deep breath, sounding so distressed that Charlotte frowned at her.

"Actually," she said, "I think I should take this chance to confess something—before you and Henry risk yourselves even more for me."

"What are you talking about?" Charlotte asked. "Of course we're going to help you. We're not just going to run away and abandon you."

"But you don't know everything," Gwen said. "You think it was your parents that came up with the idea of using their candle to get a look at Henry's face, but actually..." She finished on a rush, "Actually, it was me. When they took me out to their stables, I put all sorts of doubts about Henry in their heads and suggested the idea of the candle."

She turned to Henry. "I'm so sorry! I had no idea who you were. I thought you were working with the queen. I even thought you might have been the one to give her the bear enchantment in the first place."

Charlotte stared at her, her mind whirring. "It was you?" she cried. "Why didn't you say anything?"

Gwen winced. "When I tried to express doubts at first, you were so certain about Henry. I was worried about you, thinking you were another person being fooled and trapped by my mother. We'd only just met, so I thought you would be more likely to listen to your parents than to me. So I set up a chance to speak to them, and I poisoned their minds against Henry. It's all my fault."

"No," Charlotte said slowly. "I'm the one who took the candle into that room and lit it. Half of my anger toward my parents was because I was actually angry at myself." She sighed. "What a mess. You were right that I listened to my parents, and that was another mistake of mine. I let myself be swayed by their concerns even though they don't have a history of good judgment or decision-making." She sighed again. "You can love someone and know not to trust their judgment. I should have known better than to let myself be swayed by them. But their proposed solution lined up so exactly with what I wanted to do myself."

She looked at Henry, apology all over her face. "At the end of the day, I'm the one to blame. Everyone else—even you, Gwen— have the excuse that you were acting out of concern for me. But I was driven by curiosity and impatience."

Henry gave her a reassuring smile, taking her hand and threading his fingers through hers. She turned to Gwen with a smile.

"Henry has forgiven me my much bigger crime. You don't

even need to ask if I can forgive you. Of course I can. It's already forgotten."

Gwen's expression lightened, her whole body suffused with relief. "I'm sorry I didn't tell you sooner. I should have told you straight away when we met after Henry's disappearance. But I thought…I thought…" Tears welled, making it difficult for her to speak.

"I'm glad that's resolved," Easton said, clearly trying to hide his tension. "But I think we should talk about what we do next. Gwen, do you have any idea where the queen might have taken the rebels? If she wants to keep them locked away until the wedding, where would they be?"

Gwen sat back, clearly considering the question. "The guards have cells of various sizes, of course, but none of them are big enough for so many."

"Would she think it was dangerous to keep them together?" Henry asked. "If they could work together, they might find a way to escape."

"Together…" Gwen murmured, seeming struck by a thought. "Actually, there's one place. The servants all get locked in together every night. It's a series of connected storage rooms. They're in the basement level, and there aren't even any windows. The servants have been in there as a group for nearly ten years, and they haven't found a way to break out."

"And she thinks they're rebels as well," Henry said, catching up with her idea. "She's probably got them all locked in there together."

"Do you know where the door is?" Easton asked. "And how we can get the key?"

Gwen looked down at her paws and then back at him. "We might not need a key."

Easton grinned. "If you're suggesting you could break down the door with pure force, I believe you. But if we don't want to bring people running to investigate the commotion, we might want to find a subtler method."

"And I think we need to wait for morning anyway," Henry said. "The guards' sense of smell and hearing are too great an advantage when they're bears. We won't manage to creep around unseen or sneak into the basement rooms if they can smell or hear us from half a palace away."

Easton looked like he wanted to argue, but just like Charlotte, he'd never been a bear. She was inclined to agree with Henry, and doubly so when Gwen quickly nodded her agreement.

"Does that window open?" she asked, nodding at the largest window in the room. "I think we're all going to need some rest at some point tonight, but we'll need to take turns staying up on watch, and we should have an escape route planned. They may decide to search this whole area room by room if they guess we're the source of that stench."

Henry strode over and tested the latch on the window, peering outside. "It opens, and the jump isn't too big."

"We don't need to take watches," Gwen said. "I should do it the whole time. I'm the only one with bear senses, and I actually slept well the last couple of nights."

Charlotte and Henry exchanged a look.

"You can do most of the night," he agreed, "but you need to get a few hours' sleep. We don't know what tomorrow will be like yet, but the wedding was planned for the late afternoon, I believe, so it will likely be a long day."

"So what is our plan?" Charlotte asked. "Is the queen really going to try to go through with the wedding in the middle of all this?"

"That has been her plan, but when she realizes Henry is gone, the plan is going to have to change," Gwen said.

Henry frowned. "Should I go back to my room?"

"No!" Charlotte cried, thankful when the others stayed silent. "That is not happening. We're together now, and we're going to work this out together. No more prisoners, no more separation."

Gwen nodded, Easton a beat behind her.

"She can't have a wedding," Gwen said. "Not unless she can recapture us both and somehow force us to comply." She was carefully not looking at Easton as she said it. "But she won't want to admit weakness. And she'll still want a spectacle. The invited guests from the city and even the loyal courtiers will likely still turn up at the appointed time. Celandine will be telling herself she can recapture us in time, or else she'll plan a big demonstration with all the rebels instead, thinking that will restore order and her power, at least in the short term while she works out how to fix things. That's been her strategy until now, always a temporary fix, keeping things going while she gets herself further and further into trouble."

"So we'll still have our audience," Easton said thoughtfully.

Gwen nodded.

"In that case," he said, meeting her eyes. "We need to give them what they came to see."

"A wedding!" Charlotte cried in delight, clasping her hands together. "With no need for last minute switches. Just the two of you, getting married. As long as we can keep the queen and her guards occupied, the courtiers won't protest. They don't even know what Henry looks like, remember."

"But how do we keep the queen and her guards occupied?" Henry asked.

"We lock her up." Gwen looked surprised by the ferocity in her own voice.

"Is that even possible?" Charlotte asked.

"She isn't superhuman," Gwen replied. "She doesn't have the strength of a bear during the day."

"What about her godmother objects?" Easton asked.

"She keeps them in a hidden room," Gwen said. "The only one she carries continually on her person is the one tied to the bear enchantment. And that won't help her get out of a locked cell. Her strength comes from fear and intimidation and her guards. Stripped of those, she's just a human woman with the strength of a human woman. She can't batter down a door."

Henry slowly smiled. "So we lock her up, and then we lead her guards on a merry chase so they don't have the chance to properly look for her."

"It doesn't have to last forever," Charlotte said. "Only long enough for the captives to do their job."

"The captives?" Henry looked at her, confused.

"The wedding!" Charlotte cried, rolling her eyes at his obliviousness. "Do you think a function like that is going to magically come together on its own? The queen was planning to put on a show, but now it's our show, and we can't look less impressive than her. We have to somehow convince the captives to play the role of servants one more time and set everything up."

"So the rebels will have to lead the chase," Henry said thoughtfully. "You and I can help with that."

"The bride and groom will have to stick with the wedding preparation." He looked at Easton with a small smile, and Charlotte almost laughed. It was obvious which he thought was the better assignment, despite the danger.

From the pained look on Easton's face, he agreed. After the way they had all been treated, everyone wanted a piece of Celandine and her people. But the plan made the most sense that way, and nobody tried to argue.

Charlotte was certain she wouldn't be able to sleep. But when she lay on one of the broad sofas with Henry pressed against her back and his arms around her, she drifted off faster than she would have liked.

She was jerked awake by a frantic whisper from Gwen in the small hours.

"Quick! Someone's coming," she said.

"Wha…" Charlotte sat up, bleary-eyed and confused.

Henry woke behind her, instantly alert. "Out the window, then. I left some manure there earlier."

Easton pushed it open, and Gwen climbed through first, scrabbling with her paws for purchase before heaving herself over the ledge. Charlotte tried to hold back her impatience, glancing constantly between the door and the window, just waiting for someone to thrust the door open.

"Climb through," Gwen called back quietly. "Straight onto my back."

"Gwen!" Easton exclaimed, pausing halfway over the sill. "You can't carry three of us!"

"Yes, I can," she said stubbornly. "I'm not an ordinary bear, you know. I'm bigger, for one. And I don't have to carry you far. Just far enough to confuse them. My scent will be unfamiliar to them, especially since most of them don't even know I'm a bear at night. And I'll walk through the manure. If you're on my back, it will make it much harder for them to smell where you went."

"Come on," Charlotte said to Easton, giving him a light push. "Just do what she says."

Still grumbling, Easton dropped carefully onto her back and slid forward as far as he could go. Charlotte followed next, Henry lifting her over the sill and placing her on Gwen's back with ease. He followed last, barely fitting behind Charlotte, although he somehow managed to not only balance there but also lean back to close the window behind them.

Gwen took off at a careful walk, heading for the closest patch of concealing trees. Once out of sight, she angled toward the stables.

"If we're throwing them off with the scent of manure…" she murmured in answer to the question no one had voiced aloud.

She walked all the way into the stables, and Charlotte expected the horses to start screaming and whinnying in terror. But they must have grown used to the presence of bears in their vicinity because they barely reacted at all.

Gwen stopped below a ladder that led up to the hay loft. They took turns stepping straight onto it, climbing one at a time. When they had finished, Gwen rubbed her side against the lower rungs, hopefully covering their scent.

"But what about you?" Easton leaned over the side, looking down at her.

"There's an empty stall on the end. I'll sleep there," she called quietly back.

Easton twisted to look at Charlotte and Henry, and she could read his thoughts on his face. Thankfully, Gwen spoke before Charlotte needed to.

"You stay up there," she told him. "Don't even think about coming down to join me."

Charlotte gave him a sympathetic look as he nodded with resignation. She felt selfish, but she was glad it wasn't Henry down there, so close and yet too far. After so many stressful days apart, she wasn't ready to have him more than an arm's length away.

CHARLOTTE

*I*t took her longer to fall asleep the second time, but she managed it in the end. And when she woke, the first brush of the morning was already past.

She bolted awake, staring from Henry to where Gwen now slept beside them. Easton sat to one side, keeping watch over her.

"What are we still doing here?" She gasped and lowered her voice. "Aren't there grooms down there by now?"

Henry shrugged. "No one came. I guess the grooms are all captives."

Gwen stirred, nodding sleepily at Henry's comment.

"We needed to give Gwen a chance to rest," Easton said. "She was awake all night keeping watch over us."

"But now we need to get to the basement." Charlotte's stomach rumbled on cue, making her flush. "Ignore that. I don't need to eat."

"We should eat." Gwen sat up and stretched, yawning. "I'm sure the grooms have something stashed in their office. Let's go check."

They found a whole basket of apples and a large hunk of cheese that they divided four ways.

"I'll admit, I feel a lot better after that," Henry said, and Charlotte nodded agreement.

The day before, it had been easy to sneak through first the grounds and then the palace. In hindsight, it had been too easy, the way cleared for the rebels to walk into the trap.

Now, the grounds teemed with guard patrols. They were everywhere, even if their steps lagged, and they kept rubbing their eyes as if they'd already been on duty all night.

"Thank goodness they're all so tired," Easton whispered as they once again dove into a clump of bushes to hide. "Otherwise we'd have been caught by now for sure."

They finally made it into the actual palace, but that only meant substituting empty rooms and storage cupboards for bushes. By the time they reached the entrance to the basement level, Charlotte's nerves were stretched so tight they were about to snap.

Two guards stood on either side of the door. Their attitude was far from alert, but they were awake, and they had swords at their sides.

"There's no way to sneak around those two," Gwen said. "There are only two doors down to the basement level, and if this one is guarded, the other one definitely will be. This is the back entrance."

Charlotte looked Henry and Easton up and down. "You're a prince, Henry, and you were a courtier's son at least until you were thirteen, Easton. Do you both have combat training?"

The two men exchanged a look before nodding simultaneously.

Charlotte shrugged. "Then I think we'll need a direct confrontation this time. There are only two of them, and they won't know what either of you look like, so they won't be sure who you are at first."

"I'd rather not leave dead bodies in our wake," Gwen said queasily.

"We can raid the last storage cupboard and look for something to use to gag and secure them," Charlotte suggested, and Gwen reluctantly nodded.

Henry and Easton exchanged another look and another nod before striding forward together.

"Come on, hurry." Charlotte pulled Gwen toward the cupboard, but Gwen resisted.

"Let me get the supplies," she said. "You stay here in case they need backup."

Charlotte grimaced, unsure what backup she could possibly provide, but Gwen was already darting away. And since Gwen knew her own palace better, it did make sense to let her go.

"You there!" Henry called in an imperious voice, pointing toward the guards.

They straightened instinctively, recognizing the casual note of command in his voice and bearing that marked him as someone with authority.

"What is going on?" Henry continued. "There are guards everywhere, and my wife couldn't sleep for half the night from all the commotion. We're supposed to be attending a wedding today, but—"

One of the guards interrupted. "This area is off limits. We're going to have to ask you to leave."

Henry and Easton kept advancing, and the guards looked warily at each other before the first one drew his sword and the other followed suit. But they'd left it too late and let Henry and Easton draw too close.

Breaking into a sprint, the two men rushed the guards, lashing out with fists and feet. Charlotte gasped, her heart in her throat, but before she could even think about moving forward, it was all over. The two guards lay on the ground groaning, and the swords were in the hands of their attackers.

Henry looked back and motioned her forward, and she rushed over.

"Gwen went on her own to get something to use as rope," she said, and Easton looked up, alarmed.

But before he could go off in search of her, Gwen appeared, having managed to procure actual rope and several long stretches of torn material for gags. Henry and Easton made quick work of securing their defeated opponents, dumping the two men in a nearby room.

"Let's hope we don't have to do that too many times," Charlotte said, eyeing the closed door uneasily. Easton had tied the ropes with a seaman's knots, but there was still no telling how long it would take the defeated guards to get free.

Thankfully, they met no more guards on the basement level. Apparently, only the doors had been left guarded in order to free the others up to patrol the grounds and castle corridors.

Gwen led the way to the relevant set of rooms, having explained that while she'd never been inside, she had been to the door before. Since Gwen was no longer in her bear form, it was a good thing she'd remembered that she still had her stolen master key in her pocket. Celandine hadn't remembered to confiscate it when she'd dragged Gwen away.

"I could have just unlocked the door and walked out." Gwen looked down when she said it, apparently embarrassed.

Easton put a hand on her arm. "Didn't you say what you went through in there was important? And you don't know if this key would have worked anyway. The queen changed the lock on your room, so she might have changed that one too."

"That's true." Gwen brightened. "Both of those things are true."

"But let's hope it works on this door," Charlotte added nervously. Without a bear among them, it would take a long time to beat down such a sturdy door. She took the key out of Gwen's hand since her fingers were trembling slightly after the reminder of her recent imprisonment.

The key slid in and turned. She threw a relieved look back at the rest of them, pushing the door open and stepping forward.

"No!" Gwen and Henry called at the same time.

Henry lunged forward and caught hold of the back of her dress, yanking her backward. A length of wood, being wielded as a baton, flashed down hard on where her head had just been.

Henry gave a sigh of relief and pulled her into a quick hug.

"How did you know that was going to happen?" Charlotte blinked up at him.

He gave a guilty look in Gwen's direction. "I nearly did the same thing to Gwen when I thought she was the queen."

Someone peered out the door and then turned to shout back into the room. Charlotte tried to pull away now that the prisoners had seen the identity of the arrivals, but Henry held on.

"I think we should let them come out here," he said. "I don't fancy all of us getting trapped in such a secure location."

Easton and Gwen nodded fervent agreement, so Charlotte stayed in place, watching as people began to file out of the door. Most of them she didn't recognize, but when Lydia and Jett emerged and rushed to their son's side, she smiled, watching the reunion with pleasure. And when Emmett's crutches appeared, the boy following a swing later, she almost cried to see him unharmed. His father hovered at his shoulder, his eyes meeting Charlotte's.

He nodded at her, gratitude on his face, but she gestured with her head toward Gwen and Easton, who were already surrounded. He should save his gratitude for his future king and queen.

But when Count Oswin appeared, she hurried to his side. He hadn't been in the line of prisoners who had paraded past her hiding place, so she hadn't known to expect him there. He must have been arrested separately.

She was glad to see him, though. If he was there, they only

needed to convince one person of the rebels' new role in the day's events.

The count clasped her hand. "It's good to see you. More than good. When my son told me he'd had a glimpse of Easton, I hoped…But I wasn't sure…" He glanced at his grandson and stopped, seemingly overcome with emotion.

"Of course we had to come rescue you," Charlotte said warmly. "But we're not just here to save you."

The count looked at her sharply. "We're still going ahead with the plan? How is that possible?"

Charlotte grinned. "There have been a few amendments…"

With the help of the count and his son, they got the grateful crowd separated, the servants heading down the corridor in one direction, while the rebels followed Henry and Charlotte several yards the other way.

After they'd explained the situation, the count surveyed the small crowd. "Anyone have any objections? Anyone want out?"

The group stayed silent.

Henry gave the count a disapproving look as he stepped forward to address the group. "We only want people who are actual volunteers. You've all had a highly distressing experience, and if you need to withdraw, we won't take it as a reflection on your commitment to the cause."

Still no one spoke up.

Charlotte stepped forward as well. "In that case, does anyone have any suggestions about how we can lure the queen into a secure location? Somewhere we can lock her in?"

The rebels who had snuck in from the city gave each other blank looks. But some of the freed prisoners were courtiers whose allegiances had shifted, and several of them narrowed their eyes in thought.

"I have an idea," Emmett piped up.

His grandfather stepped forward, but Charlotte motioned for him to wait and let Emmett speak.

The boy looked back toward the room they'd just left. "Why not use that?"

Charlotte raised an eyebrow. "How do you propose we get her in there?"

"She's already planning to come," he said, gaining enthusiasm. "I spent the night talking with some of the servants."

"Captives," Henry said, and Emmett flushed.

"Yes," he amended. "The captives. They said the only reason the queen hadn't slaughtered them already was that she needed them."

The count scoffed. "That's what comes of replacing every single one of your servants with captive slaves."

Emmett shifted uncomfortably, and Charlotte motioned for him to continue.

"Apparently, she was going to come back today and collect some of them so they could finish preparing her big event. The others were going to be left here, under guard."

"She was going to threaten them in order to make the others comply," Henry said thoughtfully, clearly turning Emmett's suggestion over in his mind.

"But will she come herself?" Charlotte looked to the count as the one who must know her best. "Won't she just send some guards to collect them?"

"She'll come," he said confidently. "She'll want to make a big show to intimidate them, and she won't trust that to any of her people. It's one of her weaknesses that she surrounds herself almost entirely with subservient people. The old captain of the guard is more interested in not attracting her attention than showing any initiative. He doesn't have the personality for chilling speeches or spreading fear by his mere presence."

His son nodded. "Prince Henry and Princess Gwendolyn have both escaped her grasp. She knows she's hanging onto the situation by a thread. She won't want to risk anything else getting out of control."

"In that case…" Charlotte grimaced. "How well does she know her own guards?"

"I'm going to guess not well at all," the count said, looking bemused. "They aren't loyal to her because of a personal connection. Only because she gives them power and gold."

Charlotte surveyed the group, pointing at one man and then another. "You and you." She turned to Henry. "What do you think? I think they're the closest matches we've got."

He narrowed his eyes, examining the two men before agreeing.

"How do you feel about playing guards for a little?" Charlotte asked them.

The two looked to the count, who redirected their attention to Charlotte.

"The door down to this level had two guards when we arrived," Henry explained. "We…removed them. You'll find them tied up in a room just upstairs. You'll need to strip them and use their uniforms. Here's one of their swords." He handed the weapon over. "We'll retrieve the other one from Easton."

"The queen will likely use the main entrance," the count said. " But if she does appear, just keep your heads bowed in respect and attempt not to say anything. Hopefully no one will notice you're not who you're supposed to be."

Charlotte handed the master key to the count's son. "You go with them. The guards are locked away. Once they have the uniforms, lock them up again and bring the key back down. We'll need it here."

The three men moved off, a couple of others following to assist them.

"Won't the queen notice something is wrong when she opens the door and the room inside is deserted?" Charlotte asked.

"That's why I need to be in there," Emmett said, rejoining the conversation.

"Absolutely not," his father said instantly, and the boy rolled his eyes.

"I'm not a baby, Father. And obviously you'll need to be with me. But look at me! I'm a child, and also—" He gestured at his leg. "Do I look like a threat? I'll be in the first room, lying down without my crutches. The queen will send some guards in first to make sure no one tries what we did earlier, so when I see them, I'll start crying and wailing, saying I've been abandoned and the others are all hiding in the back rooms. But the moment the queen comes inside herself—all the way inside—Father will leap up and grab me and sprint us straight out of the room. The rest of you can be ready to shut the door the second we're out." He beamed around at them. "And if I get a chance on the way out, I'll snatch the key right out of her hand."

"I can see some things that could go wrong with that," Henry said through the side of his mouth.

Charlotte winced in agreement. But the idea did have some merits. It was true that no one else among them could possibly be as disarming and non-threatening in appearance as Emmett.

"What if it's not just his father hidden in there with him?" she suggested.

Henry gazed at the amassed rebels. "Some of you are courtiers," he said. "Do any of you have experience fighting with a blade, preferably of disarming a bladed opponent without a blade yourself?"

Four men shouldered their way through the crowd to stand before them. One had a roughly bandaged left arm, and another had a gash along one cheek.

"We can do it," one of them said.

"And would welcome a chance," added another in a low growl.

"We wouldn't have been taken so easily back there," the first added, "if they hadn't gotten a knife to the boy's throat."

Emmett looked down at the ground, reminding Charlotte of what she had overheard the evening before. He wasn't supposed to have been in the apartment at all. No wonder he was desperate to have a part in making up for his mistake. Charlotte could relate to the feeling.

"It's fairly dark in there," she said. "We should be able to conceal all five of you in there with him. You can be ready to burst out and fight your way out if necessary. The queen's not going to send her entire guard force in ahead of her."

The count tried to protest, but surprisingly it was his son who restrained him. "We have to let him do this," he said quietly in his father's ear. "If he walks away from this feeling like he was weak and helpless and at fault, it might destroy the rest of his life. He already has enough battles of that kind to fight."

Both men glanced at the boy's missing leg.

Charlotte watched them, impressed. She hadn't expected so much insight from the count's son. It was reassuring, though, after his actions earlier in his life. Maybe he really could prove a support to Gwen in the future.

Once the plan had been decided on, it didn't take long to get everyone organized. Gwen and Easton led the captive servants away, taking them out through the back door that was now guarded by their own people in disguise.

Some of the rebels went with them to hide on the next level up and wait, splitting their forces. There were only so many people who could be helpful in a single corridor.

Once Emmett and his various protectors were hidden inside, the rest of them crowded through the next door down, hiding themselves out of sight from the corridor. Once the queen arrived, they would have to move fast.

It seemed like they'd hardly settled out of sight before Charlotte heard marching boots, and someone hissed, "She's here!"

CHARLOTTE

Charlotte would have preferred to have longer to catch her breath before Celandine's arrival, but at least it sounded like she was coming from the direction of the main door. She wouldn't have passed their people in that case.

Charlotte strained her ears to hear the key turn in the lock and the door open. As expected, the first steps to enter sounded like the boots of guards.

Some low, surprised murmurs drifted out, presumably at the discovery of the empty room. Then Emmett started whimpering, his cries pathetic and weak. He spoke amid the blubbering, but Charlotte was too far away to catch his words. More footsteps sounded, and then Celandine's imperious voice demanding to know what was going on.

"Now!" Charlotte whispered and raced out of the door. Henry was a step ahead of her, two burly men from the city ahead of him.

The four of them lined up along the wall behind the open door to the prison rooms, staying as quiet as possible. A shout rang inside the room, and then the sound of a scuffle broke out. Charlotte recognized a fist hitting flesh and more shouts before the count's son raced from the room, Emmett in his arms. He didn't stop, continuing down the corridor toward the back exit. Emmett looked back over his shoulder and met Charlotte's eyes, grinning broadly. He held up his prize—the queen's key—and Charlotte saluted him.

One of the other rebels came next, walking backward, a sword in his hand and a bruise already blooming under one eye. Two of the queen's guards followed him, both on the attack, and behind them came a crush of people that was hard to distinguish, some rebels, some guards. Charlotte struggled to complete her head count of the rebels, ensuring they had all emerged. But she reached the correct number at the same time as she noted the other important point—the queen still hadn't emerged.

"Close it!" she yelled, and the two rebels against the wall heaved together, pushing the door ahead of them.

One of the guards shouted in protest, trying to throw himself into the closing gap, but Henry darted forward and shoved him hard enough to send him staggering all the way inside. The two rebels gave a final push and slammed the door closed, leaning against it to keep the guards still remaining inside from opening it again.

Charlotte darted between the struggling bodies, inserting their key and turning it before dashing away, heading further down the corridor in the direction of Emmett and his father.

From the other direction, the remaining rebels streamed out of their hiding place, joining their comrades and easily subduing the guards with their superior numbers. Charlotte counted heads again, not relaxing until she had confirmed her original count. Everyone on their side was accounted for, along with many of the guards.

She could hear screaming and shouting from the other side, but the wood was the thickest she had ever seen, and the hinges were on the outside. The guards who had ended up locked inside with the queen could pound on it for hours without breaking it down.

"Do they have any weapons left in there?" she asked one of the rebels who had been hidden inside.

"We disarmed most of them," he said. "They might have a dagger or two, but they won't get through that door in a hurry with only that."

"We're fortunate that once we sprung into action, most of them leaped to form a shield in front of the queen," another added. "It meant they unintentionally blocked her exit."

A piercing scream cut through the wood of the door. "Why don't we move upstairs?" Charlotte suggested, happy to put distance between her and the enraged queen, even if Celandine was locked away.

"What about this lot?" a rebel asked, indicating the subdued guards.

"We can take them upstairs with us. There's rope up there, and we can tie them up with their comrades."

"There must be others who knew the queen was coming down here, though," the count said. "If they come looking with a key…"

"They'll have to come through us." All four of the volunteers who had identified themselves as experienced fighters stood before them, now armed. "In a corridor like this, the captain of the guard would have to bring his entire force—split and attacking from both directions—to get through us."

A grin spread over Charlotte's face. "Then it's our job to make sure the entire force isn't available, even if they do work out where she is."

The four of them grinned back, moving to take up positions by the door. The rest of the rebels dragged their new prisoners with them up the stairs, finding a crowd on the other side of the door. The remaining rebels rushed forward to help secure the guards, having already found the rope Gwen left.

"What about Gwen and Easton and the others?" Charlotte asked one of them.

She shrugged. "They didn't stick around."

Charlotte nodded, hoping that meant the other part of their plan was succeeding as well. If the captive servants all decided they were taking their freedom and left without helping, the later parts of the plan would falter.

"You all know what we have to do now," the count said loudly. "Split up and find weapons if you can. Pair fighters with someone less experienced if possible, and I want at least one member of the court in each group. The guards will hesitate to do any serious damage to a member of the court without direct commands to do so. Our goal is to sow chaos and confusion. Find guards and then lead them on a chase for as long as you can. Keep them running and confused. We can't let them gather into a force of any size or give them time to stop and seek proper command. If you see someone else has been captured, free them if you can."

A chorus of agreement sounded, and the group spread out, breaking into smaller clumps. Charlotte looked at Henry with a smile.

"What about us?"

"We're a pair," he said. "And I don't think we need anyone else." He held out his hand, and she put hers into it.

"I've still got that master key," she said. "So I think we can get up to enough mischief on our own."

It took them several minutes of running to find their first pair of guards. The two men strolled leisurely across their field of vision until one of them recognized Charlotte and let out a shout. Charlotte and Henry took off running immediately, Henry taking the lead as they led the soldiers around in circles. When he darted through a door, he led Charlotte straight through the receiving room on the other side and out through a door in the opposite wall. He closed it behind them and gestured at the keyhole.

Charlotte locked it, and the two of them dashed back around to lock the other door while the protesting soldiers were still trying the handle of the locked one.

"There are windows, so I don't know how long it will keep them," Henry said.

"Long enough for now." Charlotte grinned back. "Let's go and find some others."

With Henry's knowledge of the castle and their master key, they managed to pull the same trick on ten different soldiers, strolling away each time to the sound of shouts and curses.

Charlotte grinned up at Henry. "Is it terrible that this has been kind of fun?"

The thrill of being chased was both terrifying and exhilarating, and if it wasn't for the exhaustion setting in to her legs, she could have gone on much longer. She glanced out a window, noting the lowering sun. They had passed several other rebel groups in the last few hours, even rescuing one as they were being escorted back toward the guard barracks. She hadn't seen Gwen or Easton or any of the servants, though. The rebels had purposely been trying to keep the guards away from the section of the palace that included the throne room.

Were the wedding preparations finished? Had the ceremony started? She wished she could be there to see her friend married, but she knew her role was too important to worry about being a guest.

Thought of guests made her wonder how the arriving wedding guests had gone. Had any of them spotted a rebel group being chased by royal guards? Had some of the guards been available to guide guests in? She hoped some of the intended guests had made it through the chaos to be the witnesses Gwen and Easton needed.

"Do you think it's—" she started to say to Henry, but a figure jumped out behind him, making her words falter.

Before he could respond to her horrified expression, the

enormous guard had his arms around Henry from behind, pinning his arms to his side and holding a knife to his throat.

A sneering courtier stepped out from the shadows, another guard at his side.

"Shall I restrain her, Lord Rafferty?" the second guard asked, looking toward Charlotte.

"I don't think that will be necessary," he said in an oily voice that sent a shiver up her spine. "I think she'll be most well-behaved." He looked toward Henry and smiled again.

Henry shook his head, but even that small movement made the knife tip prick his skin. Charlotte gasped.

"Don't listen to him," Henry choked out before his captor tightened his grip.

"All I want from you is that key in your pocket," Lord Rafferty said. "I can't find the captain of the guard, but I know you have a master key. Don't bother trying to deny it. I just watched that neat little trick you pulled. If you want this fellow here to live, hand it over now."

Charlotte's mind moved faster than seemed possible, heightened by the danger to Henry and all their plans. If this lord was after the key, he must know or guess where the queen was. But she couldn't just stand by and watch Henry be killed.

She glanced again at the window. The sun was even lower. Soon it would be kissing the horizon. She had to trust they had held out long enough.

"Fine." She drew the word out, keeping her expression downcast and fearful. Slowly she plunged her hand into her pocket and drew it out. But as Lord Rafferty reached for it, she flicked her arm back and then whipped it forward, sending the key sailing over his head and down the corridor.

He cursed, and the second guard raced after it. But Charlotte's eyes were on Henry. As the guard holding him turned to watch the hunt for the key, Henry's eyes flickered down to the man's left arm.

Charlotte jumped at him, biting hard into his left arm. The man screamed and pulled it away, shaking her off. But the second he loosened his grip, Henry's own left arm broke free, snapping up and pulling the wrist holding the knife away from his throat.

The whole thing took only a second, and Henry was free. A line of red dribbled down his neck, but he brushed it away, appearing unharmed in any serious manner. He kicked the guard in the shin, and when he shouted and doubled over, he punched him hard in the stomach. The man went down, winded, and Henry took Charlotte's hand.

For what felt like the hundredth time that day, they ran.

"Never mind them!" she heard the lord screaming behind them. "We have the key. That's all that matters."

"Should we try to get down there first?" Charlotte gasped out between panting breaths. "Try to stop them?" But when she glanced back, four more guards ran up to join them.

"I think it's too late for that," Henry said.

Charlotte nodded. "I just hope we managed to give them enough time. Should we head to the throne room in case Gwen and Easton need help?"

"Actually," Henry said. "If the queen is about to be free, I think there's somewhere else we need to be."

GWEN

As people poured out of the basement prison, the captive servants turned toward Gwen's familiar face. Alma and Miriam pushed to the front of the group, and Gwen could have cried to see the smiles on their faces. She had been afraid they would resent her after her request had exposed them to the queen.

"I told you she'd come for us," Alma said in a loud, satisfied voice, eyeing off the rest of the group.

"Thank you for your faith," Gwen murmured, tears pricking at the back of her eyes. "I just hope you're willing to have a little more because I have a final request for you."

She led the way a short distance down the corridor, relieved again when the captive servants followed her, separating out from the rebels who had clustered around Charlotte and the count.

She raised her voice slightly so they could all hear her. "I came here to rescue you, and if you want to walk away now, I understand. You don't owe me anything."

"The mountain kingdom owes *us!*" a discontented voice shouted from the back.

Gwen nodded. "I agree. And that's why if you walk away now, I'll understand. But the reality is that while you're freed from that room, you're still trapped here in a kingdom controlled by Celandine. All of us are. If any of us are going to be truly free, then we need to remove her from the throne. And I'm hoping you'll be willing to help with that."

"So that you can sit on it instead!" another scornful voice called from the middle of the crowd.

Miriam whipped around, glaring. "You all know what she told me! The princess isn't like her mother. She's not only going to free us, she's going to send us off with compensation." She turned back to Gwen. "Right?"

"Absolutely!" Gwen said firmly, remembering the chests of gold in her mother's hidden room. "I even have a way to get you home." If she had to fly each of them across the mountains individually, she would do it.

Murmurs swept through the group at that, everyone turning to their neighbor and exchanging whispers. Gwen didn't try to catch individual words, instead listening to the sound as a whole, tracking its mood. It had started with astonishment and a tone of disbelief, but as they conferred, she heard it change. A note of determination crept in before taking over completely. Alma had said they were waiting for their chance, and apparently she had been right. The captives were ready to seize the opportunity offered to them.

"How dangerous is this task you want from us?" Alma asked.

"Hopefully not dangerous at all," Gwen said. "But it's something you know best how to do. If I tried it on my own..." She grimaced. "The queen planned for this afternoon to be a grand spectacle of her power. We're planning to turn it into something else, but we still need the grand spectacle. We need to show the courtiers and the people of the city that we are just as capable and powerful as the old queen."

"You want us to set up the ballroom?" Alma sounded disbelieving.

Gwen nodded. "Down the corridor, you'll see the rebels gathered. They're going to keep the guards and the queen occupied, so I'm hoping there won't be anyone to disturb your efforts. In fact, it's likely the guards aren't even keeping up with the constantly changing situation. If they see you working and preparing in your previous roles, they won't even realize anything is wrong. I don't expect them to harass you."

"And after we've finished?" Alma pressed. "Will we be expected to prepare your evening meal when all of this is over?"

"If this day ends with me as queen, you will be free," Gwen said firmly. "It will take a bit longer to distribute the compensation, and even longer to ferry anyone who wants to go across the mountains. But I'll do it as quickly as is possible in the middle of everything else." She drew a breath, feeling like she was taking a risk. "And if anyone wants to remain in the mountain kingdom—either in the city or in a paid role in the palace—I would love for you to stay. By choice or not, this has been your home for years now, and I won't take it from you forcibly like your last home was taken. From this point on, each of you gets to choose."

She gazed over the faces, reading in the expressions that she'd said the right thing.

Alma rubbed her hands together, her face setting into lines of determination. "All right then, we have work to do."

No one argued.

"Well done," Easton murmured in her ear, his approval warming her. "You sound like a queen."

She threw him a grateful look, but there was no time for a proper conversation. The same was true with Charlotte, although from the look on her face and the brief squeeze she gave Gwen's hand, everything had gone smoothly on their end as well. The captives were ushered out the back way, some of the rebels going with them.

When she walked through the door and saw the two guards back in position, her heart seized. But they grinned jauntily and gave her an elaborate bow, and she relaxed again. They weren't the old guards but rebels wearing guard uniforms. Charlotte had even managed to find rebels who looked similar to the men who had previously held the post.

Once they were all out of the basement level, Miriam approached Gwen with a grin she'd never seen the captive woman wear before. Something had changed in her, and she was no longer tentative in Gwen's presence.

"Come on, then, Your Majesty, we have lots of work to do." She gave Gwen an exaggerated look of appraisal, running her eyes up and down her body and wrinkling her nose. Four women stood behind her, two of them chuckling.

"And you're with us, Your Majesty." An older woman and two men appeared beside Easton.

He looked at Gwen in alarm. "I'm happy to help with the preparations of the throne room in any way I can, but I'm staying with Gwen."

Alma stepped up, tutting and shaking her head.

"The preparations you need aren't in the throne room. If we're putting on a show, don't forget that you two are the star players. If you want to present an image of glory and power, it's going to take a *lot* of work."

Gwen flushed, wanting to protest, but when she looked down at herself, the protest died unspoken. She had slept the night in the stables and before that in her ruined room. She probably had feathers in her hair, and she couldn't remember the last time she'd washed. It had definitely been before the manure. With horror, she looked across at Easton's dirty, disheveled appearance. He hadn't spent hours in a state of total panic and cold sweat in the recent past, so what did Gwen herself look like?

Easton looked back at her, his expression bemused but his

eyes laughing. When she held his gaze, his look turned soft and loving, his message clear. He didn't care what she looked like.

Her panic receded but only a little. Alma and Miriam were right. She couldn't appear before the court and city in this state and claim to be their rightful queen.

She still hated being separated from Easton, but neither of them complained further as they were carried off in different directions. The servants didn't need to be told not to take Gwen to her own room, instead easily locating unused rooms closer to the throne room for their purpose.

The women around Gwen came and went over the following hours, but Miriam was always with her. They prepared a bath, somehow producing fragrant soaps for both her body and hair and lotions for her to use after. And when they'd wrapped her in a soft robe, they began on her hair.

The woman who took the lead was one Gwen knew only a little, and she'd had no idea of the woman's skill. It took a long time, but when she finished, Gwen's hair was twisted into an elaborate pile on her head, full of curls and artful tumbles. Pearls and small flowers hid in the creases, and a tiara of silver and pearls nestled at the front. Gwen had never seen anything so elegant.

They helped her into the frothy layers of her wedding gown after that, and the gown was even more breathtaking than when Gwen had worn it for the final fittings. In the back of her mind, she couldn't forget that Charlotte and Henry were out there somewhere, doing battle with the queen and her guards on Gwen's behalf. But neither could she help losing herself in the moment, thinking of Easton, who was somewhere nearby being helped into the wedding outfit originally intended for Henry. Was someone desperately making last minute adjustments, perhaps sewing it while he modeled it for them? She had to stifle a laugh at the idea of poor Easton forced to stand still for hours or risk being poked with a needle.

She had thought the afternoon would drag, her worry making the hours interminable, but instead they passed shockingly quickly. When Alma appeared to say it was time, Gwen started and flew to her feet.

"What do you mean? It can't be!" She looked out the window and realized the sun was lowering toward the horizon after all. "Did any guests arrive? Did they still come?"

Alma grinned with satisfaction. "We requisitioned those two rebels dressed as guards and added a few of our own to their number. We've had *guards* escorting guests from the edge of the palace grounds for the last hour. It looks like most of the courtiers had fled to their city homes—even they could tell something strange was going on in the palace—but none of them dared miss the wedding. The seats are full."

Gwen drew a long breath, fear fluttering through her. But it was balanced by a sense of certainty. This was the role she had been born for, the one she was supposed to fill. Whatever happened next, she was doing the right thing.

She turned to Alma and nodded, face serious. But Alma just gazed at her before smiling in an almost motherly way. "You look beautiful, Your Majesty."

Tears welled again, and Gwen quickly blinked them away. "Thank you, Alma. Thank you for everything. Your kindness meant everything to me in those lonely years after Easton's banishment."

Alma gave her another, sadder smile. "I always felt sorry for you, Princess Gwen. Some of the others thought it was foolish since you were the princess, but at least the queen didn't keep any of us close by her side day after day."

Gwen swallowed and nodded. "Just so you know, she isn't my mother. She isn't even my stepmother. She's no relation of mine in any way, just a usurper. And it's time for her to go."

Alma held out her arm. "In that case…"

Gwen took it, allowing Alma to lead her out of the room,

Miriam coming behind to fix her train. She would have liked Charlotte beside her, but she knew she was working out of sight to clear the way for Gwen and Easton's moment. And it felt fitting, somehow, that it was just the three of them.

When they reached the door of the throne room, she heard the gentle swell of music from inside as the doors ponderously opened. She gasped at the sight before her.

Rows and rows of white seats ran down both sides of a long velvet carpet. Greenery and the first of the spring flowers had been woven into the chairs closest to the aisle as well as around the columns that lined the room. Gauzy white material, like the top layer of her dress, hung from the ceiling in graceful folds, and at the end of the aisle stood Easton. His messy brown curls had been tamed for once, a golden circlet holding them in place, but his eyes were the same as ever as they stared back at her, blazing with love.

"Ready?" Alma asked softly, and Gwen nodded, unable to speak.

A rustle of movement filled the large room as Gwen stepped in on Alma's arm. She heard the faint murmur of query and alarm—presumably coming from the loyal courtiers in attendance. They had been expecting her to enter on the arm of Queen Celandine, not a woman most of them wouldn't recognize.

But Count Oswin himself—a noble who had been a close advisor to both King Isander and Queen Celandine—stood at the front of the room with the man they all assumed to be Prince Henry. And false guards stood in ceremonial positions between each pillar, their spears straight and their faces serious. The crowd settled.

The aisle felt simultaneously long and short, the moment stretching on too long and then over too soon. Alma put Gwen's hand into Easton's and the sense of homecoming was overwhelming. Trouble was coming for them—it might be almost at the door—but still this moment was exactly what it should have been.

The count began to speak, his measured voice serious and unhurried as he said the traditional words. Gwen wanted to whisper for him to hurry, but she only smiled at Easton instead. It was their wedding, but it was also a drama being enacted for the people of the kingdom, and they had to play their parts properly.

Part of her remained tensed, watching the double doors of the throne room out of the corner of her eye. Someone had closed them, but they had no bar or key.

But the other part of her still managed to lose herself in the moment and in Easton's wonder-filled eyes. He gave no outward sign of remembering their precarious situation, his heart apparently full of Gwen and their marriage.

At one point, she glanced at the audience, and her eyes caught on Lydia and Jett, standing at the back of the room. She smiled at them, glad they had managed to leave the rebels to be present at their son's wedding. And surely it was a good sign about the success of the rebels' mission.

She didn't falter when the count instructed them to face each other and weave their right arms together, circling three times with their joined arms at the center. Her eyes remained fixed on Easton's the whole time as the count spoke of the joining of their lives and futures.

Her voice didn't waver when the count asked her if she promised herself to this man as her husband and had her repeat a series of vows. She had attended plenty of court weddings, but the words had never hit her so forcefully before. And she had never been so glad that tradition dictated their names were used only at the end. Most of the audience still believed they were watching her marry Prince Henry.

When two people each carried a washtub onto the dais, she almost laughed aloud, however. In the past, she had accepted it as part of the tradition, but now all she could think of was Natalie's scorn. The girl was right. Even as a princess, Gwen had never worn such a beautiful dress. It wasn't what she would have chosen to do laundry in.

With exaggerated care, she bent over the tub, Easton mirroring her to her left. Had Easton washed his own shirts in the long years of his banishment? Gwen was relying on the hasty lesson given her when Miriam dumped several shirts into Gwen's bathwater and showed her how to scrub them.

Gwen tried not to splash her dress, even as she scrubbed as quickly as possible, her eyes on the horizon. The sun was creeping lower and lower, and at any moment, the queen might appear and ruin everything. Gwen couldn't bear if all this led to nothing, the wedding interrupted before the marriage was official.

Finally, she held up the dripping shirt that apparently belonged to Easton. It was white and clean. Easton also held up hers, and the crowd cheered. They let the clothes drop back into the water and stood, turning to face each other and clasp hands.

They were close, so close.

"You have woven your futures together," the count said, his loud voice echoing through the room like a proclamation. "You have made your vows, and you have washed each other clean, I therefore—"

Both doors crashed open. "Stop!" The queen's scream rent the room.

Chairs scraped and heads twisted as everyone turned astonished faces to the furious woman in the doorway. Guards streamed past her, racing for Gwen and Easton. Easton's fingers tightened on Gwen's, and he tugged her toward him.

"Stop this treason instantly!" the queen shouted again.

Count Oswin met her eyes across the distance of the room and shouted even more loudly into the shocked silence of the crowd.

"I therefore declare Princess Gwendolyn, daughter of King Isander, married to Easton, of the mountain kingdom. What is done cannot be undone."

As he spoke the traditional words—the ones that made the marriage final—several things happened at once.

Celandine screamed her anger, the shrill cry cutting through the crowd and making Gwen shiver. The guards along the walls sprang into motion, pouring forward to block the path of the queen's guards. The sun slipped all the way below the horizon, and Gwen looked into Easton's eyes—the eyes of her husband.

The familiar tingling itch began, but she barely felt it, her heart welling with love for the man who had stood by her through everything. The man who had just promised to stand by her forever.

And the tingling faded, dropping away into nothing. No tearing started, and no transformation followed. Night had fallen, but Gwen was still a woman.

The arrival of the queen and disruption of the wedding had shocked the crowd into silence. But nightfall sent the courtiers surging to their feet, shouting and calling. Gwen turned her head and saw people falling on each other, tears streaming down faces as they embraced or collapsed from shock and relief.

The count called again in the same booming shout.

"The enchantment is broken! All hail Queen Gwendolyn and King Easton! All hail!"

"No! No!" Celandine screamed, still in the doorway, but louder still came the roar of the crowd.

"Hail! Hail! Hail!"

Gwen turned fully to look out at them, her earlier certainty and strength returning in response to their cries.

"Hail! Hail! Hail! Hail!"

The shout seemed to swell and grow impossibly loud until Gwen realized the voices inside the hall had been joined by a roar from outside. A mob of people burst in behind Celandine,

Natalie at their lead. They streamed around the queen, who stood alone, like an island in the rippling sea of people. The crowd from the city filled every spare space in the room, their enthusiastic cries of support filling the air with a thundering noise.

The grappling of the guards had been swept away by their arrival, and Gwen was relieved to see none of Celandine's guards attempted violence against the new arrivals. They had already been confused by their unexpected opponents—dressed in identical uniforms which made it hard to tell friend from foe—and the roar and unity of the growing crowd appeared to have provided the final piece of intimidation.

Gwen held up her hands, and the shout slowly faded, expectant silence slowly gripping the crowd. Celandine still stood straight, however, her eyes spearing into Gwen's.

"This is treason!" she cried, her words whipping over the distance between them.

"No," Gwen said back, her voice projecting across the room. "Yours is the treason. You stole the throne, enchanted my people, and abused me. It ends now."

"How dare you speak those words to your mother!" the queen cried, and a soft murmur reminded Gwen that Celandine still had supporters in the crowd.

But other voices murmured back, hostile and defensive. Celandine might have her supporters in the room, but Gwen had more.

Her eyes hardened, her hands clenching. "You are not my mother. Neither are you my stepmother. If you had been, you would have given me my throne when I came of age, as the law requires." Another murmur, and this time there was only sympathy and approval for Gwen. "I was with my father every moment until his dying breath. He never married you. He never even met you. You are nothing but a usurper, and your time is finished."

A shocked cry rose at her words, heads turning between

Gwen and Celandine. Brows lowered and voices raised as the mood in the room turned ugly.

Celandine fell back one step and then another, horror twisting her face as she surveyed the angry crowd. Gwen stood steady, not removing her gaze, and Celandine was the first to look away. Turning, she fled.

Gwen looked at Easton, wishing Celandine's desertion was the end. If only the woman would run and not stop running. If she disappeared into the mountains, it would all finally be over.

But Gwen knew her too well to believe she would give up so easily. Celandine's guards and position had not been her only source of power. She had one last move to make.

"She'll go to her objects," she said to Easton. "We have to stop her."

He nodded, the same anxiety she felt showing in his eyes. It wasn't over yet.

Gathering up her skirts in both hands, Gwen leaped down from the dais and ran after Celandine.

INTERLUDE

CELANDINE

Celandine ran, hatred and anger and fear twisting in her gut and burning in her throat. She had to get to her objects. She had to let them drain away the awful emotions. Once her mind was clear and sharp, she would see her way out of the mess the ungrateful princess had created.

There would be a way out. There had to be. Celandine had worked too hard and for too long to see everything stripped from her. She would destroy everyone rather than become weak and vulnerable again.

A man jumped out to block Celandine's path, and she recognized him. How dare her own courtiers turn against her! She had given this man everything, and yet his wife had smiled to Celandine's face while behind her back she whined endlessly about babies. Being pregnant, having a baby—they were things that made you vulnerable. Didn't the woman realize Celandine had done her a favor?

No matter what she did for them all it was never enough.

They were always poised, ready to betray her, ready to seize power for themselves. Just like that brat.

The man lunged for Celandine, but her fury lent her strength. She sidestepped him, spinning as he passed, and smashed her fist into the back of his skull with all the force she could muster.

He went down, hitting the floor hard, and she resumed her flight. As she ran, she shook her hand, which pulsed with pain. She should have drawn her dagger instead of lashing out with her fist. This was exactly why emotions were dangerous. It was too hard to think clearly while in their grip.

She reached the door to her exclusive wing of the palace and slowed. There was no sign of the guard always stationed there. Fresh fear gripped her. Her standing command was that no matter what happened in the rest of the palace, that post was never to be deserted. Seeing it empty was a fresh blow.

She quickened her pace again, not quite to a run, but she couldn't keep herself to an appropriate cautious speed. What if the rebels were already ransacking her objects?

Celandine reached for the closed door of her bedchamber only to be grabbed from behind.

"You're under arrest for treason to the crown," a rough voice said, this one unfamiliar.

She drew her dagger in one fluid movement and stabbed backward. It plunged into some part of her captor. She didn't care which part since all that mattered was that he let her go, staggering backward. She released the hilt and reached for the door instead.

Someone else was behind her—shouting angrily and rushing to help the injured man—but she didn't care. All she could think of was her objects.

She shut the door behind her, her eyes flying to the tapestry. It had been pulled back, revealing the portrait. She snarled at the sight of it, taunting her. She should have slashed it to pieces days ago. From the moment Henry broke his enchantment, the image had changed. It now showed his human state, smiling out at the world with his arm around the golden-haired girl. But worse than the two of them were the new arrivals in the portrait.

The portrait of the mountain princess had disappeared along with the castle that was a mirror of the mountain palace. But instead of ceasing to exist, the image had appeared beside the happy couple. And now, the mountain princess was no longer alone. One of her arms twined around the waist of the traitor, Easton. The boy she should have killed ten years ago.

While she stared at the image—fresh, dangerous fury rippling through her—someone spoke.

"We thought you might come here." Prince Henry stepped out of the shadows to stand in front of his portrait.

His wife stepped forward to join him, the two of them mocking her with their double appearance.

"It's over, Celandine," she said. "Gwen is queen as she should have been long ago. But she's nothing like you, so if you surrender now, she'll show you mercy."

Celandine growled, eyeing the hidden latch. If she lunged for it, could she get it open before they stopped her? Could she get to her objects?

"Is this portrait the only information you had about us?" the girl asked, apparently unable to help herself.

Celandine refocused on her. Why was she wasting both of their time on such irrelevant questions?

"I didn't need any other information," she said coldly, trying to regain her usual manner. "I saw when the prince found himself a foolish girl to become his wife, trying so hard to free himself from my enchantments." She laughed, but the sound was weak and thin.

The girl's brow furrowed. "Then how did you know? How did you know I would betray him and look at his face before the three months?"

Celandine laughed, the sound fuller. "You really have to ask that? The more infatuated you clearly became, the more obvious it was."

"But…why?"

The girl must be even more foolish than she appeared.

"Because trust is as much an illusion as love," Celandine snapped, her eyes drifting back to the hidden latch on one side of the portrait. "No one truly trusts any other person. Of course you would want to see his face—to be sure he was who he said he was. Love and trust are both illusions that make you weak and vulnerable—and easy to manipulate."

The girl paled and stepped back, but the prince caught her around the waist, steadying her.

"You're wrong." He looked at Celandine without flinching. "Fear is what cripples us. Fear is what makes us vulnerable. Love is what gives us the strength to throw off fear. You discounted love and trust and that has been your undoing. Gwen and Easton never wavered, and now they have taken back everything that is rightfully theirs."

Celandine cried out, feeling his words like a dagger straight to her chest. Done with analyzing, she threw herself forward, her fingers reaching for the latch.

She found it, tearing the portrait open and revealing the dark space beyond. The prince shouted and tried to grab her, but she slipped from his grasp, darting forward into her most treasured place.

She didn't hesitate, her hands reaching for the object that would destroy them all.

CHARLOTTE

Somehow Celandine slipped through Henry's grasp and fell into the room behind the wall. Charlotte cried out, both of them scrambling to follow. They had been trying to find that latch when they'd heard Celandine's arrival. If only they'd known where it was, they might have been able to intercept her before she got inside.

Night had fallen outside, but enough light came through the room's windows and spilled from the lanterns in the bedchamber beyond to illuminate the scene before them.

The chests that overflowed with gold lay neglected along the walls, the focus of the room on the many plinths that were scattered through the middle of the room. Each one held a different object, except for the empty plinth in the middle where Celandine stood. Her hand was clasped around something that looked like a short scepter, and her mouth was turned up in a smile that held no true emotion.

All the anger, fury, and fear that had danced over her face earlier were drained away, leaving her terrifyingly cold and empty. How was it possible to change so quickly? Was it due to the object in her hand?

Both Henry and Charlotte stopped warily just inside the room, but Henry began to advance slowly forward again, his eyes on the deposed queen.

"There's no point to any of this," he said. "Put down the object, and we can report that you cooperated."

Celandine laughed, mirthless and high. "You have no idea how hard I worked for the power I hold. I will never choose to lay it down."

Henry took another step forward, his eyes on the object in her hand.

"What is that?" he asked, his voice reasonable and calm, although Charlotte knew him well enough to recognize the underlying note of tension.

"I was going to flatten the path before Gwendolyn with this," Celandine said. "She claims I'm so awful, but I was going to give her everything. I was going to flatten the mountains for her."

Charlotte gulped, staring at the winking jewel on the tip of the scepter. Could that small thing really do so much?

"But Gwendolyn doesn't want what I can offer," Celandine said. "And she has turned my people against me. Now she will see what happens when I turn the mountains against her."

"You can't do that," Henry said. "You *shouldn't* do that."

"You think I'm lying?" Celandine's lips curled upward, and she thrust the scepter toward one of the windows. "This object can do even more. She thinks the sunset saved her, but I will steal the sun away. See who will follow her when the sun never returns."

As she spoke, dark clouds rolled across the sky, too quickly to be natural, stealing the last of the dusk light and obscuring the stars and moon. The only light left in the room was the lamplight coming in from the bedchamber.

Charlotte shifted uneasily, staring at the stark blackness out the window. Surely Celandine's words were empty boasts. She couldn't really steal the sun, could she?

Celandine cackled. "First the sun, and now I'll take her

precious mountains. I was going to flatten them for her, but instead I'll send them crumbling on her head."

Henry lunged toward her, reaching for the scepter, but she jumped backward out of reach. A rumble began outside. It sounded like thunder except it built and built until Charlotte could feel it rattling through both the stones beneath her and her bones.

She staggered toward the window, gripping the sill and trying to peer outside. Were the mountains collapsing toward them? It sounded like it.

Henry lurched, the ground beneath them shaking and disrupting his footing as he tried to chase Celandine through the plinths. She evaded him, her knuckles and fingers white around the scepter.

The rumble grew until Charlotte pressed her hands to her ears, her eyes watering. Celandine was going to destroy them all, not caring that she would destroy herself in the process. And what about the valleys and the kingdoms beyond them? Celandine would destroy everything if she blocked the sky and brought down the mountains.

Charlotte dropped her hands, using them to brace herself against the wall instead as she took in the room. Celandine was dashing between the plinths, Henry in pursuit. But somehow she always slipped from his fingers. Should Charlotte help? If she tried to circle from the other direction, they might be able to trap her and force the scepter from her hand.

Or maybe Celandine would bring the ceiling down on their head before they could. The palace was already creaking alarmingly, and they were three stories up. If the wing collapsed, none of them would survive.

Her eyes swept over the room until a beam of lamplight coming through the open portrait caught on a round, smooth golden surface. The one familiar object in the room of plinths. The golden apple.

With a jolt, Charlotte remembered the moment Gwen had first placed it in her hand and her explanation of its purpose. Gwen had arranged for it to be placed here with intention. If there was something in this room that could stop Celandine, the apple would tell Charlotte what it was.

She pushed off from the wall and ran toward the apple, swerving to avoid Celandine's path on the way. Thankfully, the deposed queen swerved to avoid her as well, unaware of Charlotte's intentions.

She staggered the final steps to the plinth, the floor unsteady beneath her. Her fingers fell on the apple, and even before she had fully picked it up, her mind warmed with the awareness of multiple familiar objects all around her. It was nothing like her previous experience with the apple, not only because of the affectionate familiarity she felt toward the objects but because of their number. They overwhelmed her mind.

She gasped, whirling to look at all the objects with her eyes, trying to match them with the sense of their presence in her mind. Her eyes landed on a small golden whip, sitting alone on a plinth near the door. As she focused on it, her awareness of the other objects in the room muted, receding slightly to bring this one to the front of her mind.

It was the pair to the golden halter in her pocket, the tool Celandine had used to fight Gwen's travel on the wind—a tool that had leveled a village and nearly sunk a fleet. It was no good to her inside the room when the halter wasn't in use, but it called to her because it was familiar.

She tore her eyes away, forcing her mind to the next object along. But there were too many objects in the room, and the rumbling was growing even louder. She could barely hear anything above its sound now. If she examined the objects one by one, she might not find anything of use in time.

Instead, she squeezed her eyes closed and filled her mind with the apple's awareness. Even with her eyes closed the objects floated in her mind, no longer attached to their plinths. She let her mind drift over them, releasing her conscious thoughts to let the instinctive layer of her mind take control.

There! Something flashed past her awareness, and she seized on it, focusing in. The object was a jewel, cut to fine points and polished to a high sheen. Its outside was cold and hard and clear, but inside it roiled and pulsed with an intensity that took Charlotte's breath away. Anger, sadness, love, joy, hatred, envy, excitement, anxiety, disgust, all mixed together and contained beneath the smooth surface of the jewel.

And Charlotte knew—thanks to the apple—the meaning behind what she sensed. This object removed emotions, sucking them from anyone who touched it and storing them inside the jewel instead.

Charlotte had noticed the change in Celandine after she entered the room and wondered if the scepter was responsible. But Celandine must have touched the jewel on her way past. How often had she come into the room to hold the jewel? From the store of emotions inside it, she must have come countless times.

Celandine didn't believe in emotions—she had made that clear. She saw them as weaknesses, so it made sense she wanted to purge them from her system. But that meant she had never learned to deal with them, to feel them. She had never learned how to let them wash over her and recede. If Charlotte could break the jewel, would the emotions return to their original owner?

Her eyes snapped open, and she scanned the room, looking for a jewel that matched the one in her mind. Her gaze caught on a red stone thanks to the lamplight that made it gleam.

She ran toward it, ducking past Celandine as she went. Celandine was in the middle of lunging away from Henry, and her body slammed into Charlotte's arm, knocking the apple from her grip. It flung halfway across the room, rolling out of sight.

But it didn't matter now. Charlotte already knew what tool to use.

She reached the plinth and snatched up the jewel. Instantly her body calmed and her mind felt clearer and easier, the terror and anxiety she had been feeling sucked away. She could see why the object had been appealing to the former queen. But it had become a crutch.

Lifting it over her head, Charlotte threw the jewel with all her might at the closest wall. It sailed through the air, winking as it arced high. It caught the attention of the others, and they both paused, turning to look. Celandine let out a wordless cry of protest, but it was too late.

The jewel hit the stone wall and smashed, shards flying in all directions. A wave of fear and anxiety hit Charlotte so strongly she staggered backward as her fear returned to its original owner. Gasping, she barely kept her balance, spinning to find Celandine.

If the returned emotions had hit Charlotte so hard, what would they have done to Celandine, who had stored decades' worth of every emotion in there?

Celandine's head was thrown back, her face twisted with heightened emotion, her eyes wide and staring. She fell backward, colliding with a plinth and taking that down too, its object toppling off and bouncing away in one direction while the scepter flew from Celandine's hand in the other.

Celandine curled into a ball, sobbing. Her arms wrapped so tightly around her knees it must have hurt, her sobs turning into a keening that rose higher and higher.

It was hard to turn away from the horrible effect of twenty years' unchecked emotion, but the floor was still shuddering, the rumble in the air still vibrating in Charlotte's bones. The scepter had flown in her direction, so she dropped to her hands and knees, searching the floor for it.

"There!" The tip showed from between two chests, fallen gold coins lying atop and around it, obscuring its presence.

She stretched out, wrapping her fingers around it and pulling it back toward her. The second she touched it, her mind expanded, taking in not just the room or the palace but the mountain range in every direction and the sky above her. Holding the scepter, she could shape her environment however she wanted. The thrill of power ran through her, but following behind was the fear. It was too much. No one person should be capable of re-forming the land itself.

Charlotte nearly flung the scepter away from her, only just stopping herself. Her fingers remained wrapped around it, but she looked up, pleading wordlessly for someone to help her.

A figure holding a lantern appeared in the open portrait, another dark shape behind her. Charlotte's mouth fell open at the magnificent sight of Gwen in an enormous wedding dress, the filmy layers falling around her and the train disappearing behind, her hair piled high and the tiara on her head winking in the light.

Gwen paused for one second as she took in the room—Celandine balled up and keening with Henry hovering beside her, and Charlotte sprawled across the floor on the far side of the room, a scepter gripped in her outstretched hand and terror on her face. She met Charlotte's eyes, seeming to read the plea for help there, and handed her lantern to Easton behind her.

But she didn't run toward Charlotte. Instead, she gathered her skirts and darted in a different direction, stooping to retrieve something fallen on the ground.

For a stupefied minute, Charlotte's consciousness hovered between the mountains outside—whose peaks were beginning to crumble, enormous boulders rolling down their sides—and her friend. Was Gwen retrieving the object Celandine had just knocked loose? Charlotte hadn't even seen what it was, but surely it wasn't important in the middle of such danger.

But when Gwen straightened and turned toward Charlotte, it

was the apple gripped in her hand. She ignored Celandine and the plinths and the rumbling outside and walked straight toward Charlotte, the apple gripped in her palm and her eyes on the scepter.

Understanding washed through Charlotte, followed by relief. If Gwen had the apple, she would know how the scepter worked. She would know how to wield it and how to undo the damage Celandine had already done.

Charlotte pulled herself to her knees, holding the scepter toward Gwen. When her friend reached her, she dropped to her knees at her side. But when she wrapped her hand around the scepter, she didn't pull it away from Charlotte.

"Two will be better than one," she shouted over the rumbling. "It will only respond to strength. We have to force it to obey us."

Charlotte could feel Gwen beside her through her normal senses, but she could also sense her through the expanded awareness the scepter gave her. Charlotte tried to follow Gwen's lead, forcing her will on the scepter, instructing it to roll back the clouds and rebuild the mountains.

It groaned, the sound more felt than heard beneath the volume of the thunderous rumble. But it didn't obey. More of the mountain tips crumbled, the broken boulders rolling further down, heading toward the city in the valley below.

"No!" Gwen shouted. "I will not let her destroy our mountains! I will not let her steal even one more bit of light from me."

Gwen's will merged with Charlotte's, their unified voices commanding the same thing. Together they shouted into the deafening noise and chaos around them, building a mental picture of a clear sky and whole mountains and forcing the shape of that command onto the scepter.

"You. Will. Obey. Us," Gwen choked out, speaking through gritted teeth.

The rumbling quieted.

Charlotte drew a gasping breath, her fingers squeezing forcefully around the scepter. The rumbling quieted further and then still further. New light stole into the room as the sky cleared, revealing the moon and the last of the light from the sunset.

In the distance, blocked by the walls, Charlotte sensed the boulders rolling back uphill. The mountain peaks re-formed as if they had never been touched, even the life on their slopes returned to its original state.

She slumped down, every muscle trembling with the aftereffects of her exertion. They had done it.

Gwen swept her into a hug, crying into her shoulder and croaking out her thanks. A shout sounded behind them, followed by running feet, a crash, and then a high-pitched scream that made her blood stop.

The girls pulled apart and looked across the room. Henry was taking the final two strides toward a broken window. He looked back at them with a pale face.

"I tried to catch her," he said, "but…"

"She moved too fast." Easton's voice shook. "We were both watching you, and…"

Gwen stood, swaying on shaky legs. Easton hurried to her side, putting an arm around her for support, and she leaned against his shoulder.

"Perhaps, she…" She swallowed and tried again. "When I fell from an upper-story window, the wind—"

Henry poked his head through the broken window, careful to avoid the remaining shards of glass. When he pulled back into the room, his face was drawn and he shook his head.

"I'm sorry, Gwen. There wasn't any wind to catch her."

Gwen swallowed. "I could have…I should have…"

"No." Charlotte stood more slowly, speaking the word with force. "You were busy saving entire kingdoms—busy undoing the work that woman set in motion. Everything about her life was a tragedy, but none of it was your doing." She moved around to meet her friend's eyes. "This isn't your burden to carry, Gwen.

You'll have enough burdens undoing the damage she caused in your kingdom."

"Listen to Charlotte," Easton said. "She's right. At the end, Celandine made her own choice. It wasn't your fault she wasn't in her right mind."

Charlotte looked sadly toward the plinth that had supported the jewel. "I'm not sure she had been for a long time."

She looked down, realizing she still held the scepter. She wanted to drop it. She wanted to never touch it again. But she couldn't risk anyone else getting their hands on it. She gripped it in both hands, raising it high and pulling up one knee. But just before she brought it down, she paused, the scepter hanging in midair.

Her eyes slowly rose, meeting Gwen's.

"Perhaps," she said, "there's one thing…"

Gwen's blank look transformed to understanding, and a smile spread over her mouth. "Just one," she said.

She stepped forward and gripped the scepter along with Charlotte for one final time. Connected through the scepter, Charlotte knew they had indeed had the same thought. Together they bore down on the scepter, forcing their will on it.

Distantly, the sound of grating stone drifted through the night air, making Henry turn back to the window. But there was nothing to see in the gray dimness of early night.

Within a minute, both girls relaxed, grinning at each other.

"A small change like that won't do any harm to the mountains or their environment," Gwen said, letting go of the scepter.

"But it will do us a lot of good." Charlotte smiled.

Once again gripping the scepter's length in two hands, she raised it up and brought it down hard on her knee. It snapped in half with a sound like brittle wood.

She looked down at the two lifeless shards she held in each hand and nodded. No one could touch the mountains now.

Gwen nodded approvingly, and Charlotte let the pieces fall to the ground, overwhelmed by a rush of exhaustion. Henry's arms slid around her from behind, and he guided her back against his chest. She collapsed against him with a sigh of gratitude, letting her eyes drift shut.

"What did you do?" Henry asked. "At the end there?"

Charlotte didn't open her eyes although a smile curved up her lips. "Nothing too significant."

"We just made sure we'll always be able to visit each other from now on," Gwen said.

"You made a permanent pass?" Easton asked eagerly. "One that doesn't require bear form?"

"The mountain kingdom isn't cut off from the other kingdoms any longer." Gwen sounded satisfied. "And I won't have to fly the captives home one or two at a time. We can set up proper trading routes too."

"An excellent first act as ruler," Easton said, sounding a little awed.

"I thought so," Gwen said smugly before sighing, her voice turning rueful. "I'll have to explore the rest of these objects later. I think there are some wedding guests who are waiting to see us."

Charlotte's eyes flew open, taking in her friend's appearance for a second time.

"Your wedding!" she cried. "Did it succeed? Are you married?"

Gwen nodded almost shyly before looking up into the face of her new husband and beaming. "Celandine tried to stop it, but she was too late. And I exposed her as a usurper before everyone."

"We broke the enchantment, too," Easton said.

Charlotte gasped. "Of course you did! You're not a bear, Gwen!"

Gwen gave a relieved laugh. "I'm very pleased to know I never will be again. I'm quite happy to keep my normal human body from now on, even if I can't break down doors with my hands."

"I'm so happy for you both." Charlotte wasn't sure if the tears in her eyes were from joy, relief, or exhaustion. "I just wish I could have been there."

"It was beautiful," Gwen said. "The captives outdid themselves."

"*You* look beautiful," Charlotte said.

"We weren't able to be there for Gwen and Easton's wedding," Henry said, "but I hope Queen Gwendolyn and King Easton will grace our wedding with their presence."

Charlotte pulled away, twisting to look up at him. "What are you talking about? We've been married for months."

"In the valleys," he said. "But Celandine pointed out to me that it might be more than a year before Master Harold registers it officially with the Rangmeran authorities. And in the meantime, she was convinced I could register a different marriage elsewhere. So as soon as possible, we will be married again and officially registered here in the mountain kingdom. I don't want anyone to ever question that you're my wife again."

Charlotte laughed. "Are you expecting a steady stream of people trying to force you into unwanted marriages?"

"Maybe I just want to give my beautiful bride the wedding she always deserved." He smiled down at her.

Charlotte had only one answer to that. She reached up on her tiptoes and kissed him.

EPILOGUE

CHARLOTTE

Charlotte stared at herself in the full-length mirror. Her dress wasn't as elaborate as Gwen's had been, but it was far fancier than the dress she had worn at her first wedding. And —more importantly than either fact—it suited her perfectly. The clean lines of the satin gown exuded an elegance befitting a princess without overwhelming the woman inside the dress.

She met Gwen's eyes in the mirror, and her friend smiled knowingly.

"It's hard to see yourself as a princess—or queen—and also yourself. But it's possible. If I can get there, so can you."

Charlotte smiled tremulously. Gwen of all people knew exactly what she was going through. She could never have guessed that the woman in the portrait would become her best friend and the most amazing support. She was only glad that the mountains were no longer a barrier between them.

"Promise you'll come and visit," she said, trying not to sniffle.

"Of course I will!" Gwen hesitated. "Although I understand

you'll have your sisters with you in Arcadia. You might not have as much need for—"

Charlotte shook her head firmly, turning to give her friend a pointed look. "You've met my sisters. While I'm glad I can offer them a new life in Arcadia—the kind of life they've always wanted—their presence can't make up for your absence."

Gwen's smile grew stronger. "I'm actually curious to see Arcadia. I've read about it in books, and it sounds beautiful."

Charlotte glanced out the window at the mountains. They were visible from any direction, their peaks white with snow despite the warm sun that shone into the enormous valley housing the mountain kingdom.

"I'm going to miss the mountains," she said. "I've gotten used to having them always there in the distance. There's something solid and calming about their presence. It was one of the things I liked about my old life in the valleys."

"Do your parents love the mountains as well?" Gwen asked. "Is that why they're not going with your sisters to Arcadia?"

Charlotte hesitated. "I don't think it's the mountains exactly." She sighed. "My father dreams of new horizons and new frontiers. He loves the idea of building a life from nothing. So how could he turn away now that a true new frontier has opened up?" She gestured at the mountains outside.

Gwen grimaced guiltily. "I suppose we only made that worse by having the first courier through the new pass go straight to his door with instructions to bring your family here without delay."

Charlotte chuckled. "Maybe a little. He already has grand plans for the trading route he's going to set up. But Henry and I appreciated it so much."

Gwen laughed along with her. "Poor Henry was so impatient. He could barely wait for your family to get here as it was. I almost pulled out the halter to get them here more quickly."

Charlotte's eyes widened. "Do not let my father get word of the possibility of riding the wind!"

Gwen nodded solemnly. "Noted."

Charlotte relented. "My relationship with my family was so broken at my first wedding, and they won't be part of my daily life in Arcadia going forward. I couldn't have a second, proper wedding without them. Henry understands."

"Have you really forgiven them for everything?" Gwen asked, and Charlotte could hear the echo of another question behind it. Had Charlotte really forgiven Gwen for her role in the candle disaster?

Charlotte smiled. "I have forgiven them for everything. I don't want any resentment hanging over the new life I'm about to start. But I haven't forgotten. Henry and I have already discussed it, and we're going to set my sisters up in a comfortable house in the Arcadian capital but not in the court itself. They're family, and I want to do what I can to support them in building a fulfilling life for themselves, but I can't build my own new life with them too close."

"What about your mother?" Gwen asked. "Is she upset your father is insisting they stay?"

Charlotte considered the question. Her family had only arrived the day before—thanks to Henry's determination to have a proper wedding as soon as possible. But she had spent the evening with them, and her mother had seemed content with the plans being made.

"I think she would like Arcadia," she said. "But she would never leave my father, despite his flaws."

She and Gwen's eyes met, and they shared a look of silent understanding. They were both newlyweds themselves, and they understood what it meant to enter a marriage. It was inevitable there would be times when one member of a couple would have to compromise for the other. That was part of being a team.

"Their new house disappeared, you know," Charlotte added, trying not to laugh at the thought. "It was created for them by the bell, so when Henry broke his enchantment and the castle and bell disappeared, everything else it had created disappeared with them."

Gwen's eyes widened, but Charlotte continued to smile. "I think it worked out for the best, though. They fled to my aunt and uncle's house, and since the last of my cousins has just become betrothed, my mother and aunt realized they enjoy living together. Henry is going to give them the gold he originally promised, and they plan to use it to expand my aunt and uncle's house. When my father—and probably my uncle with him—are traveling through the mountain pass, my mother will still have company. I think she'll be happy enough in that life."

"And you'll be happy having some distance from them," Gwen murmured.

Charlotte grimaced, not denying it. "Some relationships improve with some distance. We'll be very happy to see each other when we have a chance to visit." She hesitated. "My family is far from perfect, and they've hurt me, but I know it doesn't compare to your situation. Even if Celandine had been your true birth mother…" She hesitated, shaking her head. "Some relationships can't be salvaged."

Gwen's smile didn't waver. "Don't be sad for me. Not on your special day. I have a new family now. Lydia and Jett are already the parents I always wished I could have."

Charlotte impulsively embraced her friend, and Gwen hugged her back. She wished she could have Gwen as her attendant, but she understood that Gwen's new role as queen precluded it. At least Gwen and Easton would be present in the front row, which was better than Charlotte had managed for their wedding.

She had been prepared for her sisters to throw fits at not being included in the wedding themselves, but they seemed to accept the excuse that there was no time to organize the necessary outfits. It probably helped that they were still in shock at the discovery of Henry's true identity and the coming changes in their lives.

"Are you ready?" Natalie bounced into the room, looking beautiful in a gown of deep gold. "I had no idea it took so long to get ready for a wedding!"

Gwen threw a speaking look at Charlotte. "Are you regretting your choice of attendant yet?"

Charlotte stifled a laugh. "Never."

Natalie joined her beside the mirror, surveying herself with satisfaction. "How could she regret it? I was clearly born to wear a dress like this."

Gwen and Charlotte exchanged looks of concern at the disturbing light in Natalie's eyes. There was something both terrifying and exhilarating about never knowing what outrageous plan the girl would get into her head next.

At least her inclusion in the event had succeeded in raising her spirits. Ever since the revelation that her brother Baden had been the one to reveal the rebels' plans to the queen, she had been unnaturally downcast. Charlotte was just glad the job of sorting out that particular delicate situation fell to Gwen, not her.

Natalie herself was above reproach. Even without her brother's assistance, she had managed to rouse the city's youth, leading them to gather their families and storm the palace in support of Gwen, arriving at the crucial moment.

Natalie finished her perusal of her reflection. "Well? Are you ready, Charlotte?"

"She is," Gwen said with a smile. "She's perfect."

Charlotte laughed. "Perfectly happy, perhaps."

"Come on, then." Natalie opened the door. "You don't want Henry to think you're not coming."

Gwen shook her head. "I think Charlotte, of all people, has proven her devotion. She came all the way to the mountain kingdom to find Henry. She's not going to run away now."

"Will you really let me visit you in Arcadia?" Natalie asked Charlotte as they walked through the corridors toward the throne room.

"Of course," she said before hastily adding, "Once you're a bit older, and if your parents give permission."

Natalie nodded absentmindedly, but Charlotte wasn't sure she'd actually heard the last part.

They reached the double doors of the throne room and found Charlotte's father waiting for them, a beaming smile on his face.

He leaned in to kiss her forehead, his eyes gleaming. "I've never been so proud of you, Charli-bear."

She smiled back. "Just don't let Henry hear you using that nickname. I think he's had enough of bears for a lifetime."

Her father laughed back. "If anyone deserves to become a crown princess, it's you, my daughter."

Charlotte shook her head but didn't protest aloud. It was no use trying to convince her father how unqualified she was for the role. He believed in her, and she would have to believe in herself as well.

As Natalie took up her position in front of them, ready to enter first, Charlotte caught a considering look in her eye. When Charlotte glanced at Gwen, she saw she'd noticed it too, but whatever Gwen's thoughts on the matter, they were clearly swept away when Easton appeared, the golden circlet from his own wedding glinting among his brown curls. His eyes moved quickly over Charlotte to land on Gwen.

They lit up at the sight of his wife, regal in frothy layers of deep blue. Charlotte sighed and smiled. In just moments she would be standing at Henry's side. She couldn't wait to see the same look in his eyes as Easton wore when he looked at Gwen.

The doors creaked open, and Easton offered Gwen his arm. She accepted it, and the two of them walked into the throne room. The audience rose at their entrance, bowing or dropping into curtsies, sending a rippling wave through the room in line with their progress.

Only when they were seated at the front of the room did

everyone else resume their seats, craning their heads toward the door as the wedding music began.

Natalie stepped out confidently, making her way slowly down the aisle. Charlotte took her father's offered arm and let him lead her behind her lone attendant. She had insisted that the room's decorations be kept simple, given all the tasks facing the palace in the wake of the transfer of power. But just the presence of Henry was enough to make the whole room beautiful in her eyes.

He didn't take his gaze off her from the moment she appeared, and as soon as she reached him, he squeezed her hands.

"You're beautiful," he murmured.

She smiled back, forgetting both the pain of their past and the anxiety of her future role. In that moment, she was free to do nothing but celebrate this reminder of their vows. They had already promised with both word and action to be loyal and to love and be loved. But she couldn't wait to make the same promises again.

Some elements of the ceremony were unfamiliar, but she succeeded in weaving their arms together and circling without tripping over her small train, grateful for their several practice runs the day before. But when they brought out the tubs for washing, she made the mistake of meeting Natalie's eyes.

The look on the younger girl's face made it almost impossible not to break out into giggles, and Charlotte spent the entire time she was scrubbing trying not to let them burst free. Henry kept shooting her amused glances as he struggled through the task himself. He had more experience than most princes his age, but apparently scrubbing shirts wasn't part of his skill set.

Eventually they both had the garments clean, however, holding them up proudly and enjoying the cheers of the crowd. When Count Oswin proclaimed the final words of the ceremony, declaring that what had been done could not be undone, Henry and Charlotte gazed into each other's eyes, feeling the special weight of the words. No one could dispute their marriage now.

Henry pulled her close and kissed her, leading to more cheers, and Charlotte's cheeks were flushed by the time she pulled back. Henry grinned down at her unrepentant, though. He hadn't stopped smiling since she had entered the room and just seeing him gave Charlotte a swell of happiness. How long would it be before she stopped feeling that way every time her eyes fell on his tall form?

The party following the ceremony continued long into the night. Charlotte and Henry had allowed Gwen and Easton to choose the guest list, knowing they wanted to make use of the invitations. There was far too much politics involved in setting up their new court to miss such a valuable opportunity.

Charlotte didn't mind all the unfamiliar faces. Her family was there, along with the new friends she had made, and Henry was at her side. Nothing else mattered.

But when Gwen had finally finished circulating—having needed to talk to every one of the guests—she collapsed into a chair beside Charlotte.

"Did I know being queen would be so exhausting?" she moaned.

Charlotte grinned back. "If you're trying to terrify me, know that nothing will ruin my mood today."

Gwen straightened in her chair. "Of course I'm not trying to do that! I'm sure you'll love making polite talk with every single person at all those future Arcadian parties."

Charlotte snorted but didn't retort since Natalie bounded up to them at that moment, her eyes concerningly bright.

"I've been thinking," she said ominously.

Gwen and Charlotte exchanged a look.

"What are you planning now?" Gwen asked in an even more exhausted voice.

"Charlotte said I can visit Arcadia in a few years, but why stop there?" Natalie gazed into the distance dreamily.

"What do you mean?" Charlotte asked warily.

"It hit me during the ceremony," Natalie said. "You're a queen, Gwen."

"Queen Gwendolyn to you," Charlotte said sternly. "At least in public."

Natalie waved a hand dismissively. "But you were born a princess, so it's not surprising. But Charlotte on the other hand… She's going to be a queen one day too, but she was born into a family just as ordinary as mine."

Charlotte winced. Was Natalie's introduction to Charlotte's family responsible for sparking this train of thought?

"So if Charlotte can become a queen, then I'm going to become a queen too," Natalie finished cheerfully.

"You're going to become a queen?" Gwen asked incredulously. "How would that work, exactly?"

Charlotte could see the connection, though. "By marrying a crown prince, I suppose," she said.

Natalie nodded. "Exactly. Did you know the old crown historian is one of the guests today? He's absolutely ancient, but he's the one who's been updating the official records since the traders reestablished contact with the Four Kingdoms. I've just had a very interesting talk with him."

"Don't tell me…" Gwen said weakly.

Natalie continued on, unheeding. "It turns out," she said triumphantly, "that Crown Prince Frederic of Lanover has a son who is sixteen years old and who will one day be king of Lanover."

Charlotte wracked her brains, trying to remember the royal family trees she had learned as a child in school. "You mean Prince Leo?" she asked.

"That sounds right," Natalie said. "Or Leon, or Luca, something like that. Anyway, as soon as I'm eighteen, I'll come to Arcadia to visit you, Charlotte, and then I'll continue straight on to Lanover. It's perfect."

Gwen and Charlotte stared at her, rendered equally silent by the matter-of-fact plans. Natalie eyed them both as if they were the strange ones before shrugging and bounding off again, perhaps to regale someone else with tales of her glorious future.

"You don't...You don't think there's any chance she might actually succeed, do you?" Gwen whispered in the silence after her departure.

"Let's hope not—for Lanover's sake," Charlotte said back with feeling, and then both of them dissolved into helpless laughter.

Their laughs had finally subsided to the occasional chuckle, and they were wiping at their eyes when Henry appeared, eager to steal his bride.

Gwen sent them off with a wave, and Charlotte went joyfully. As lovely as the day had been, she couldn't wait until it was just the two of them again as it had been all those weeks in their castle.

Henry pulled her into a shadowed corner and wrapped his arms around her, gazing down into her face. "I talked to Easton. He and Gwen are lending us their lodge for two weeks. He said it's their wedding present."

Charlotte's face lit up. "The one right on the edge of the valley?"

Henry nodded. "I told them we don't need any servants. I think we can survive two weeks on our own, even without the bell."

Charlotte nodded fervently, overwhelmed at the thoughtful offer from their friends. As happy as she had been already, the knowledge they would leave so soon for Arcadia had been a slight shadow. Knowing she would have some time alone with Henry before she had to face his family and the Arcadian court made the whole prospect easier to bear.

She sighed and leaned against him.

"It will be nice to have some time to ourselves before we head home," Henry said, echoing her thoughts. "And I hope you don't mind, but I suspect we'll have to have a third wedding when we do eventually reach Arcadie. I am their crown prince, after all, and you'll be their queen one day. We might be well and truly legally married now, but my people will want their own celebration."

Charlotte swallowed. She didn't mind another ceremony. It was what it signified that scared her.

"How can I be a queen one day? I'm just an ordinary girl."

Henry threw back his head and laughed. "An ordinary girl? You are far from ordinary, my beautiful wife. Who else could find their way to the palace east of the sun and west of the moon? Who else has ridden the wind, stolen back the sun, and helped defeat the mountain queen? I've never met anyone less ordinary." He paused. "Unless it's my mother. You know she was born a woodcutter's daughter, right?"

Charlotte nodded, the vague memory of Alyssa's history coming back to her. But everyone said the Arcadians loved Princess Alyssa—or Queen Alyssa as she must now be. Was it possible they could accept Charlotte in the same way?

Henry smiled down at her, reading her thoughts on her face. "They're going to love you just like they love her. You're not only beautiful, you're intelligent, kind, and considerate of others. And my mother will love you most of all. You don't have to worry. Queen Alyssa is going to approve of the newest princess of Arcadia."

GWEN

Gwen's stiff smile remained in place until the door closed behind the latest supplicants. Some days it felt like their time consisted of nothing but meetings from sunup to sundown. Hands appeared on her shoulders, firmly kneading at the knots. She closed her eyes and sighed, welcoming the momentary release of pressure.

"It won't be so bad once everything is more settled," Easton murmured. "At least that's what my parents have assured me, and the count agrees."

Gwen opened her eyes and smiled up at him. Reinstating Lydia and Jett to the court had been an easy decision, and they had already turned out to be better advisors than most of the people who held the title. She was thinking of giving them the official appointment soon.

She stretched, bending her head from side to side in an attempt to erase the crick in her neck. Charlotte and Henry's current days at the royal lodge were looking more and more idyllic with every passing hour. But Gwen and Easton had promised each other they would have their own visit there once matters settled down in the mountain kingdom. She just hoped it didn't take much longer.

At least both the court and city had accepted Count Oswin's reinstatement as Chief Advisor thanks to the combination of his longstanding position at court and his role in the rebellion. Unfortunately, the new positions given to Patti and Dane weren't so uncontested.

Gwen sighed again. It was only a minority who insisted the whole family should take the blame for Baden's treachery, but their last meeting had contained several of their number. Of course it had also included a few who represented the majority— people who argued in favor of the valuable role in the rebellion undertaken by Patti, Dane, and even Natalie. Thus why the conversation had been heated.

Thankfully, those who were wavering in the middle had been mostly convinced by Natalie's participation in Charlotte's wedding. Seeing she still held royal favor had swayed all but the most entrenched. But those who were most entrenched in their opinions were also usually the most vocal.

And she and Easton would have to make a decision about Baden himself soon. She had been putting it off for Patti and Dane's sakes—and to a lesser extent Lydia and Jett's. As betrayed as they all felt, they had argued passionately that he had only done it out of fear for his family, believing the old queen too powerful to be overthrown. They had pleaded for clemency, and Gwen and Easton had put off any decision at all, not wanting their reign to begin with something so contentious.

Celandine's guards had been easier to manage, at least, since no one had spoken in their defense. Those known to have committed casual cruelties in the city were handed over to be tried as civilians, and the others had already been marched through the new mountain pass. According to Easton, there were sea captains who would be both willing to take them and capable of keeping them in line. Some of them might even become productive citizens.

"Do you think they accepted Patti and Dane's new roles as spokespeople for the city?" Easton asked, gazing at the closed door. "Even if they didn't like it?"

"They certainly didn't like it," Gwen agreed. "But there's no one we could appoint who would be loved by everyone. I'm sure they'll come around when they see what a good job they do." She groaned. "But what are we going to do about Baden?"

"Actually, I've been thinking about that," Easton said. "And for once, maybe we can follow in Celandine's footsteps."

Gwen's head snapped around to face him. "What?"

"She misused her power, but she did manage to maintain it in the face of opposition for twenty years. She knew something about balancing opposing interests. And when faced with a rebellious youth whose parents had influence, she chose banishment over a more confronting punishment."

"You only challenged her!" Gwen cried indignantly. "You didn't put anyone's life at risk. You weren't a traitor to your own family and people! Her reaction was outrageous."

He shrugged. "That's a matter of perspective. Celandine certainly thought of me as a traitor. I'm sure if she'd had her free choice, she would have executed me for daring to challenge her. But she recognized the effect that would have on every parent in the court. So she solved the problem by removing me from view."

Gwen forced herself to consider the option with an open mind. "If Baden is banished from the mountain kingdom, he'll be out of sight, and hopefully mind, of everyone baying for his blood. But his parents and sisters will know he's physically unharmed and able to build a life for himself."

"Exactly," Easton said. "I, of all people, know it's possible to do. And he's three years older than I was when I was banished. He's certainly old enough to work and provide for himself in a town like Ranost. I've had several long talks with him, and I agree with my parents. He did it out of fear for his family's safety. He won't be a danger to anyone else if we set him loose in Northhelm."

Gwen's shoulders slumped. "Patti and Dane won't exactly be happy, but you're right. I think it's the best we can do. And now that the mountain pass is open, they can probably pay him some quiet visits in a few years' time, which is better than your parents could hope for."

"You don't feel the punishment is too light?" Easton asked curiously.

Gwen rubbed her temples. "He's still a youth. Of course we can't ignore something so big, but I don't want us to start our rule by handing out harsh punishments. These weeks have been difficult enough as it is." She groaned. "I can't say I thought I would be taking Celandine's example in anything, though."

"No one is completely wrong all the time," Easton said. "Just like no one is right every time. I've been spending every spare minute reading the histories, trying to absorb all the records of how past monarchs handled the issues that arose. I haven't found one who was perfect yet, but there's always been something to learn from each of them."

"And this is why you are just the husband I need." Gwen stood and wrapped her arms around him. "I think you're better at this than I am."

He shook his head. "No, we just make a good team."

He leaned down to kiss her, but a knock on the door made them pull reluctantly apart. Alma backed inside, a tray held in her hands.

"I knew you'd need something substantial after that lot," she said, placing it on the enormous desk. "So don't even think about starting another meeting until you've eaten everything on there."

She fixed them both with a stern look, and they grinned back at her. Gwen had already said farewell to Miriam and most of the other captive servants, but she had been beyond delighted when Alma decided to stay.

Gwen had immediately given her the official role of house-keeper, and Alma had already sourced paid servants for most of the needed roles. From what Gwen had seen, she was training them thoroughly and ruling with a firm but fair hand. Gwen was just relieved she didn't have to attempt the task herself. She had enough on her plate already and very little idea of the daily practicalities of running a palace building.

"What would we do without you, Alma?" Easton asked, settling in to eat with enthusiasm.

"That's what I asked myself," she said, watching him eat with satisfaction. "What was the point of returning to Northhelm when there was no family waiting for me? That was why I was snatched in the first place, after all. Here, on the other hand, there's plenty needing my attention."

"And you have family here now," Gwen said firmly.

When they had both eaten, and Alma had taken the tray away —having watched them sternly the whole time—Gwen finally sank back into Easton's arms.

He managed to kiss her successfully this time, but when he pulled back, they both sighed simultaneously. Their stolen moments were always too short.

"After our trip to the lodge, I want to take a trip to Ranost," Gwen announced. "I want to learn more about your life in those years when you were gone."

Easton smiled. "And I want to share all my stories with you. I think you'll love the sea as much as I do if you get the chance."

He glanced toward a locked drawer in the desk. A drawer whose only key was on a chain around Gwen's neck.

"In ordinary circumstances, I would say we won't have the opportunity to get away very often," he said. "But thankfully I married a queen who can ride the wind. We can manage a day trip to Ranost if that's all the time we have."

"Oh yes, let's!" Gwen said instantly. "Surely we can manage at least a single day away soon."

"We'll be able to visit Charlotte and Henry more easily with your halter too," Easton said. "The more I think about it, the more advantages there are. I'm sure there will be plenty of difficult decisions in our future, but at least we'll always be able to manage brief trips away to clear our heads."

Gwen smiled at him and turned her face up for another kiss. "Just having you at my side is enough for a happy life. After everything we've been through, it isn't something I'll ever take for granted."

"I want more for you than just me," Easton protested, his eyes soft as he smiled at her. "And thankfully that's true already. And we'll continue to build even more together." He nodded decisively. "I think we can have a very happy life riding the wind together."

NOTE FROM THE AUTHOR

Thank you to everyone who has joined me for so many adventures in the Four Kingdoms. Although those adventures are now drawing to a close, new fairy tale adventures will be beginning. If you enjoyed the Four Kingdoms stories, discover the new fairy tale kingdoms found in Kingdoms of Legacy, where not only the characters, but the kingdoms themselves, are shaped by classic tales. (Although also kept an eye out for a future Four Kingdoms novella since Natalie is a heroine who needs a story!)

Or if you missed discovering the Four Kingdoms, try the rest of the Four Kingdoms books, starting with the very first book, The Princess Companion: A Retelling of The Princess and the Pea, or if you prefer to skip ahead and meet Charli as a child, try the final book in Return to the Four Kingdoms, The Abandoned Princess: A Retelling of Rapunzel.

To be informed of my new releases, as well as new bonus shorts, please sign up to my mailing list at www.melaniecelli er.com. At my website, you'll also find an array of free extra content in my Four Kingdoms world.

Thank you for taking the time to read my book. I hope you enjoyed it. If you did, please spread the word! You could start by leaving a review on Amazon or Goodreads or Facebook or any other social media site. Your review would be very much appreciated and would make a big difference!

ACKNOWLEDGMENTS

When I started writing To Steal the Sun, I intended for it to be my last book in the Four Kingdoms world. However, it proved impossible to write a character like Natalie without finding myself imagining what she might set out to accomplish after the story was over. So while I don't know when it will be, I hope to come back to the Four Kingdoms at least one more time. And I'm especially glad at the prospect because of all the readers who take time from their busy lives to tell me how much they love the Four Kingdoms. I know I've said it before, but thank you to everyone who has embraced these series and this world alongside me. I appreciate you all so much.

And I am also beyond thankful to my whole team. You know who you are, and your support in my writing and publishing journey is the only reason I'm still going.

A final thank you to God, who is with us in every dark place and is always leading us back to the light.

ABOUT THE AUTHOR

Melanie Cellier grew up on a staple diet of books, books and more books. And although she got older, she never stopped loving children's and young adult novels.

She always wanted to write one herself, but it took three careers and three different continents before she actually managed it.

She now feels incredibly fortunate to spend her time writing from her home in Adelaide, Australia where she keeps an eye out for koalas in her backyard. Her staple diet hasn't changed much, although she's added choc mint Rooibos tea and Chicken Crimpies to the list.

She writes young adult fantasy including books in her *Spoken Mage* world, her *Mage's Influence* world, and her various *Four Kingdoms* and *Kingdoms of Legacy* series that are made up of linked stand-alone stories that retell classic fairy tales.